THE FIFTH SEASON

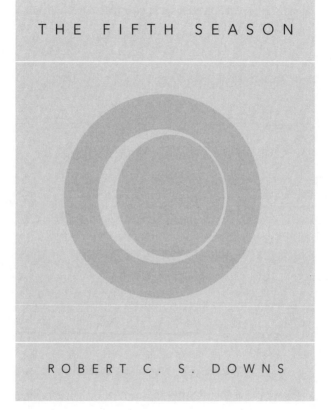

THE FIFTH SEASON

ROBERT C. S. DOWNS

COUNTERPOINT

WASHINGTON, D.C.

Library of Congress Cataloging-in-Publication Data

Downs, Robert C.S.

The fifth season : a novel / Robert C.S. Downs.

p. cm.

ISBN 1-58243-134-5

I. Title.

PS3554.095 F55 2000

813'.54 21—dc21

99–045924

Text design by Victoria Kuskowski

Printed in the United States of America on acid-free paper
that meets the American National Standards
Institute Z39-48 Standard.

Counterpoint

P. O. Box 65793

Washington, D.C. 20035-5793

Counterpoint is a member of the Perseus Books Group.

10 9 8 7 6 5 4 3 2 1

THE FIFTH SEASON

At five-thirty on this early October afternoon my ninety-two-year-old father, Able Neel, lies in four-point restraint in Bed Two in a room on the fifth floor of Broward General Hospital, his cancerous left kidney gone as of ten-thirty this morning. Drugged, his eyes settle on me no more frequently, nor with any more interest, than they do on the closed venetian blinds next to the bed or on the small spires of his feet under the loose blanket. Now and then he tries to move a foot toward the center, but the gauze around the ankle says no. The surgeon, Dr. Erg, late thirties, bearded, a head shorter than I, said a half hour ago that he's going to be all right. "Home in a week, maybe ten days 'cause of his age." In the first few moments in the room, I told Able this, his eyes clear and straight ahead as I stood to the side of the bed, and he responded by thumbing the morphine pump in his right hand as if it were a buzzer in a game show. Then his eyes rolled back and the lids came down.

I've been here an hour, sitting in a low chair with wide flat arms, watching him go in and out of sleep. So far I've seen three myoclonic jerks, the first a soft spasm, the other two powerful enough to wake him, his eyes wide and fierce with surprise. The room and hall are quiet after the dinner scurry. Bed One, empty, has stiff fresh sheets and a pillow as smooth as white marble. I asked the nurse who came in just before dinner why Able was restrained and she said he'd thrashed around right after they brought him back from the ICU. She turned his left arm slightly so I could see the inside of the elbow and the patch of black under the skin where he'd torn out the first IV. She said patients as old as Able often get disoriented, that restraint is the best thing for them. She winked and said, "Us, too," then added that this time tomorrow he'd be much better, they'd have him up and sitting where I am.

Quite suddenly he speaks, his voice as clear as years ago, and asks for Lillian, my mother. I take the few steps to the edge of the bed and say everything's fine. Through his teeth he says, "I have to take care of her." Then he raises his hands a few inches, as far as the ties will allow, and looks at them. I tell him he pulled out an IV and his eyes roll back and he says, "Lil?," then goes to sleep again. I step back as the evening nurse swishes through the door and across the room to bend down at the end of the bed and raise the sheet slightly to look at the dangling collection bag for his urine. She turns it in her hand once, then follows the clear tubing up under the sheet. Her face tells me that what she's looking at she doesn't like, and when I ask if there's a problem she says, "There will be if the bag stays empty." His output, she says, is key, and when I say but the right kidney's just fine she says sometimes the one that's left shuts down sympathetically. Then she takes a stethoscope from her pocket and listens to his chest, says, "Bueno," then snaps the ends from her ears and says, "You're the professor, aren't you?" I nod, say my name, Ted, and she tells me that last night when they were prepping him Mr. Neel told her about my brother and me. "At some length," she adds, and I smile and shake my head and softly say I know how he can go on. "You've written three books?" she asks, and I tell her all on Tennyson. Then there comes the familiar vacuum in the conversation when someone not academic kindly mentions my work, about which there is not a shred of general interest. It's the same effect my brother, Benny, gets in conversation when someone asks what he does and he says psychology: one can just about hear the silent *Oh* in the person's mind. The nurse says how fortunate for my father that I have a sabbatical and can be here.

After she leaves I go out the door and turn in the opposite direction to walk down the hall to the balcony where patients and staff smoke. Outside, the sun is stuck behind a long bank of clouds to the west, a couple with mean thunderheads in them, but a few miles north great shafts of sunlight strike the ocean.

I have not been here to Fort Lauderdale for a year, but when I got to their apartment yesterday about noon it was as if a decade had sped by, as if their telephone voices had been careful facades, what I'd heard at best exaggerations, at worst lies. I knew my mother's short-term memory wasn't good—she'd ask about my daughters, Melissa out of college and working, Rebecca a junior, and ten minutes later would ask again—but otherwise the quality of her voice and her quick laugh was the same. But the real problem, which I discovered two hours after I was in their apartment, is that her vision is in serious decline. I found this out on the eleventh-floor balcony of their U-shaped ocean-side building, a place where over the years as my children grew up my family had spent some very pleasant times. When I remarked that down below by the pool, shuffleboard courts, and putting green I could see Bill and Margaret Nicely, ten years younger and their friends of eighteen years, my mother leaned forward, her bright blue eyes in a sad search, and finally said, "Oh, I believe I do, too." I shot a look at Able and realized he'd ignored the exchange. Although during lunch—cold cuts and macaroni salad bought from O'Donnell's Deli—I hadn't noticed anything, now I realized she could hardly see.

When I mentioned it was getting close to admission time, Able, reclined on the chaise, suddenly looked like a man losing his way, as if in what pillars there'd been in his life he could now hear and feel the sounds of core friction, as if he could actually see cracks wiggling along the surface. His small close-set eyes grew large, as though possibly in his anxiety about the coming surgery he'd had the brief thought that this might be his last afternoon. His hands were folded across his small belly, and his shoulder bones stuck up like two knuckles under the cream-colored sports shirt.

Next to me in the white metal chair with plastic stripping, Lillian let her hand rest along my forearm, and her fingertips lightly, absently pressed into the flesh at the back of my wrist, as though sending a signal she was not aware of. She observed that the Florida weather isn't what it used to be, that it's gray and cloudy now a lot, and when she turned slightly to ask me why I said I didn't know. "Global warming," Able said, watching me.

"I've heard of that," she answered and turned away, her mind as calm and soft as pudding.

When I go back to Able's room I find he now has a roommate, a man in his thirties who doesn't look very sick, but who tells me, along with his name, Danny Ramsay, that he's just come up from detox with pancreatitis. He's a tall man who takes up the whole length of the bed, and whose stubble, unkempt hair, and scabby hands support his history. When I ask how long he was downstairs he says he doesn't know, could have been a couple of days, maybe even a week, then asks if I have a cigarette. I shake my head and say sorry, and then he startles me by turning toward the door and hollering, "Nurse, get in here." I expect her appearance within seconds and when no one comes I turn away to Able to see him deeply asleep. "Your old man?" Danny asks.

"My father," I answer, nodding.

"Is he croaking?" I tell him no, explain what's happened, and he says, "Jesus, I got to have a smoke." I pull the curtain along the space between the beds so there is the feeling of privacy and look at Able. Suddenly, his eyes snap open and he says, "Call your mother." I do on the phone on the small night table next to the curtain, and right away it's pretty bad. Lillian has forgotten where we are and she's nearly weeping she's so glad I've called. When I tell her Able's just fine, he

wants to talk to her, she says, "Oh, is he all right?" I say just a second
and lay the phone next to Able's head on the pillow. He tells me to
take these goddamn ropes off his hand so he can at least talk to his
wife. I loosen the slipknot and get the hand free and he takes the
phone, all the time his eyes on me like a weight. His pupils are
hugely dilated. I'm astonished and scared that right away he tells her
to drive down here, he's going home tonight, the place is filled with
crazy people. "You can't go home," I tell him, "you just had surgery."
I reach for the phone but he turns his head away, his grip on it like
steel. Finally, I get the phone from him, his arm drops like it's dead,
and I tell Lillian that he's not himself, he's talking through his hat. To
this she says if she can find the car keys she'll come and get him, and
it's like she hasn't heard a word. "Listen," I say, "it's after six. Watch
the news or something. I'll be there." When I hang up, Able's looking
straight at me again, his lips in a solid line, and he's almost squinting.
"Why are you making this so hard on me?" he says.

"It's for your own good," I tell him. For a second or two he seems
to consider what I've said, then turns his head away. I take the gauze
loop, slip it over his hand and tighten it loosely around the wrist.
Right then a nurse comes in, the third different one I've seen, nods at
me, then checks the urine bag. It's still empty. As she makes a note
about it, the IV monitor begins to beep, and when I look over I see
that blood has begun to back up into the tubing. The nurse sees it,
too, takes the few steps to it, flips a small switch, and then walks
around past me to the other side of the bed and closely examines the

needle in his arm. She says something under her breath and then walks out of the room. I don't know if he hears me when I tell him I've got to go to make certain Lillian's okay, but when I rest a hand on his knee and start to tell him again he says, "Give me that thing." I put the morphine pump in his hand and watch as he presses down on the button as hard as he can.

The drive from Broward General to North Ocean Boulevard was forty minutes in this morning's traffic, but I make it back in twenty-five, park my rental on the north side of the building, hurry through the lobby to the J Tower, and am relieved to find that the elevator's only one floor down in the garage. When it does not respond it's my guess that some-one's propped it open to bring groceries from their car. It takes four or five minutes before I hear the door close and the elevator start up. When the door opens, a small, thin couple who look to be in their early eighties stands side by side, two pull carts filled with groceries in front of them. They stare at me. I smile, get in, and press 11. The elevator stops at 10 and they get off, each with the same difficulty with the cart, as if they have to get it over a curb. I have my key out and go in the door almost without stopping. To my great relief I hear the television in the den, but when I get there the room's empty. It doesn't take but a few seconds to realize that Lillian's gone, but even as this registers some-thing makes me call out, "Mother, mother?"

Right away I'm back in the elevator heading for the garage, know-ing I'm going to find the old Cadillac gone, and it is. I stand in the space feeling useless and very afraid. God knows where she is, I think, and pictures of her in trouble run through my mind. I go back to the apartment to wait in the den by the phone and the call comes within a half hour: the police tell me Lillian's at the Galleria down on Sunrise, sitting on a bench near a bus stop, the car parked so awkwardly it's taking up two handicapped spaces. When the officer finds out I'm her son he tells me I ought to take better care of my mother. I tell him he's absolutely right and that I'll pick her up as soon as I can get there. I call a taxi and go down to the west entrance to wait for it. The doorman, Joseph, is on evening duty. I've known him for all the years my family and I have visited. He shakes my hand and says it's good to see me and asks how my daughters are. I tell him fine and he frowns and asks how Mrs. Neel's doing. For an instant I wonder how he knows she's lost, but then he says, "With her hip, the therapy." I answer vaguely, feeling my way, that she seems pretty good, and it works when he says, gesturing to the steps outside, that it was a hell of a tumble she took, a wonder she didn't break a leg or something. "Oh, yes," I say, "that."

At the Galleria I thank the cop and he's quick to leave. Lillian doesn't recognize me until I sit next to her on the bench and put an arm around her. She's softly crying, her lips wet and trembling, and when I say things are going to be all right she answers, "Oh, good." In the car on the way back I ask where she was going and she turns and looks at me and says give her a minute, it'll come. "To see Able?" I prompt, and she says, "Yes."

"He's in the hospital, you know," I tell her.

"It's the cancer," she says, eyes once again ahead.

"He's going to be okay," I say. "The doctor said he'll be all right."

"Which hospital?" she asks. I decide to keep the car keys with me from now on.

When we get back to the apartment, Lillian goes straight into the den and sits on the end of the couch to watch television. I tell her I'll make us something for dinner, but when I go into the kitchen I can feel the heat from the oven over the stove. It's set between 425 and 450, and when I open the door there are two Stouffer's frozen dinners, lids still in place, bulged out and so charred that even the pictures are scaly and dark brown. I turn off the oven and take the dinners out, pot holders on both hands, and walk them to the door of the trash chute next to the refrigerator. They make almost no sound as they disappear down the wide, drafty space. Next I turn on the ceiling fan to dissipate the heat that's built up, and then open the freezer door of the refrigerator to see if there's something else to eat. Oh, there is, all right: probably thirty to forty Stouffer's frozen dinners are stacked in five rows, each row a different entrée. I go into the living room and call to Lillian in the den to ask what she wants. Her response is to say *Jeopardy!* is on and I should come watch. "Tell Able," she adds. For an instant I cannot get my breath, and I think where is my mother, where did she go? I tell her I'm going to make dinner and she calls back, "That's nice."

I see right away when I open the refrigerator why there're so many frozen dinners in the freezer: There is no room on the shelves for anything larger than a thimble. Glass and food containers are stacked side by side, from half-finished Pepsi cans to special nutritional drinks capped with aluminum foil, to GLAD-wrapped saucers of leftovers long forgotten, to small and medium-sized bottles of medicines I've never heard of with expiration dates of nearly a year ago. I go back to the den to ask her what she and Able have been doing with the refrigerator, and if they eat anything but frozen dinners, but my irritation is instantly gone when I see that she's lying back on the couch, feet up, her head resting on a small pillow on the padded arm at the end, sound asleep. Her hair, thin and nearly orange from the beauty-parlor rinses, lies like a cloud of cotton candy high on her forehead, her hands are folded across her middle, and her tiny diamond engagement ring, the stone so dirty that it gives off no light, is held upright by two fingers of the other hand. A tall woman, she takes up most of the couch, the soles of her white oxford walking shoes nearly touching the other arm. It's possible, I think, judging from how worn and rounded the heels are, and the tiny splits along the sides, that she's had these shoes now for eight or nine years. She is, I realize, in the same white blouse and aqua slacks that she wore yesterday and that each has smudges of food and, in places, light fingerprints, as though from picking off crumbs.

Back in the kitchen I order two takeout spaghettis from Nick's, the Italian restaurant a few blocks down on A1A, then get a roll of plastic bags and pull up a chair in front of the refrigerator. The food and medicines go in the bags, the glass containers and the Tupperware onto the counter above the dishwasher. So packed is the refrigerator that it seems as though it's been a careful project over many years. They've been saving food—a last slice of cake, a thin cut of melon, a half-eaten banana tucked down in the skin, a months-old slab of meat loaf, milk with a date from last summer, and on and on it goes until I have eight five-gallon bags on the floor next to me, the dishes and glasses all over the counter. Just as I open the fresh-produce drawers at the bottom and see two heads of brown, shrunken lettuce in decayed plastic wraps, ooze all over the place, the spaghetti arrives from Nick's. I pay the young man, who thanks me in broken English as if I'm royalty for the two-dollar tip, and set the package in the oven and turn it to warm. Then I go back to the den to tell Lillian that dinner's ready. She's awake and staring at a *Seinfeld*. When I tell her what we're eating she brightens in a way I haven't seen since I got here, gets up too quickly, and for a moment has to steady herself on the end of the couch. When she finally pushes upright and shoves off, she's very unsteady and I have to cup her elbow as we walk. She thanks me and says it must be these old shoes.

At the table she asks where Able is and I tell her he's in the hospital. She turns and looks out the window right next to her, the last of the evening light casting pink reflections in her eyes. I cut the spaghetti and put some on a plate for her, dice the large meatball, and then sit to watch her move the fork through the food, then raise to her mouth what she's been able to catch. About half the time she gets a regular, normal portion, the other half only a few clinging strands. She remarks on how good the spaghetti is, says she hasn't had a meal like this in so long, and then asks not only how my daughters are but where they are. I say they're fine and tell her again. Then there's something about her that relaxes visibly—her shoulders slump, her head goes down as though to stretch out the muscles at the back of her neck, and she says again how good the food is. Her face is slightly flushed. When I say a salad came with the spaghetti she says, "Oh, I'd like that. Italian dressing?"

As I'm pouring the dressing over the lettuce and red onions and mushrooms, Lillian asks if I ever hear from Benny. I answer that from time to time we talk on the phone, and then she says he lives in California now, doesn't he? "Santa Barbara," I tell her, then add, "He's the psychologist to the stars." This is an old, friendly line from years ago when Benny used to joke (or so we thought) that what he wanted from life was wealth, fame, and glamour, and that he was going to the coast to open a practice and become a talk-show celebrity. While he's not a regular for anyone, he has gotten in front of the camera on the Fox psychology half hour four times and has said privately that he did two behind-the-scenes consults for O.J.'s defense. Lillian smiles at the remark and says Benny can do anything he wants, then adds, "You, too." She turns in her chair, her chin propped on her hand, and looks at me about ten feet away at the counter, her eyes as though I'm only a memory, and starts to talk about the times when I had my first teaching job and Elaine and I would bring the girls for a week, how we'd stay a block away at the Villa Caprice and walk over to the apartment along the beach. She asks if I remember how mad Able got when Elaine lost one of the sets of keys he gave us and I answer, "I sure do." Her whole face is alive, and an erectness comes into her posture and she leans back and lets her fingertips rest along the edge of the table. For a moment she looks as though she's going to start to play the piano like she did when I was a kid. Her fingers move a little, as in an involuntary twitch, and then she sets her hands together in her lap.

As we eat our salads she says several times how wonderful this tastes, and when I ask her what she eats beside the Stouffer's in the freezer she says those are just for the nights she and Able don't go to the club. I ask how often that is and she stops jabbing at the lettuce and thinks hard for a moment, then says it's not so regular anymore. The confusion on her face tells me I've done her no service by asking such a question and right away I change the subject to one of our visits years ago when Melissa, then four, accidentally locked herself in the bathroom and Able had to break the lock with a screwdriver. Lillian remembers this like it happened only an hour ago.

Outside, the last of the light has gone, and down by the pool and around the walkways by the putting green there're burnt umber rings on the concrete where the high-security lights have come on. A few couples walk the perimeter of the area, one holding hands, another striding purposefully for the exercise, one with the man some yards ahead as though they've had a dinnertime argument. They are smooth, dark cutouts against the strange light. I remember when Lillian and Able first came here thirty years ago, just after his retirement from Union Carbide, and each evening they did the same as those I now watch, two people more carefree at sixty-two and sixty-one than it's probably possible to tell. I'd just finished my course work and, for my dissertation, I was reading more seriously than I ever had. My first marriage, loveless and childless, had just come apart; I was an eastern intellectual snob in the foreign land of Iowa City, then with a population of less than twelve thousand in a squared-off bunch of blocks set down in an ocean of corn. When I visited to tell them Janet and I were separated they seemed, in their secure bliss, to register only passing concern, as if in their move from White Plains to here something final and difficult to name had been left behind. The aura they had about themselves for their first years here—somersaulting in the surf, joining the Coral Ridge Yacht Club, eating what and where they pleased, sometimes all three meals out at fine places, wallowing in huge chunks of empty leisure time—was immortality. They were entering a stage of life I had no knowledge of.

The kitchen phone sits on the counter right behind Lillian, and now when it rings she turns automatically in her chair to answer it. Her voice is as light and fresh as it was in middle age, and when she says hello it's like back then. "How are you?" she says, and I think it's a friend calling to ask about Able, but when she follows that with "Where are you?" I know it's Able. There's a pause and she says, "Oh, yes," to his answer, then follows that with "When are you coming home?" Another pause and she hands the phone to me and goes back to the dregs of her salad as if there'd been no call at all. "Jesus, where are you?" Able says. "How long's a guy got to wait?" Slowly, I ask him what he's waiting for and he says to come the hell home, what do you think? I answer he's not going anywhere, he's staying right there, and he says, "Who says so?"

"The doctors," I tell him. "Everybody."

"I'm all packed," he says. "I'm sitting right here on the side of the bed. Bring an umbrella, okay?" Chewing, I ask if he knows the Series was tied up last night, but he's not buying diversion and repeats again that I'd better get down here, he's coming home if he has to call a cab. I tell him finally okay, no problem, I'll be there as soon as I can. "And bring your mother," he says. "I want to have a good look at her."

"Okay, for sure," I answer and hand the phone back to Lillian, who hangs it up, then asks if he's all right, and when I answer he's just fine, the doctors and nurses know what they're doing, she says, "It's the cancer, isn't it?" I start to repeat what I told her just hours before but then stop myself and say, "He'll be all right." She smiles, her eyes somewhere around my chest.

When she's back in front of the television I go to the kitchen and call the hospital and ask for Five East. A nurse answers and I introduce myself and tell her I just got a call from my father that I don't understand. She asks what room he's in and when I give the number she turns her head away from the phone and says something in Spanish, then laughs, then asks me what the trouble is. I tell her I feel like a fool saying that my father told me he's coming home and I want to know if he's all right. "He *called?*" she asks, but before I can answer she talks again in Spanish to whoever is next to her, then tells me to call back in an hour and hangs up. Next I call the hospital again and ask for him, there's a pause and then the extension rings. Just as I assure myself he can't get to it, the receiver's picked up and he says, as if he were still a Carbide executive, "Able Neel speaking." I tell him it's me and that I just wanted him to know I'm on my way. In the background I hear his roommate shout as loud as he can, "*Nurse, nurse.*" Then, "Goddamn it." Before Able can say anything I hear the nurses come into the room and ask him how he managed to get out of the restraint and he says, "What restraint?" and then the same nurse I just talked to takes the phone and asks who I am. "Is he all right?" I ask and she recognizes my voice and says he's just fine, thank you, and I should come during visiting hours tomorrow. I ask what she thinks is wrong with him and she says he's just an old man confused from the surgery and I should come tomorrow during visiting hours. Then she hangs up.

Back in the den, Lillian's sitting on the end of the couch, bent over, one arm down trying to get under it. I ask what's the matter and she says, "Have you seen my purse?" I tell her no and she says she's got to have it, everything important is in it. I ask if she had it when we came back from the Galleria and she says of course, she always has it with her, everything important is in it. She gets up, holding onto the end of the couch, and leans over. Satisfied it's not there, she goes to the other end of the couch and does the same thing, then says, "Oh, dear." I tell her to sit down, I'll find it, and she complies, her eyes dreamily on the television. I walk back through the living room and then into the kitchen and see her purse on the counter next to the phone. I take it back to her and put it on her lap and it's like I've saved her life. She looks up and thanks me, then puts both hands on the sides of the purse and says, "Well, good." She massages the sides as though trying to feel for something through the leather, then opens the top and starts taking everything out: a small stack of index cards held together by a rubber band, on which she writes her grocery lists, is followed by a hairbrush, a large red wallet, a compact, several lipsticks, two small packages of Kleenex, two medicine bottles, a post-card-size map of Fort Lauderdale, and a balled-up scarf for her head. From the sides she takes several envelopes, one of which is still to be mailed, the others bills, flyers, and junk mail stuffed in there I don't know how long ago. I pick up the envelope and see that it's some kind of card, then see the address is Benny's. I ask if she wants me to mail it and she says, "Oh, would you? It's his birthday." Benny's birthday is in April. I tell her I will and put it on the desk next to the television. Remarkably, then, Lillian stares at the stuff in two piles to either side of her and then methodically puts it all back, and when I ask if she's missing anything she says, shaking her head, "I don't think so." She looks up at me and smiles, then says, "What do you usually watch?"

"It doesn't matter," I answer.

She asks if I'll put on one of the new sitcoms, she can't remember which, that she and Able always watch, and slowly, so she can make out the characters, I change the channels with the remote. "There," she finally says, happy, and sits back in the corner of the couch and crosses her legs.

When after a few moments she's looking at the television as though she can see everything on the screen, I say I promised to call Elaine and tell her how the operation went. She nods, her eyes on the television, and says, "Give her my love." I go straight through the living room and past the kitchen to the balcony door. As I open it there's a rush of warm wind that's like a hand on my face. It billows the curtains to either side and then is gone. It's as if I've broken some fragile seal around the apartment. The lights from the hundreds of windows that have a view of the ocean are just enough to give the tips of the small lazy waves a white glow. Each curls on itself and dies on the sand with no sound. The pool is still lighted and there's a man in a white cap right in the middle doing the sidestroke. He looks to be making no progress at all, as if he's swimming against a current he can neither see nor feel.

When I go back inside I realize right away that I should have stayed with Lillian. She's on the phone in the den explaining that Able has cancer and that he's lost a kidney and may never come home. I think she's talking to one of her friends in the building or from the club until she says, "Why, right here," and hands me the phone and says it's Benny. I tell her I'll take it in the kitchen, that I don't want to interrupt her television, and she puts the receiver in her lap and looks toward the sound. I pick up the phone and tell Lillian I've got it, she can hang up, and after a long silence she does. Benny says he's between appointments and has only ten minutes but wanted to find out how things went. I ask how long it's been since he's visited and he pauses and says, "Four, five years. Why?" I tell him that Able's out of his mind and, from what I can tell about Lillian, she no longer has one. He tells me he had a clue or two about her losing short-term, but that when he talks with them on the phone—they're always both on at the same time—Able covers up for her beautifully. Then he starts to tell me that there're six stages to Alzheimer's, and he's not finished with the third one when I say, "And what should I be doing about that?" He doesn't answer directly but asks if she's having any trouble with dressing or the toilet. I tell him she wore the same stuff today she had on yesterday and he says check it out in the morning and I say I will. Then he says that she must be all right in the bathroom, otherwise I'd know by now. "They still see Armstrong?" he asks, the reference to their longtime doctor. I tell him I don't know and he says I should find out pronto, then adds that I should check Medicare backup to see what Able's carrying for coverage and to get a handle on any long-term hospitalization policies he's got. There's a pause then, and finally he asks if Able's all right after the surgery. I repeat that he's out of his head—"'Disoriented,' the nurses said"—and then I remember the empty urine collection bag and tell Benny that. He says Able's got maybe forty-eight hours to kick in the kidney or he's a goner. "What do I do with her?" I ask, and before he can answer I tell him about her getting lost this afternoon in the car. "Watch her like a hawk," he says, "and we'll have to see what happens to him. Depends." Then he says his next patient's just arrived and he's got to go. "Any chance you can come?" I ask.

"All that way?" he says.

While I've been on the phone, Lillian's gotten ready for bed and sits on the end of the couch, leaning forward toward the television. She still has on her shoes, and her knee-hi stockings are rolled down to her ankles. She asks if I remember the day Elaine and I got married, and I say I sure do, a cloudy humid afternoon in September, and she says, "Yes, it was," and asks how Benny is. I tell her he's okay and she says, "We never get to see him." Then she gets up and goes into the master bedroom just outside the den and on into the bathroom, lights on everywhere. Just as I sit down and pick up the remote, she calls to me to come for a minute. Even before I get halfway across the bedroom I see she's standing at the sink in front of the open medicine cabinet, one hand up in front of it, motionless in indecision. "What is it?" I ask as I come up beside her.

"I don't know what to take," she says. The bottom two cabinet shelves are full of prescription medicines with her name on them. I take the bottles one by one and read the dates and directions. Those out-of-date I put back, their labels to the wall, and the others I set on the counter. Lillian tells me she takes a blue one at night, and another that she thinks begins with Z. "'They're so expensive,' he says," she tells me. There's no bottle in the cabinet that begins with Z, but when I see *Xanax* I know what she means. I ask her who gave her these and she says Dr. Gandhi, and I say but don't you see Dr. Armstrong. "Oh, no," she answers. "He died."

"Who's Dr. Gandhi?" I ask, holding the two pill bottles.

"He's a handsome young man," she answers. "Right over on Commercial."

"You like him, then?" I ask.

"Oh, yes," she says.

I see the Tuinal is only 15 milligrams and let her have that, but tell her I don't know about the Xanax and how the two might not be good in combination. She takes the Xanax from me without a word and puts it in her mouth with the Tuinal, takes a small sip of water and snaps her head back. Then she looks at me in the mirror and says, "That's better. Thank you." As she leaves the bathroom she glides toward her bed along the far wall of the room, her house coat flowing behind her, her steps measuring the exact distance to the bed. As we say good night I ask her how long she's been taking those pills and she says, "I don't know." Then she asks if I'll leave the bathroom light on and the door cracked a little, and when I tell her it's that way now she says, "Thank you," and pulls the blanket around her shoulders and turns to the wall.

I go back to the den and sit in my father's recliner next to the couch and stare at the television. What am I going to do with her, I think, if he dies? A quarter of my salary and what Elaine makes nursing part-time goes to pay on the long-term loans for our daughters' colleges; I can't get hold of my retirement money for six years; our house has a second mortgage to pay for having to rip up fifty-five feet of concrete in the basement four years ago to replace decayed terra-cotta sewer pipes. I cannot take care of her. Suddenly, I find myself angry at Able because I know nothing of his finances. This is by design. Never has he let either Benny or me or Lillian know even a general idea of what he made for a salary, and he's never given any indication of how he's been able to live the last thirty years in what has always been a comfortable way. I do know that the apartment was paid for by the sale of our house, but beyond that I have no idea what his pension and investments are. Once, after Able required a detailed budget for my senior year in college, I asked Lillian about their money and she smiled and said that Able took care of all of that. But I pressed her, said she ought to realize that married women in this country will live alone for an average of thirteen years, either through divorce or having been widowed. She looked at me and said, "Able takes care of all that." It wasn't a move on her part designed to keep me in the dark. She neither knew nor wanted to know, her faith absolute.

I take the remote and turn the volume off, the silence in the apartment like a church at midnight. Then I hear Lillian softly snoring, her breathing deep and young, and I know that she's safe in there. I go out again to the balcony and this time there's no one below, the pool like a square, empty eye in the darkness, the warm wind off the water as though scented with some vague rich powder. The tops of two palm trees lean with the wind in a fine slow dance. Across the way, in the other wing of the building, about half the apartment lights are still on, and for a moment I watch men and women, some in night clothes, some fully dressed, move among their rooms. On the horizon there are two small white lights from a dead slow freighter.

In the morning I know I have to take Lillian to the hospital when I go to visit Able. She says it'll be so good to see him. Then I tell her I called Elaine late and filled her in and she sends love. I play it down from what it really was. At first Elaine had trouble understanding what I told her, then was adamant that I had to do something. When I asked her exactly what, she said I had to get some help in here, someone. I said maybe when Able comes home but that right now it was going to be day-to-day, even hour-to-hour.

"When are we going to get her down here?" Lillian asks. In the morning light her eyes seem especially bright. Then I realize she's wearing what she's had on for the last two days and I ask if she wants Able to see her in the same outfit. "This?" she asks, her hands high and flat on her chest. She thinks for a moment and then says Able likes her in slacks and a blouse. As we finish eating, I ask if she wants any help finding something, and she says she sure does, that closet's the darkest place she knows. I pour her another cup of decaf, put some Equal in it, and then go back to the bedroom to her big walk-in closet. At least half of the dresses, blouses, skirts, and slacks are brand-new, their tags from the Galleria stores still dangling. Along the wall are mostly new shoes carefully set side by side; there's a grouping of three new purses over one hook in the rear, and two shiny, creased raincoats hang next to them. Right near the front is a white blouse-slacks combination and as I take it out and lay it across her bed I see that it's just as spotted as what she's got on, like she's worn it a week straight. I put it back and take out a light floral print dress and, after I see it's clean, put it on the bed. Next I take out a pair of shoes that look likely to give her support and put them on the floor next to the bed. In the kitchen I tell her I think the white outfit's maybe not quite right and tell her what I chose. She says Able likes that dress, too, and she smiles at me. Then I ask her where she got all those great new clothes and she says Able bought them for her. "We shop all the time," she says.

As I clean up the few dishes and put them in the dishwasher, Lillian rises and goes out of the room toward the den. "Don't forget to change," I call after her, and she says she will in a while, right now she's going to take a bath. I sit down with a half cup of coffee and look out. There's early activity both on the beach and around the pool, and I remember the times Elaine and I brought our children here when they were very young. Two years ago they flew down on their own. When the phone rings I answer it and hear Margaret Nicely say, "Ted? Thank goodness. Able said you were coming." Politely, I ask how she and her husband are but she wants nothing to do with small talk, and right away asks how Able is. I say okay, the operation was a complete success, and that in an hour or so we're going down to see him. Then, tentatively, she says, "And how's my Lillian?" I answer as honestly as I can that she's not as good as when I was here last year. "She needs to get out more," Margaret says. "Able ought to take her to the club more." I ask how often she's seen them there and she says it's certainly been a month, maybe two. "You tell him that for me," she says, then asks how my wife and daughters are. I tell her they're fine and she says I'm to tell Lillian she called to ask if they could do anything for them until Able's back on his feet. I tell her I will and she asks how long I'm going to be here. "I don't know," I answer, then say probably a few days, until I can get some help in. "If you need anything," she says.

"Margaret," I say, "when did her eyes get so bad?"

"Able said she needs new reading glasses," she answers. "Thank goodness it's not something to worry about." Her voice gets close to a lilt and she adds, "At our ages we have enough, don't you know?"

"He actually said that?" I ask.

"He takes such care of her," she says, and without so much as a breath changes the subject to Bill's new pacemaker and how it's monitored by the doctor's office over the phone. "What'll they do next?" she says. Then, "Give my love to Lillian," and she hangs up. For a moment I sit perfectly still and listen to the wind racing up and down the trash chute. A few boxes go by, some glassware, then something so large it sounds like a body.

When I go back to the den, Lillian's sitting on the ottoman in front of the television in what she wore yesterday, staring at the stock market tape across the bottom of the screen. She's just able to make out LLY and she follows it from right to left, then says, "Lilly's up." Eli Lilly's in Indianapolis, where they were both born, and met and married. When I ask if Able has some of that stock she says she doesn't know but six months ago he gave her a hundred shares. She sounds like this is all the money in the world. I tell her that Margaret called. Lillian asks how she is, then tells me Bill had a pacemaker put in, when she doesn't exactly know. "But he's all right," she says. Her eyes search for another LLY quote as if she's at a slow-motion tennis match. After a moment she says she's ready when I am, and I say she promised to wear the dress for Able, not the slacks and blouse. For not more than a second she's upset by this, but then says, "He did ask that, didn't he?" and she rises, puts a hand on the end table, and goes into the bedroom. I take a couple of steps and reach my hand inside the door to put on the overhead light. She doesn't seem to notice it.

In the elevator, her head bent over severely, she looks through her purse for the car keys, then says we'll have to go back up to the apartment, she's forgotten them, and when I hold them up, she reaches out. "Let me drive," I say, and she drops her hand and says why that'd be fine, thank you. "But be careful," she adds, "you know how Able is about his Caddy."

I do, indeed. It's ten years old with twenty thousand miles on it, a Seville he proudly paid cash for, and it's his baby. He's a jerk behind the wheel, his personality altering when the engine turns over. He sits, right hand on the top of the wheel, left elbow jutting through the open window, as if returning to some randy outing of his youth. He also has the annoying and sometimes scary habit of turning in the seat to talk to whoever's in the back. Although his eyes are all right, he can't stay between the white lines on the road, and even though he concentrates on what's ahead there's an inevitable drift to his driving that requires constant correction. The last time I drove alone with him was two years ago when we took a friend of his from the building to the airport. Getting there was no problem, but getting back sure was. When Able's behind the wheel he's right and the rest of the world isn't. Dismissing my directions that he shouldn't take I-95 to get home, he powered up the ramp and we suddenly found ourselves in car and truck traffic easily going seventy-five to eighty. In what could only have been a moment of arrogance, Able dove into the middle lane and kept our speed at forty-five. Then came his drifting, mostly to the right, and twice the outside mirror on my side nearly touched the wheel of a semi. Heart pounding, I said if he'd pull over on the shoulder I'd drive, to which he responded that it was Lyndon Johnson who built these damn highways anyway. Horns and lights flashing behind us, some to the sides, he managed, however, to get to the shoulder just in time to take an exit. At the end of the ramp, more drift to the right, and when two blocks later he finally stopped in the parking lot of a church he said maybe I should drive us home. As I got out to go around to the driver's side he said it was a long time since he'd been on the interstate.

In the hospital parking lot a transformation comes over Lillian. Walking toward the main entrance, she pulls her shoulders back, her chin comes up, her right arm across her middle with her purse dangling from the elbow so that she looks as proper as Queen Elizabeth. With the other hand she holds my arm, her eyes straight ahead. She stumbles at the first speed bump, and I can feel from her weight that if I weren't there she'd have gone down. As if he were a doorman, she says good morning to an African-American with dreadlocks who's smoking outside the entrance. "You, too, ma'am," he answers with surprise. Inside, she leans her head toward me and says the people in Florida are so nice. As we walk toward the elevator bank she gestures toward where a small McDonald's has been built into the enormous lobby and tells me that's where we'll have lunch, she's eaten there a lot and it's very good. I then realize that when Able was in the hospital three weeks ago for the tests that discovered his kidney cancer that she had driven back and forth and taken care of herself for three days. That she neither crashed the car nor took a terrible fall is a benevolent act of God. In the elevator I ask if she had any problems coming and going and she thinks for a bit, then looks at me as if to say what a strange question.

When we go into the room I realize I don't have an explanation for my not having driven down last night to take Able home, but I see right away that I don't need it. He's lying in bed, now with a Posey vest on, a chest-and-arm restraint, his head our way, staring at the door. It takes a few seconds for him to recognize us and then he turns his head and looks at us as if we are in a dream. As we pass the foot of Bed One, Danny says, "Your old man had a hell of a night talking to the ceiling." Lillian turns her head and smiles at Danny, but we go right on by. "I'm up from detox," he says and then is quiet as I pull the curtain. Able's eyes search over every part of Lillian as if he's trying to place her from somewhere, then says, "Good morning, Lil," like he's just come in to breakfast. It's as if he hasn't seen me at all. Lillian lets go of my arm and walks the few steps to the bed, leans over, and kisses him on the mouth. He responds by trying to raise his arms to embrace her but the Posey holds them down. She raises up a little and puts two fingers on his mouth and says, "You need a shave, you know that?" Then she sees the restraint on his right arm and puts a hand around it. Confused, she turns to me and asks what it is. When I tell her the doctor said it was for his own good she accepts the reason with a blank stare. It's then I see that greeting us has been a huge effort for Able and he closes his eyes and his head rolls back to the center of the pillow. I move a straight-back chair to the side of the bed for Lillian and she sits in it, one arm on the mattress, her hand covering his. He opens his eyes about halfway and they look at each other as if they are the only people in the universe. I turn and sit in the low cushioned chair at the end of the bed, and just as I cross my legs I see that the urine bag is still empty. Instantly I search Able's face for some sign of deterioration—a color change, an inability to focus, some kind of tremor—but nothing's there except fatigue and age, like he's been beaten on by small, invisible fists.

It's then that Danny calls from behind the curtain that he needs a bedpan and would someone, anybody, for Christ's sake, help him out. I ignore this, thinking that surely a nurse or orderly will fly through the door and all will be well. It doesn't work out, and within a few seconds there's a moan from Danny and then a stench in the room like a backed-up sewer. Neither Lillian nor Able seems to have heard him nor does either take any notice of the smell. So overpowering is it that I leave right away to report it to the nurses' station, a huge U-shaped chest-high block of wood down the hall between the two aisles of rooms. I introduce myself to a nurse I haven't seen before and tell her what's happened. "Five-o-two," she says and looks at the light board behind her where it's easy to see that Danny's already called. I sense something I don't like and ask the nurse how long the light's been on and her response is to shrug and say in a Bahamian accent that Philippe, the orderly, will be along to tend to things and how I'm not to worry. When I ask again how long the light's been on, she says she doesn't know and moves away to one of the three desks at the center of the station, lifts a phone, and then I hear Philippe's name called softly over the loudspeaker system. Almost right away he's there and the nurse gestures toward me as though that's all the communication needed. I shake hands with Philippe and then tell him what's happened. He smiles and says 502 is the "b.b. room," and when I stare at him he wastes no time saying that means bad boys. As we walk down the corridor, he tells me that Bed One is the junkie, Bed Two the crazy old man. When I ask what's wrong with Mr. Neel it's as if he doesn't give a damn that I've identified myself. "All night long," he says, "yelling and crying out," as though he really doesn't need any more support for his first statement. He looks at me and says he was here working a twelve-hour shift at midnight and if I want the truth nobody wants to go near the damn room. I ask him why in the world my father was crying out and he says nobody knows but he thinks it might be the morphine making him crazy, he's seen it happen like that before. Then I remember that twelve years ago when Able had a pacemaker put in, he mentioned in passing that he'd had a strong reaction to whatever drug it was they'd given him. "Made me loony," he said.

Back in the room Philippe pulls the curtains tightly around the bed and says to Danny that it looks like he's been a bad boy again, to which Danny answers, "You bet your ass." As I step around the curtain, I see Lillian standing beside the bed, one set of the metal bars on the side of the bed lowered. Astonishingly, Able's sitting up, the restraints dangling from where Lillian's untied them. He's breathing heavily, his smock barely covering his middle. I step in front of Lillian and put my hands on his shoulders and look into eyes that are nearly dead. He raises his head a little and stares at me.

"Lie back," I say, my hands with a little pressure to his shoulders. The strength of his resistance amazes me, as though the power with which he holds himself steady comes from a source not physical. Without a word Lillian moves to the chair at the end of the bed and sits. Right then the nurse who I've just talked to comes in, says, "Whew, Danny's been at it again," and waves a hand in front of her face. When she sees Able sitting up she smiles at me and goes around to the other side of the bed to take his shoulders and tip him back to horizontal. All the way down his eyes stay wide and determined. As she covers him I ask her how long she thinks he'll stay confused, and she shrugs and says, "Maybe forever."

"Could he be allergic to morphine?" I ask.

"Possibly," she tells me, tucking in the light blanket and sheet. "I'll make a note of it for the doctor." She turns to look at Lillian and, with a smile, Lillian acknowledges her. Behind the curtain in Danny's space I hear several short hisses from a can of air freshener, then Danny says, "Get that out of my face, goddamn it."

"You're Mrs. Neel?" the nurse says to Lillian, whose smile broadens as she nods. "Well," the nurse says, "he's going to be all right. Don't you worry."

"Oh, I know," Lillian answers. In her face and voice there is no possibility that something might happen to Able, that she might one day be alone. "We've been married sixty-seven years," she tells the nurse, who glances at me as if to say such longevity is utterly beyond comprehension. As the nurse comes around the end of the bed and squeezes through the space between it and the chair, I tell her that I remember my father's drug reaction when the pacemaker went in. She asks if I'm sure it was one and I say what else could it have been. "A bunch of things," she says as she turns away. She glances at Danny as she starts out and then at the door says again that she'll make a note of it for the doctor.

Philippe shoves back the curtain with a great flourish, rolls his eyes at me, and, holding the bedpan, spins on one foot and leaves. Danny, hair pointy and shiny, hands locked behind his head, grins at me. He tells me his pancreas hurts like hell. Lillian says, "I'm so sorry," but he doesn't take his eyes from me. "Sometime this morning," Danny says, "will you get me a pack of Camels?" I have no trouble hearing that if I don't say yes he's threatening to mess the bed again. His smile widens as I say, "Sure, how about two?"

"You're a nice guy," he answers.

"Pull that damn curtain," Able says. Danny ignores him and rolls onto his side. Able sounds as coherent as the day before the operation. He beckons me closer and then looks straight at my mouth and tells me as long as I'm here I should see his dentist. I answer there's nothing wrong with my teeth, I had a checkup just last month. He raises one finger, points and says I've got missing teeth. I shake my head and tell him no, but he says, "You do, right there." He jabs a finger at two places in the air. Then he spreads his lips as wide as he can in a proud, grotesque smile and, jaws clenched, says, "See these, see these?" I nod and he says, "All mine, every single one." I glance at Lillian, who's smiling at him as if she, too, is proud of his teeth.

At a little after eleven, obviously late in his morning rounds, Dr. Erg sweeps into the room with two nurses and Dr. Gandhi, a man about my age. We shake hands and he asks Lillian how she is; the response, "Just fine, doctor." He turns away quickly to stand behind Dr. Erg, who's just asked Able how he's feeling. When there's no immediate response, Dr. Erg raises his voice and says he wants Able to sit up so he can look at the incision. Without waiting for an answer, he takes Able's hand and pulls a little, then slips the other behind his shoulder and brings him forward so that he's bent over. The butterfly bandages are along his flank in military precision, the dark line under them smooth and straight. Clearly, Dr. Erg is proud of his work and compliments Able on how good-looking the incision is, then says that the nurses are telling him that he's not behaving himself. "What's up?" Dr. Erg says. Able, eyes perfectly clear but still with pupils like dimes, looks at Dr. Erg as though he's only a voice far away. Dr. Erg then tells Able that he can't start making a fuss just because he's a kidney light, and that he's to follow orders to the *tee*, you hear. "Also," he adds, as though it's no more than an afterthought, "you're going to have to void soon." Able's face shows no comprehension and again Dr. Erg raises his voice and says, "Pee. Hear me?" I glance at Lillian to see that she's diverted her eyes to the floor, as if in her head she's gone somewhere to visit a friend.

As Dr. Erg leaves, Dr. Gandhi stops in front of Lillian and again asks how she is, to which she says, "Fine," her eyes upturned and bright blue, and then he looks at me and says how good of you to come. When I answer I'm on sabbatical he asks what my field is, then says, "That's nice," and turns to leave. I catch up to him in the hall and he turns but does not stop when I ask if there's anything I can do about my mother. "What about her?" he says and glances at his watch. I tell him her memory's terrible and I don't think she sees well at all. "Not many ninety-year-olds around, period," he says and smiles. He stops by the elevator bank, punches the down button with the knuckle on his middle finger, and says for me not to worry, he gave them their annuals last spring and all's well. He smiles as he looks up at the floor indicator above the elevator. "I think my father's allergic to morphine," I say and he nods and says well, that would explain a lot. "Dr. Erg didn't seem to care," I go right on, but as the door opens and he gets in all he can manage is the statement, "He's like that." I wait while the door closes and just as it does he lifts a hand and says he'll give him a call about it. I wonder how long it will take for the information to route all the way back to Able, or if it will.

Back in the room Lillian's gone. I'm utterly frozen for a moment, all kinds of thoughts in my head, and right away I ask Danny when she left and he says a couple of minutes ago. I think how could I have missed her in the hall, and raise a hand to thank him and then go out to look for her. The emptiness of the hall has the same quiet terror as last evening, the same evil loss of control. Which way to go, who to ask, what to say. Even when I try to remember what she was wearing it doesn't come right away. For all I know she could have walked the other way around to the elevators and now be out wandering in the parking lot. Just as I start down to the nurses' station, I see her come out of the ladies' room four or five doors down. She doesn't see me right away and is confused as to which way to go, then chooses the wrong one. I catch up to her quickly and take her by the arm. I tell her she wants to come back this way and she says of course she does, what was she thinking. She puts her arms out a little to the side to help her balance, and briefly she looks like she's thinking of flying. Back in the room she holds the end of the bed to let herself down into the chair.

"Take my bride downstairs for some lunch," Able says, his voice perfectly clear. Lillian rises up in the chair to look at him, smiles, and says we'll go to McDonald's and bring you something back. "Quarterpounder, well done," he answers. "No cheese." Lillian leans over and gets her purse from the floor, then digs into it for her index cards and a small pen to write down his order. I see then that the switch on the morphine pump is off, that Able's coherence is growing. Then he asks me what I'm doing here and when I tell him I came down for the operation he looks around as though he's surprised he's not in his own living room. As he begins to put things together, a slow landslide of pain gets in his way. "This is pretty bad," he says. "Wow." I have never heard him use that word. I reach over to the night table and press the call button for the nurse. Her response is almost immediate and she comes in with a syringe on a tray, says it's Demerol and worth trying because of his allergy to the morphine. Gandhi, I conclude, has a cell phone.

In not more than five minutes Able's asleep again and Lillian, as though it's rehearsed, rises with her purse and says it's time to go to lunch. She takes my arm, once again her back straight and her head up, as we walk slowly to the elevators. Two bells, one on either side of the hall, go off almost at once, and the choice of elevators confuses her. It's only when I turn to go into the nearer one that she relaxes, as though it's good to be led. As we get off the elevator and she sees the bright lights of the McDonald's, she says, "I don't know what I'd do without you here." We go to a far corner of the small room—everything in the place is about a quarter the size of a regular McDonald's—and she sits and says she'll have a medium Coke, quarter-pounder, small fries. "You're not going to go anywhere, are you?" I ask. She says she's too tired to move and then I say, "You'll stay right here for me?" and she nods and looks across the room through the glass to where a steady procession of people—doctors, nurses, orderlies, visitors—passes both ways along the huge hall. They move like seconds, minutes, and hours.

The food seems like something more than food to Lillian, as if it has a center of sweetness and vitality only she can access. She eats slowly, with small deliberate bites of the quarter-pounder followed in turn by two fries, a sip from the Coke and a napkin-touch to her lips. Then she asks again when I think Able will be coming home and I tell her what Dr. Erg told me yesterday. She nods and says of course, I already told her that. Her eyes tear from the food to the point where it looks as if she'll cry, but she doesn't notice it. "He's going to be all right, isn't he?" she asks, and for an instant I struggle with telling her maybe yes, maybe no, depends on the other kidney now, but finally I smile and say again when the doctor said he'll be coming home.

Suddenly, right on the other side of the glass doors, a fight breaks out between two young men, both shouting at each other in Spanish, one pushing the other in the chest with both hands. The head of the shoved man slams so hard against the door that I think the glass is going to break, but then he punches the other in the mouth and they wrestle to the ground. Two large black men from security race over and go to their knees to separate them, one with a headlock, the other with a huge hand gripping the back of the other's neck. As they take them to the front door, one of the young men tries to kick the other. Outside, the one whose head hit the glass door sprints off into the parking lot. When he disappears, the security men let the other go, but he does nothing but fix his hair and say something rude to the men, one finger pointing. Lillian has seen nothing of it, lost as she is in the taste of things.

I look at her, her eyes over my shoulder on something or other, or perhaps nothing at all, and I wonder what is going to happen to her and Able. I suddenly miss my daughters, who know nothing of what's going on, who couldn't imagine a life like this, and my wife, whose voice I want to hear badly. A plan comes to me: if Able dies we'll bring Lillian up to Pennsylvania to live with us. A good idea, a voice says in my head, but how fair would it be to snatch her away from everything familiar when she can hardly see anything, to put her down in a house with stairs, two cats, a big dog, everything strange. But I know I may have to do just that.

Back in the room there's a splendid quiet, Danny and Able both asleep, and Lillian goes right over to her chair at the foot of the bed, sits down, crosses her legs at the ankles, and holds her purse firmly in her lap. She sits looking in Able's direction as if she's gone on duty. She settles back in the chair as though it will be for as long as he needs her. It's right then I see that in the bottom of the urine bag there's a thin line of dark amber. The kidney has kicked in. I tell Lillian this and her eyes search for the bag, then she stares at it for a moment and says, "Is that what that is?"

"It means he's going to be all right," I tell her.

In the car as we go back to the apartment through rush hour, Lillian's head nods in light sleep. One moment she's staring through the windshield, the next her eyes are closed, her neck loose, head slightly down. It's as we come over the Intracoastal on Commercial that she snaps her head up and, fully awake, says we ought to get some dinner sandwiches at O'Donnell's Deli so we don't have to order out. "That was expensive last night, wasn't it?" she asks. I tell her it was worth it, it was the best pasta I've had in years. Then I try to joke with her and say you and Able can afford to order out if you want. She gives this some thought and then says of course they can, it's just that you wouldn't want to spend so much every night. When I say it was only twenty dollars she snaps her head toward me and says that's quite a lot. As I drive down A1A, we're quiet for a few blocks, the late afternoon sun like a huge spotlight straight in the eyes. "We know people," Lillian says, "who've run out of money." I glance at her and see that the sunlight has no effect on her, that she's staring almost straight into it. "Who?" I say, and when she asks if I remember the Jameisons I say who wouldn't, they had twin Lincoln Town Cars. At the same time, I realize I haven't seen either of them in at least five or six years. Lillian tells me that Howard died three years ago and it was then that Hilda found out they'd been living on their savings and stocks and bonds. She says Hilda was down to the last thirty thousand and she gave it all to a home in Pompano that took her in for however long she has left. I turn onto the small street where O'Donnell's is and park in one of the slots opposite the store. There's plenty of shade from a low palm tree. Lillian's still staring through the windshield as though she doesn't know we've stopped. "And then there was that man who lived in our building, oh, what's his name," she says, "the one Able called Mortimer Snerd because that's what he looked like."

"Dwayne Coolidge," I say. "Who'd forget him?"

She tells me, as clearly as though she'd heard it an hour ago, that after Dwayne's second wife died, their agreement left him only the use of the apartment but not, she emphasizes, any of the furniture, and that her daughter swept in from Buffalo and stripped the place clean. He had to rent a bed and TV, she says. I tell her I thought he was in real estate in Scarsdale, and she says that's what everybody thought. She pauses and adds, "Maybe he was."

"And he didn't have any money?" I ask.

"Apparently not," she says. "Or he spent it." I ask what happened to him and she says nobody knows, but that the daughter finally sold the apartment and he had to leave.

"Maybe he had children; maybe he went to live with them," I say.

"Well, then he did that," she answers.

In stores like O'Donnell's, where Lillian's been going for years, she's Mrs. N to everyone. She asks Albert, the owner, if he remembers me, and he says he sure does and how's the professor doing. I ask if business is good and he gives thumbs up, says never better, then asks Lillian what he can do for her. She points at a block of cheese and says she'd like a tuna sandwich on whole wheat, then another block and says macaroni salad, too. I ask for Polish ham and Swiss with Dijon, what I've had at least once each time I've visited, and a kosher pickle, quartered. For drinks we get two Arizona iced teas. For a few moments it feels like years ago when my daughters were small children and a place like this was a feast, when Nanna would bring them and say, "Sweeties, whatever you like, but save room for Häagen-Dazs." I turn to look out the front window, partially covered by a lowered awning against the southwestern sun. There are so many metal surfaces the sun hits that it looks like someone's scattered diamonds. Up at the end of the counter when Lillian pays, he tells her it's $14.80. She takes her wallet out and gives Albert two twenties. He holds them for a second or two, confused, then hands one back without a word. Lillian looks at it for a moment, then says, "Thank you," and tucks it back in her purse, but not in the wallet. Then he gives her the change. I pick up the plastic bag and as we leave she takes my arm and we walk very slowly across the narrow street to the car.

In the apartment Lillian goes straight to the den, sets her purse next to her on the floor, and then lies down on the couch facing the television. Her hand finds the remote on the small coffee table next to her and she turns the set on. CNBC instantly fills the screen, the final stock quotes on the tape marching across the bottom. "Tell me when we get to the Ls," she says, then closes her eyes and puts an arm across them so that the elbow juts straight up. Just before she falls asleep, she says she wants to know how Lilly did today. "I keep up on that," she says.

I make a gin and tonic in the kitchen, then begin to set the table for our sandwiches. Still wrapped, I put them on the plates. The six o'clock sun is down behind the building, and dark, hard shadows lie across the pool area and putting green. But there's still sunlight on the beach and out over the ocean, a thin autumn light that seems watery even here in the tropics. I know that at home the oaks are just coming into high color, that hard morning frosts are not far off.

Over the next three days Able's progress is slow, then on the third day dramatically better. Lillian and I already have something close to a routine of coming to the hospital, lunch at McDonald's, then picking up something to eat on the way back to the apartment, her nap, then dinner, then in a few hours her pills and sleep. Yesterday afternoon I knew Able's mind was clearing when he asked me to bring his reading glasses and the copies of the *Wall Street Journal* he'd missed. Today, when Lillian and I get back from lunch, he's sitting up in the chair at the end of the bed, a blanket over his knees, reading an article. It's strange to see him not in bed, as if some small part of his energy has been suddenly, if only briefly, returned to him. Lillian leans over awkwardly, holding onto the top of the chair, and presses the side of her head against his. At the same time, as if it were a private declaration, he reaches out to shake my hand. "I've been sitting here," he says, "waiting for lunch." It is almost two o'clock and his order last night, he says, was not included in those sent to the kitchen. It's right then that an aide comes into the room, sees him in the chair, and does a U-turn so swiftly that she doesn't slow down at all. She's back in less than thirty seconds carrying a tray, and Lillian and I step out of the way as she sets it down on a small table, then wheels that in place in front of him. "It's what we can do for now," she says, then adds that she made sure dinner had been properly ordered. The plate, cellophane-wrapped, contains pale liquids: broth, a glass of juice I can't tell the flavor of, saltines, and an almost transparent Jell-O. Able is so weak that he can't get the plastic fork and spoon out of their sealed wrap. I reach over and take it from him, push the end down on the table, and the utensils pop out the top. Able's first spoonfuls of the broth are shaky, and he has to lean down close to the bowl to get any of it. That more than half spills back into the bowl bothers him not a bit, his scooping motion as steady as a metronome, and little by little the level of broth is reduced. It's as if Lillian and I have disappeared, and when he's finished with the broth, only tiny grains in a splash of liquid in the bottom of the bowl, he moves on to the juice, which he takes slowly, a sip at a time, until it's gone. He goes at the saltines as if they are an entrée. At first he can't open the package, and when Lillian reaches out to help he pushes her hand away and bites open the top with his front teeth, shakes the crackers onto the plate, and then eats them with his eyes closed, as if there's great pleasure in hearing each mechanical crunch. Last is the Jell-O, spongy and glistening, that delights Able with its evasiveness. He moves the spoon around after individual chunks, finally using the forefinger of his left hand to shove them onto the spoon. His face is flushed, his eyes watery from the small sweet explosions in his mouth, and he is clearly disappointed and nearly childlike when the dish is finally empty. He sits back in the chair and closes his eyes, his lips and tongue alert to every shred of aftertaste. "Wonderful," he says softly, eyelids fluttering.

Pushing a wheelchair through the door right then is a large black man, about thirty, with an easy, certain smile. He stops and rubs his hands together as if he's just finished washing them, then looks directly at Able and says, "Physical therapy." I think this is either a mistake or a cruel joke. Lillian looks from me to Able and back again. I ask the man if he's sure he's got things right, tell him my father's only been up for an hour or so, and he takes a folded piece of paper from his shirt pocket and says there's no mistake, then asks Lillian and me to step into the hall. She stands with one shoulder leaning against the wall and I watch as he unplugs the catheter from the bag, clips it, then moves the IV pole to the side of the wheelchair. Then, remarkably, he simply lifts Able out of one chair and into the other. As Able's wheeled out I ask the attendant when he'll be back and he says probably an hour. "What will he do there?" I ask.

"Walk," the attendant says.

Lillian looks at me as though with a wave of my hand I can stop it all, then turns to watch Able as he goes around the corner. She and I wait in the room until Able comes back, a soap grinding away on the television on the wall opposite the bed. Lillian watches it on and off, but from the expression on her face it doesn't seem to make any sense to her, either. Able's exhausted but excited when he's wheeled into the room, and he reports, with the attendant's pleased nodding, that he's managed to walk—unaided, he adds—the length of the therapy room four times. The attendant raises his eyebrows in admiration. "The man is something," he says.

"How old do you think I am?" Able asks him. The man smiles, his expression one that says he knows, then tells Able that he ought to be proud of what he did in the therapy room, that *he's* proud of it. He puts Able into bed, one large hand in full support of the incision area on Able's back, then steps away, says he'll see Able tomorrow, and leaves, the wheelchair gliding soundlessly in front of him.

Able breathes deeply, gathering himself, assessing his weakness, then asks if I've heard from Benny. I tell him he called once and I called him last night to say how you were doing. He thinks about this, then looks away to the thin lines of sunlight between the closed slats of the venetian blinds. "He's okay, then?" he asks, and I answer, "As far as I know." With his thumb he gestures to the phone and says for me to give Benny his room number here, and when I tell him I already did he says fine, that's good to know, then his eyes go back to the blinds. Briefly, he's so utterly lost it's as though his soul leaves him and returns. Then he asks me two things: one is to take Lillian to the club for dinner—it's Friday night, he says, and they'll be serving the seafood buffet—and to bring him his old bedroom slippers, which are on the bottom shelf of his closet.

"I shouldn't go without you," Lillian says, but Able ignores her, reaches out a hand to hold my wrist, and says it's what he wants more than anything. "Have all the shrimp you can," he says and smiles a little. Then it's suddenly clear that the physical therapy has nearly done him in. His breathing's shallow and a bit fast, as though only now has his blood signaled a need for new oxygen, and his hand slips off my arm. He looks at Lillian like a schoolboy with a crush, then barely whispers to her, one hand slightly beckoning in invitation, "Come here." She leans over and he tries to kiss her but he cannot raise his head enough. His pursed lips get nothing but air and then his head drops back on the pillow. Lillian realizes right away that this is her fault and she bends further to kiss him on the lips. They hold each other that way for a moment and then she straightens. Able tells her he loves her, then says to have a good time with me at the club. He is near tears as we leave.

On the way back to the apartment, Lillian tells me it's been at least six weeks since she's been to the club. She thinks for a moment and then nods and repeats, "Six weeks." She tells me that it was that Saturday night when they got home that Able went to the bathroom and uri-

nated blood and they got right back in the car and drove straight to
the emergency room. She's telling me this as though I've never heard
it. Nervously, her hands hold tightly to each side of the purse in her
lap. Occasionally, the fingers knead the leather. Then she mentions
the four days he was in for the tests and that he told her every night to
double-lock the doors and how she always did it as soon as she got
home. "We do love the club," she says from nowhere. Then she looks
at her watch, holds the left wrist with her right hand, and brings it up
to within a few inches of her eyes. She asks if it's four yet and when I
glance at the clock on the dashboard and tell her it's twenty to she
says we'll just get home in time to see the market close. When she
asks what we ought to do for dinner I remind her that Able wanted
me to take her to the club. She tells me that as soon as we get home
she'll call.

A few minutes after she does, she's in the den, shoes off and feet up
on the couch, a glass of Pepsi on the small coffee table, as we watch
the market close. When I give her the last quote on Lilly she says it's
doing very well, then asks what it was yesterday. I tell her it was the
same. "I always try to remember for Able," she says. She looks down
to her feet and watches as she wiggles her toes, then presses the end
of the right foot over the left to stretch the arch. She says those hospital floors are awfully hard. Then she's asleep almost at once, as if it's
come on her without warning, without even the slightest drowsiness.
I watch the tape on the screen for a few moments, and then when the
closing summary rolls by I look at it dumbly. I know what some of the

indices are, but only the major ones like the Dow, S&P, American Exchange, and the Nasdaq, but most of the others are like word salads, the string of abbreviations little more than a baffling code, the meaning of which I've never been able to keep in my head for longer than ten minutes. Even when over the years I've asked Able what they mean, and he's explained carefully, my retention was minuscule because it just didn't interest me. Certainly, I think, this is an area in which I have disappointed Able, who's spent his whole life in finance and has no relative with more than a third-grade appreciation of what he knows. Part of this, though, is his fault because, when Benny and I were growing up, dinnertime was often spent on his telling us what a debenture was, how you could make money on Wall Street when the market went down—still a concept that mostly eludes me—and how you judged companies on price-earnings ratios. This to a fourteen-year-old who knew most of "Tintern Abbey" by heart and wouldn't tell anyone. I catch myself smiling as I think of how Benny and I would put him on by asking questions to which we hadn't the slightest interest in the answers, then later in our room mimicking the seriousness of his lengthy, boring responses. One thing I did get from Able, though, was an understanding that if you invested in a mutual fund, "and left the damn money alone," as he said, I'd one day have a generous retirement fund. It's worked, and I know that although my wife and I live mostly paycheck to paycheck we will, when the time comes, be well off, hardly rich, but okay. It's a good feeling I owe to that single piece of advice from Able.

As I glance at Lillian, I remember Able's request to bring his slippers and I get up and go into his closet, a long narrow room with a weak ceiling light, his clothes on hangers along either side. The slippers are exactly where he said they'd be, on the bottom shelf of the shoe rack. As I pick them up I see that next to them is a large loose-leaf binder. A white label with a red border on its front says *Holdings*. The slippers in one hand, I squat and slide the binder out. It makes a small dull sound as the top edge hits the floor. I know, of course, that this is his private business, but I cannot help myself and open the binder. In his perfect accountant's hand, numbers fill the pages, each numeral so exact in size that it looks to be in type. I don't think I've ever seen a page of numbers so perfectly spaced, so artistically arranged, as though there was as much pleasure in putting them down as in the information they contain. Each page is divided into columns for bought, sold, dividends, and capital gains, and every page, I begin to see, has one blue-chip stock: General Motors, McDonald's, Du Pont, Merck, Carbide, IBM, Procter & Gamble, and on it goes. It takes a few moments to page through the binder but then it hits me that what he's collected over the years, so far as I can figure, is nearly all of the thirty components of the Dow Jones Industrial Average. At first it's a muddy picture, inexperienced as I am in reading pages that contain numbers exclusively, but at the back of the binder there are other pages, from their headings kept quarterly for nearly fifty years, that tell the whole story: Able, I realize, is rich beyond any sum I'd imagined. Over and over, with a date next to each figure, there's one word, *NET*, and as I go through the final pages I see it increase almost geometrically until, on the last page, as of this past September 30, it says $1,412,582.99. I realize then that in squatting my feet have gone to sleep, and in my unsteadiness I rock back, lose balance, and smack my butt on the floor. I sit there, legs out, the blood roaring back, staring at the binder between my knees.

It's then that the bedroom light snaps on and Lillian walks by on her way to the bathroom. "Hello," she says with no more than a glance, as if where I'm sitting is entirely normal. I manage a weak "Hi" and slowly get up, slide the binder back, and then take the slippers, one in each hand, out to the small foyer and place them on the chair next to the door for tomorrow. She comes out of the bedroom and as she walks across the living room she looks at the chair, then goes over to it and looks down to see the slippers. "That's a good idea," she says and then goes into the kitchen. The idea of Able having more than a million dollars drills into my head. I realize, with enormous relief, that Able can afford anything he wants, that even if something happens to him, there will be enough money to take care of Lillian. I go back to the den and sit in his chair to watch the alphabetized stock symbols march across the ticker like a line of faithful soldiers.

After a few moments I realize I've lost track of Lillian, and I get up and go to the kitchen. She's sitting at the end of the small table by the window, holding the telephone, staring into the middle of the floor more lost than I've yet seen her. Just as I step forward, though, she asks for Eduardo, says she's been on hold for ten minutes and wants to speak to him. She says, "Thank you," in a way that's curt and most unlike her. There's another lull and she finally says, "Eduardo? Good," then says she's Mrs. Neel and wants a reservation for seven o'clock. Her eyes come up and she makes me out across the kitchen by the door. She smiles and raises her hand in a little wave, then says into the phone, "Oh, why that's right, isn't it? And thank you so much," and hangs up. She rests her hand on the phone for a moment and then looks up again and asks if I made reservations for us at the club. When I say no she says how odd, it must have slipped her mind.

She prepares for dinner out as though she were on a first date: bath, humming just before she runs in the water; careful makeup; several new dresses laid out on the bed waiting for a decision, three different kinds of shoes tried on; jewelry matched painstakingly. While I'm on the phone with my wife to tell her about Able's progress, Lillian comes into the kitchen in her slip and stocking feet, sees me across the room where she was, and asks if I'm making the dinner reservations. "It's all taken care of," I tell her and she says that's good, because on Fridays it's hard to get seated right away without a reservation. "We'll be okay," I say and smile. She turns as though she's suddenly thought of something she has to do elsewhere and leaves. My wife asks me what that was about and I tell her it's just Lillian's memory again. She says it must be hard for me to watch her in such decline and I wait a moment to answer, then say it's just about the worst thing I've ever seen.

The Coral Ridge Yacht Club backs up to the Intracoastal Waterway, and access to its front entrance is through a short maze of small, residential streets. This is the first time I've driven here—always in the past either Able or Lillian has been at the wheel—and I am anxious now that Lillian will forget the way. Not only is she precise in her directions, but she anticipates each turn so well that I don't even have to ask her one question. When she greets each of the two carhops at the door by name and tells me on the way in that I should tip when we leave, it's like an important part of her has been returned for the evening. Eduardo, the maître 'd, an immaculate Cuban with a thin black line for a mustache, gets the same treatment, and when we walk across the small dance floor at the front of the dining room to our table she takes my arm and looks around and smiles at groups of people already eating. Seated, menus in front of us, she says to remember that this is the seafood buffet night and that I'm to help myself to all I can eat. It's as if this were the first or second time I'd been here, twenty-five years ago now, when, in my thirties, I still occasionally ate like a teenager. Her smile and the way she looks at me says that I should tell her I intend to empty the shrimp bowl and clean off the platter of crab legs, all in preparation for the oysters. I return her smile as the waiter comes to take a drink order.

It's then, just as we're settled, that some of their friends stop at our table on the way to and from the buffet to ask about Able. I have known these people since the first year Able and Lillian moved here. Warm, pleasant people, they always ask about my family and say they'd love to see my daughters sometime, and how's Elaine. I can tell, though, by the exchange each has with Lillian that they all know she's got Alzheimer's and they don't want much to do with her. Lillian tries to cover up gracefully, but time and again her memory refuses to supply the name of the person coming our way. In response to questions about Able, she says he's doing well but, you know, it's the cancer, and she nods gravely. I notice, too, that of the ten or twelve people who stop by during the meal that there are many more widows and widowers than I can ever remember from past times here. When I ask Lillian about this couple or that one she answers either he died or she died or, in one case, the Millers, who have always been at the club, that they both died.

When the three-piece band—piano, sax, and drums—starts to play, Lillian looks up as if for an instant she cannot place the sound, then relaxes and a pleasant smile comes to her. Then I see her and Able on the dance floor years ago, my daughters ten and seven, in rapturous stares as they two-stepped to "Blue Moon," "Unchained Melody," "Those Were the Days," and so on. Able would dance with each of them, then with Elaine, and I'd take Lillian onto the floor and we'd manage a scaled-down Lindy or, several times, at her request, a brief Charleston. As couples now come onto the floor it's as if the sight is inspiring to her, and although I'm certain she sees only dim shadows, they make sense to her and there's much joy in her face.

In the buffet line, while I'm getting Lillian a small slice of Key lime pie and myself a salad, Margaret Nicely comes up, embraces me as best she can since we're both holding small plates, and then says how good it is to see me. She's got too much makeup on, and from the water in her eyes it looks like she's had a lot to drink. I say it's nice to be here, and thank her for her call the first night. Then she sways slightly but recovers and says Lillian's in bad shape, isn't she? I answer that I had no idea when I got here what was going on. "Able," she says, "could be kinder to her." We step out of the line and over near the wall. I ask her what she means and she glances in the general direction of where Lillian's sitting and says even when she's asked him about her condition he's stonewalled her. "He won't admit there's a problem with anything," she says. Her mouth makes a tight line and she shakes her head. "Makes Bill and me mad as hell," she says.

"He's been through a lot himself," I answer.

"Is he dying?" she asks. Her eyes snap to mine.

"No," I tell her. "He'll be home in less than a week."

"And when you go back what'll happen?" I tell her I don't know, that depends on Able. "They ought to be in Lighthaven," she says, the reference to a plan Able had ten or twelve years ago when they were supposed to go into residential care when they reached eighty-three and eighty-one. When I nod, she asks why didn't he do that and I tell her he told me back then it wasn't the right time. "Nor was anything wrong with their health then," I tell Margaret. Her answer is to say that although they're in good health, too, she and Bill have a down-payment in and that's where they're going next year, come hell or high water. Her gaze shifts toward the area where Lillian sits alone at the table, shadows from the dimmed lights making her nearly invisible. "Your mother," Margaret says, "is a lovely woman."

"Thank you," I answer.

"And Able's a jerk," she says, then pats my arm and says never mind her, it's just the cocktails talking.

I get the pie and go back to the table. Lillian asks if everything's okay and I tell her everything's just fine, I was talking to Margaret and we've solved the problems of the world. She smiles at this and then puts her fork into the middle of the slice of pie and pushes down hard enough that it splits in two, one piece sliding off the plate. I don't think she sees me put it back. Then the band starts in again and we have decaf and listen to "The Girl from Ipanema" and a cha-cha version of "Downtown." Only two couples, each around seventy, are on the dance floor, both quite expert and highly practiced. Lillian watches for a while as though they give her great pleasure. I think that this is one of those places that doesn't change. There's an airless, permanent quality—the service, food, band, lighting, furniture all in a pleasant denial of time. Here there's a sleepy comfortableness, as though each moment is not a moment gone.

I ask Lillian if she remembers some years ago Able talking about Lighthaven, and right away she says she certainly does and what a nice place it was. Then I ask her why they didn't go there and she says because Able decided not to. "What about you?" I ask.

"He didn't want to," she says, her eyes fixed hard on the dancers as they spin away and reel each other in. Her head swings a little in my direction but she does not look at me. "We would have given up so much," she says.

"Like all those Stouffer's dinners?" I say, then immediately regret it. She smiles and tells me those dinners are wonderful, and so easy to make. "And nutritious, too," she adds. With her fork she finds the last of the pie and, after pushing it around on her plate trying to spear it, she holds it with two fingers of her left hand and catches it on the end of the fork that way. Finished, she looks around as if she might be able to see if anyone was watching. "What I don't understand," I say, "is what he would give up." As I repeat the high points of Lighthaven, sounding like a talking brochure, she nods politely, and when I'm finished she says, "Privacy, for one," then adds that he said he wanted nothing to do with going to a hotel for people sick and dying. "And I don't blame him," she says.

"It's not like that," I tell her.

"I know," she says and smiles, then raises a hand slightly to ask for the check.

We aren't ten minutes back in the den, watching a sitcom I've never seen or heard of, when Lillian gets up and goes into the bathroom to throw up. Because of the laugh track it takes a moment or two for me to figure out exactly what's going on, but when I do I hurry across the bedroom and knock lightly on the bathroom door and ask if she's all right. For a second or two there's no response and I think I'll have to break down the door or something, but then it slowly opens and she says everything's okay. Her eyes are watery, nose runny, and there's a Kleenex in each hand. I ask if she thinks the crab cakes were bad and, as though she would defend the club food to her last breath, she says, "No, no, that couldn't be." I ask her why and she says because she's been doing this off and on now for a few weeks. "Ever since the cancer came," she says. There's a relief to her face, as though the episode has had a strong, cleansing effect, and she seems almost instantly ready for sleep. "I will take my pills now," she says, and when that's done she goes into the bedroom and I go back to the den. In not less than ten minutes more, when I go back to check on her, she's already deeply asleep, the blanket and sheet over half her face, her clothes across the end of the bed. I turn on the light in her closet and slowly, careful to make things straight on the hangers, put them back where they were.

Four days later we bring Able home from the hospital into the biggest, saddest mess I've ever seen. I don't understand what the hospital stay's taken out of him until, ready to go, his walker's brought in and I see him stand behind it for the first time. He hasn't said anything about it in all the time we've visited, as though it were something with shame to it. He uses it at the hospital entrance to go from the sliding doors to the car with agility and confidence. He helps me fold it and put it in the trunk, then gets in the passenger side of the front seat without help. He's also now just strong enough to give orders again, and coming across Commercial he tells me he wants to go in the west entrance of the building and walk through the lobby. When I try to argue a little with him by saying it's twice as long to the elevator as the north entrance, he says he knows that, it's why he wants to do it, it's what's going to make him strong faster.

The west entrance fronts on A1A, shielded by high hedges and a row of dwarf palm trees, and it's not until I'm fully committed to turning in that we see the two ambulances and three police cars, their lights like small controlled explosions. Joseph comes down the steps and waves us around the small landscaped circle to the north side. His usually cheery wide face is pale, his eyes extra large. As we slowly turn the corner Lillian says, leaning forward, that someone must be sick. Able's response is to say it's something more. He looks at me and explains that the service entrances and elevators are always used by the undertakers. As soon as Sidney, the doorman on the north side, opens Able's door and greets him with a "Welcome home, Mr. Neel," Able asks what's the matter. As he opens Lillian's door he says that Dr. and Mrs. Schermer, as far as anyone can tell, committed suicide. This stops Lillian in mid-rise and she sits hard and awkwardly on the edge of the seat, her dress up above her knees, her feet splayed. "Doris?" she says. "Doris?" Her eyes run up and down the side of the building in a wild search. Able hangs onto the door for support, unable to get to Lillian. I've known the Schermers for years—not well—but to say hello to in the pool and to ask how their daughter is, whom I've met and who's about my age. They have always seemed in good health and spirits. Sidney gets Lillian on her feet, and I see that she's in shock and just short of tears. She reaches out to get Able's hand and, together, they get over the curb and to the steps that lead into the building. I take Able's bag and walker out of the trunk and Sidney tells me to leave the car, he'll park it. Just as I turn, I see I've made an error in judgment: Able has started up the stairs into the building as if he were just coming back from the beach, one hand on the railing, as erect as he can be. Even in his weakness he's much quicker than Lillian and she tries to follow too quickly, trips on the bottom step, and goes down, hands out, face to the side. Able does not notice until I call out and he turns around and looks back from the top of the stairs. Lillian lies on her side on the steps for a long second or two until Sidney gets to her and begins to help her up. "What a silly thing to do," she says. There's a white emptiness to her face, her eyes large and jerking around. She looks up to Able who reaches out a hand to her, as though to tell her to keep moving, there're things to do. Sidney asks if she's all right, and she blinks hard a few times and then says she's just fine, it wasn't any-thing. By this time I've gotten to her, Able's bag in one hand, the folded walker in the other, and Sidney takes them from me and I get hold of Lillian's arm and put the other arm around her waist. There's not much, if anything, left to the muscles of her back. I look up to the top of the steps where Able has turned around and stands, feet slightly apart, steadying himself only with a couple of fingers on the end of the railing. He nods and says, "Come on, Lillian," his voice calm, soft, and more determined than I've ever heard.

Sidney gets us to the elevator and it's there, after the door closes, that the shock of the suicides hits Lillian. She leans back against the brass handrail and looks up at the indirect ceiling lights. Able, as if he knows precisely what's on her mind, says, "Fools."

"Were they sick?" I ask.

"Even if they were," he answers and glances at Lillian. She has great tears in her eyes made all the more prominent by the soft reflection of the lights. She looks like she has little stars in them. "Nothing wrong in being sick," he adds.

I get off the elevator first, carrying the bag and walker, and Able waits for Lillian, who doesn't seem to know where she is until he says, "Eleven, dear." Unsteadily, she comes into the small hall, but just as Able follows her the door starts to close. He doesn't see it until it smacks him flush on the back of the shoulder, and then it's as if he's been hit by something a good deal more powerful. The force makes him lose balance and stumble awkwardly into the hall. It's as if under his trousers his legs have been turned to sticks, the arm and back muscles beneath his light windbreaker and shirt of no use at all. He grabs the edge of the wall next to the call button and with his fingers hangs on to stop his fall. Then it's simply as if nothing has happened: I take out the door key and open it and they go in ahead of me, Lillian straight to the bathroom, Able, using the walker over the high carpet, into the den. Within a few minutes he's got the television on to the market quotes, and even though there must still be a good deal of soreness in his back he sits in his chair as though it's the softest thing he's ever touched. After a few moments Lillian comes in and sits on the couch and leans forward as if that will make it easier to see the television. "Lilly was up while you were gone," she says.

"So I see," Able answers, then turns to me and says he gave her a hundred shares last year. I say I know but he doesn't seem to hear me. He's watching her, tired as he is, so intently that it feels as if I'm hardly in the room. When I ask why he thinks the Schermers committed suicide he says again, this time very quietly, still looking at Lillian, "Fools."

"What do you want for dinner?" Lillian asks him.

"What's there?" he says.

"I'll go see," she tells him and gets up from the couch and goes into the kitchen.

I hesitate for a moment, trying to judge his strength and whether or not I should talk to him about her right now. I open the subject by saying I've been here ten days now and I was thinking of when I might be leaving. His answer is to nod in a way that clearly says he's given the situation much thought. He looks away from me and back to the television and then says what the social worker at the hospital has already told me: that tomorrow the Medicare nurse will come along with the physical therapy people and get him started on a program they talked about in the hospital. He pulls up the trouser on one leg all the way to the knee and shows me the calf muscle, or, rather, what's left of it. It looks no larger than a teenager's arm. The trouser leg then drops straight down and he looks at me and says he's like that all over, the hospital took everything out of him. "When I leave," I say, "you're going to need someone to help you out."

"You're on sabbatical," he says. "Why the rush?"

I tell him I've got to be in England for a month just before Christmas, and then I mention the two libraries I'll be visiting in the spring. England gets some interest out of him and I tell him I've gotten access to some of the family's private letters. "I also have a wife," I say and smile. He puts the topic away by saying we'll talk to the Medicare nurse tomorrow and see what the time frame is for being back on his feet. Just then Lillian comes back into the room and he says, "There's the light of my life." They exchange glances as though they are at a high school dance. But then all that's gone on seems in an instant to catch up to both of them, especially Able, and his initial surge of energy at being home leaves like a dying breeze. For a moment or two his head and upper body appear frozen, even statuelike, his mouth hangs slightly open as though for the first time he now must breathe through it, and he looks as close to death as I've ever seen him. Actually, I think, this *is* a moment of death, that if there are a thousand of them leading to it, this must certainly be one of them. He asks then for Lillian to help him into bed and before she can get up he's shoved the walker around in front of his chair and now makes every effort to stand. Amazing to me, and him, too, is that he simply cannot do it. Elbows out, hands on the arms of the chair, he has no strength and, worse, the angle created by the walker is much too steep for it to be of any support and it slips away on its tiny feet. He brings himself forward to the edge of the chair, reaches out an arm to me, and says, "Give a hand now," which I do, and as he rises he quivers all over from the effort. He grips the walker so hard his knuckles go white and then as he pushes it ahead of him he bends over as though there's a sudden extra weight he must now carry. But after a few steps, when he feels control, his chin comes up and he looks across the hall, his mouth in tight determination, into the bedroom.

After we get him into bed he looks up at me and takes one of my hands and says, "I'm going to be all right, just give me some time." Then he turns over slowly, careful of the incision in his back, and goes to sleep.

"I'll be right here," Lillian tells him and pats his shoulder.

As we go toward the kitchen she tells me she's going to make his favorite dinner, Salisbury steak, then looks at me and says it's so good to have him back. "It's going to be like always," she says and opens the freezer door and takes out five or six of the frozen dinners before she finds what she wants, the steak for him, a chipped beef for her and, after she asks, the same for me. I watch as she hacks at the ends of the packages with a long serrated knife, the frost on the counter like a small pile of gray sawdust. When I ask if she'd like some help, she shakes her head, then to be more emphatic says she always gets his dinner. She smiles at me and then there's a dark sadness that comes over her face. "Did something happen to the Schermers?" she asks. I tell her yes and she nods as though that's all she wants out of me.

"And it was bad, wasn't it?" she says. I say it was and she goes back to the frozen dinners. "I'll ask Able when he wakes up," she says.

In his pajamas, promptly at six o'clock, Able appears in the kitchen doorway, the walker awkwardly in front of him. As he comes toward the table, which Lillian has set while I've gotten the dinners out of the oven, he tells me it's awful damn good to be home and smell the food. He sits in his usual place in the chair by the window that has the ocean view and leans forward to look out. He watches the ocean, then his eyes shift to the pool and the putting green. "My million-dollar view," he says and straightens up to allow Lillian to set the Salisbury steak in front of him. The odor from it is full and pleasant enough that it seems to overpower him—his eyes close and his mouth starts to move as if the food's already in it.

Lillian sits down, having forgotten her own dinner, and I get both hers and mine and set them on the table. Able looks over everything, then asks for ketchup, which I get. As I place it in front of him he says, "What happened to me in the hospital?"

"It's the cancer," Lillian says, her fork wandering into the creamed chipped beef.

There's just the slightest flash of anger that crosses Able's face and he snaps his eyes to mine and says he doesn't mean the operation, it's afterward he's talking about. "I lost a few days," he adds. I tell him about the morphine and his eyes stay on me hard, making sure he takes in everything I say. Then he nods and cuts the Salisbury steak in half, then again, and finally gets a piece that's just right. It looks to me as if it's the best bite of food he's ever had in his life. After he swallows he says, glancing out the window again, that he'll have to remember that. I remind him that he had the same reaction when the pacemaker went in and he nods and says it wasn't like him to forget something like that. Then he looks at Lillian, who's using a half slice of wheat bread to get the food onto her fork, and he says, "They got all the tumor, dear. Every last smidgen of it."

"I know that," she says without looking up.

It's an awkward moment between them in which each seems to have stepped over an invisible boundary: his anger, hers fear. It's just like it was when Benny and I were growing up and there was a significant disagreement between them: she had her say, he barked, and she backed off. Now, though, it's as if everything is in miniature, only the feelings still the same. I break the cloud between them by saying to Able that I think it might be a good idea to consider what they're going to do when I leave. Able bristles at my bringing this up again so soon and he looks at me and says, "We'll get along."

"You could have someone live in," I say. "Help out with shopping, laundry, even cook."

"I've thought about that," Able says quietly, eyes on his plate.

I glance at Lillian, who's staring at him, mouth open, as though truly he is her salvation. "We could go to Lighthaven," she says.

"We're not going anywhere," Able says and Lillian goes back to what's left of the chipped beef. He turns slightly and looks at me, then out to the ocean, and says, "Know what someone like that costs?" I shake my head and he smiles and says, "You couldn't do it on a professor's salary."

"You can't do anything on a professor's salary," I tell him.

He mentions Mrs. McAvoy, a woman in her mid nineties in the building who's had round-the-clock care for ten years now and he says, "She pays fifty dollars a day, eighteen thousand two-fifty per annum." His financial mind never sleeps. He shakes his head slowly, self-pityingly, and starts to say, "Where am I going to . . . ," then stops and instead says, "It'd be a drain, I hope you know that." He looks at me as if I'm the one who's caused the problem.

"If you want," I say, "I'll call Mrs. McAvoy and find out what agency she uses."

"She had a stroke in September," he tells me. "She can't talk."

"Did something happen to the Schermers?" Lillian suddenly asks.

As I start to nod and get ready to explain it all again, Able says to her: "They're all right, dear. Just fine." She nods and smiles, relief everywhere.

Right then Benny calls for Able, and Lillian hands the phone to him across the table. Able is clearly delighted and it appears that all along he's had a hidden reserve of energy. He says he's fine, no problems, just a matter of getting back his strength, and then as though for some days he's been readying a set of questions, he asks Benny how his practice is, if he's got any more TV coming up, what other public appearances he's making, is he seeing any particular woman, and how the IRS audit went. Then, as though the weight of the phone has suddenly quadrupled, Able runs out of strength and tells Benny he's tired and hands me the phone. "Old fart's immortal," Benny says.

"So it seems," I answer and then Benny says that he knows it's a bad moment and could I call him at eight tonight, West Coast time, to fill him in. I tell him I will and hand the phone back to Lillian. She puts it to her ear but it's clear that Benny's already hung up. She is puzzled but then realizes what's happened and, hurt, turns in her chair to put the receiver back in the cradle.

When I call Benny at eleven he tells me his last two patients were no-shows, which was just fine with him, he hasn't had a proper cocktail hour in a week. When Benny's had a few drinks he warms up to the world but also wishes to advise it on all matters of importance, and now is no exception. As if he's been thinking about it for the last five hours, he tells me that Able and Lillian belong in a nursing home, and that he's done some telephone research for me and here's a list of the places I ought to look into. I let him talk and when he gets down to Lighthaven I tell him I brought it up and Able dumped the idea fast, said he wasn't going anywhere but maybe he'd have someone come in to help out. Then, as though he hasn't heard the last part, Benny says something right on the mark: "That's not fair to *her*." I agree, relieved at what he's said, and then ask if he has any suggestions concerning the changing of the mind of the world's most stubborn man. "That's your job," he says. "How'm I to do that from here?"

"You could call Dr. Gandhi," I say. "Get him in on this."

"*Who?*" he asks. When I explain, he asks whatever happened to Armstrong, and I say he died, or at least that's what Lillian said. "They've got an Indian doctor?" he says and I tell him I met him, too, and that he seems okay, even got Able off morphine. "Know where those guys go to medical school?" Benny asks, then answers his own question with "Thatched huts." I try to steer him back to the issue but it's only after he says he hasn't met one worth his salt and watch out for the herbs, brother, that he settles down again and says that what's important is for me to get the best possible help in here that I can. "You've got to shop around," he says. "The home care biz is full of sleaze, druggies, and thieves."

"Considering the vast experience I've had," I tell him, "no problem."

He ignores what I've said and tells me that he's got a contact or two in Miami, he'll make some calls, and get back to me in a couple of days. Then he asks how long I'm staying and I pause and tell him apparently as long as I'm needed. He says he's grateful for that and that if he lived closer he'd be there in a minute. Then he says, "They can't make it alone, can they?"

"From what I've seen," I answer, "not for long."

The Medicare nurse, who introduces herself as Gloria Porter, is a thin, highly efficient black woman, who has two aides, one Jamaican, one Puerto Rican. She has large perfectly white teeth, and a very warm smile. In the den she sits on the couch next to Lillian and does paperwork while the others take Able's temperature and blood pressure, check his incision, and then help him stand so they can take him in for his shower. All the while Gloria asks Lillian questions that, although she tries, she really cannot answer with any accuracy. Able, even with the thermometer in his mouth, corrects her about every other answer, and when Able's finally out of the room that task falls to me. At first Gloria is irritated, but then in a flash of confusion about when Able was admitted to the hospital the first time she glimpses Lillian's dementia, and as she looks at me across the room behind Able's chair her eyes grow large. Although the room has a good deal of indirect sunlight Lillian tells Gloria several times that she ought to turn on the lamp next to the end of the couch. But it's when Gloria asks Lillian for Able's Medicare card that Lillian looks at me and her mind shuts down with anxiety and uncertainty. I go to the bathroom door, open it slightly, and ask Able. As I get the card from the top drawer of the small desk in the den, I notice it's right on top of an Aetna Long-Term Health Care policy. Able's stubborn, I think, but not stupid.

The paperwork finished, Gloria, needing only Able's signature, turns to Lillian and looks at her as if she were her own mother, a tenderness and understanding for her that makes me feel as if I'm not alone. Gloria tells Lillian that she looks to be in good health and Lillian nods and smiles and says she's hardly ever been sick a day in her life. "If you have your health," Lillian says, "you've got everything." Gloria looks over at me and smiles, then reaches up and turns on the light. "Thank you," Lillian says, "that's much better."

Able, exhausted and back in his chair in the den, signs the papers and Gloria says they'll be back Mondays, Wednesdays, and Fridays, then leans over and shakes his hand. Able nods but does not really look at her. When I go out to the front door with them, I ask Gloria how long she thinks my father's recuperation will be and she asks me what I mean by recuperation. "When he's back on his feet," I answer, "the way he was."

"A hundred percent?" she says. "Hardly happens." When I say nothing she adds, "People drop down a notch, if you know what I mean." Then she gives me a warm smile and says it's nice they've got folks to look after them. I blurt out that I'm from Pennsylvania and I'm looking for someone to come in and help them out. She gives her head a small quick shake and says she works for the government and ought not to recommend agencies. I say I understand but as she gets into the elevator she steps forward a little and says, "Sunrise Home Health. You ask for Matildy." Again the smile as the door closes.

The physical therapist, Derek, arrives about twenty minutes later, a Nordic-looking fellow whose blond hair has been dyed more blond and who's wearing an old-fashioned heavy I.D. bracelet with his first name in block letters. He and Able hit it off from the beginning, when Derek asks if the Medicare people have been there and Able nods and says, "First the shower, then the exercise."

"Isn't it the way?" Derek says, helping Able to his feet with both hands. Holding on to the walker for balance, Able looks to have shrunk five or six inches, and when Derek takes the walker away and asks Able to stand straight for him I'm surprised that his old height returns. Although he sways a bit he's able to stand perfectly straight, a fact that seems to impress Derek, who asks his age, then whistles softly at the answer. Clearly, Able likes the attention from Derek and he complies with everything he's told to do, even the overhead exercises with his arms that leave him breathless. It's right then I realize I don't know where Lillian is, and turn and leave the room. She's in the kitchen sitting by the window with the entire contents of her purse spread out on the table. What amazes me is that so much could fit into such a small space. I go over and take a chair at the end and turn it so I can cross my legs comfortably. She glances at me but in some way I don't understand my presence is of much less significance than what's on the table. She regards the contents of her purse the way someone with poor vision might study a chessboard, hands folded in her lap, head halfway to the table. When I ask if I can help with anything, she says, "Emery boards." I answer I don't see any, and she says, "Yes, they're here, they're always here." I have never known her not to have three or four tied with a rubber band in her purse and I'm surprised they aren't on the table now. "This isn't fair," she says, then, "Who was that woman with Able?" I tell her and she looks over toward the door and says she thinks it's possible she took the emery boards. When I softly ask why, she ignores the question and says that the next time the woman's here she's keeping her purse right in her lap. Yes, sir.

At that moment Able appears in the doorway of the kitchen with his walker in front of him, Derek just behind, and Able tells Lillian to watch what he's just been taught. Proudly, with each small step, Able raises the walker off the ground so he's straight up, then sets it down as he comes forward. He looks like an old large toy that can do only one thing. "It's for the arms," Derek says to us over Able's shoulder. When Able gets halfway to where we are, he turns and starts out of the kitchen as if in search of another audience. As they leave Derek says to Able that he's going to have to put some weight on, that he's got a big job of work ahead of him. "Did you meet my son?" Able asks and Derek says yes. I glance at Lillian and see that she's taking each item from the table, examining it, and then returning it to her purse. Her mouth's set in a tight line and although she's not saying anything my guess is that she's already tried and convicted Gloria of stealing her emery boards.

After Derek leaves, Able is flushed with excitement from the exercise and he and Lillian go out and sit on the balcony while I start lunch: tomato soup, Ritz crackers, and ice cream sandwiches I shopped for yesterday. Able has not said so much as one thank you to me since I got here and, as the soup starts to boil around the edges, I think that he can't bring himself to do that because it would mean an admission of weakness and dependence. So long as I do these things, I know he's going to let me do them, and I decide that while we eat I'll confront them with the fact that I have to leave as soon as they can bring in someone to help out. After I set out the soup and crackers and make myself a chicken salad sandwich, I go into the living room and start over to the balcony door. I see that in going out a while ago one of them has pulled back the curtains along the windows and that Able and Lillian are sitting side by side in the two webbed chairs looking out to the left at the ocean, holding hands.

At lunch, the shower and exercise Able's had now makes him nearly feeble with fatigue. The soup hangs on his lips, his jaws work the crackers as if he's got an ill-fitting set of dentures, and his eyes are pasty. Lillian sees none of this and chatters on about the last big party they went to at the club, how the Andersons took the whole place over on a Monday, the day the club is closed, and invited what must have been 250 people: open bar, full menu, everything, she says. Able's eyes rest near the middle of the table. When I ask when that was, Lillian says it must have been July Fourth weekend, but Able corrects her with Labor Day. "So it was," Lillian says.

Able can't eat most of the ice cream sandwich and leaves it to melt on his plate in the early afternoon sun while Lillian, delighted with food she can pick up, licks around the edges, then takes a small bite, then licks again, like a schoolgirl. One hand out for support along the side of the table, Able watches her as though he's enjoying what she's doing more than she. Then, finally, when he can no longer support himself, he drops his head and asks me to get his walker and help him to get to bed. So exhausted is he that he can hardly speak. I get the walker and help him up, then set it in front of him. I walk beside him as he shuffles across the kitchen and then into the living room, where it's much harder to lift the walker because of the rug. He sits hard on the bed, and then goes over onto his side, his breathing heavy from the work, and then by himself gets his legs up. I take off his slippers and cover him and he puts half a hand out from under the top sheet and moves it ever so slightly, as if to say he's all right now. As I reach to turn out the light on the small table between their beds, Lillian comes in and goes around the foot of Able's bed, then around hers, and finally sits down on the bed and takes off her shoes. She stands, then pulls back the one thin blanket and sheet, gets in, and covers herself almost exactly like Able. Without a word, I turn off the light and leave.

In the small hallway just outside the den, the silence of the apartment nearly overwhelms me, as though it is eternal, as though the door I've just closed is to a tomb. I go straight to the top drawer of the desk in the den to get the long-term health care policy, sit down, and begin to read it. The policy carefully states that it will pay fifty dollars a day for in-home care when there has been a *diagnosis and treatment furnished by a physician.* My relief is profound. He's covered and I know he can afford the difference. I go straight into the kitchen and call Sunrise Home Health Care. I say a Medicare nurse named Gloria recommended them and could I make an appointment to interview some prospective aides. Without a word I am on hold, the end of Sinatra's "My Way" suddenly blasting in my ear, and then a woman introduces herself as Ms. Wilson, asks my name and the nature of my request, and I repeat everything. From the small throaty sounds she makes I know she's writing. Then she says it would be most helpful if I came to the office so she could explain in detail the charges involved and sign a contract. We agree on tomorrow morning at ten-thirty and I hang up. It's right then I feel a weight the likes of which I've never known, as if I'm able to glimpse eternity and it is a yellow room with blue flowered wallpaper and a small, narrow bed. I look down at the pool area and watch the older people coming and going, some chatting in groups, others, alone, dozing under cabanas, their legs and feet shiny with oil in the slanting, weak sun.

My depression goes as quickly as it came and I decide to leave Able and Lillian a note saying I'll make chicken tarragon for dinner and that I've gone to the Publix for what I need. As I leave the building, Sidney tells me in vivid detail what happened to the Schermers: the doctor, he says, ordered himself up a bunch of Seconals, about a hundred, and then he and Mrs. Schermer took all but two, leaving those in the bottle by the bed so the medical people would know what had done the job. No note, no nothing, just turned out the light and went to sleep like it was any other night. Sidney shakes his head and asks how my father's doing, says he's a fighter, then asks about Lillian, his big eyes sad, and finally how long I'm staying. I tell him I don't know, maybe another week, ten days. As we talk, people walk through the lobby to the mail room or come and go from the pool area. I look at each one as though he or she could help me.

Dinner doesn't work out. Even when I cut Lillian's chicken in small pieces, the sauce makes it hard for her to see where to put the fork and, finally, she changes it for a spoon and holds it in her fist like a child and eats. Able, in spite of sleeping and resting until the market closed, is no better than at lunch, as though all the hours of rest have only kept him even. I offer to cut his food, too, but he waves me off with the knife and saws away. Each eats about a quarter of what I've made and then, Lillian first, they stop as if the same part of their stomachs have been sewn shut. Able looks across the table at Lillian and says, "I think we need someone to come in." Lillian stares at him expectantly. Able turns to me and asks if I'll look into hiring someone and when I tell him I'll start tomorrow he nods and says, "Someone nice for your mother. No jigs."

"How can I guarantee that?" I ask.

"Try," he says.

Then, as though Lillian's just come into the room, he asks if there's any Milk of Magnesia and says he hasn't had a bowel movement since the fourth day in the hospital. Lillian tells him she'll go look right away and gets up and leaves. Able looks at me again, smiles like he did before, and says, "Try." Lillian comes back holding two bottles of Milk of Magnesia and sets them down on the table next to Able's water glass. "They were right there," she says.

They are both in bed and asleep by nine and I go down to the pool area for a look at the ocean and to feel the sea breeze. Standing at the railing, it's almost a wind, the sound through the palms like knives flying through the night. I see a woman about my age thirty or forty feet away, elbows on the railing, her face in her hands, sobbing. Although I haven't seen her for almost fifteen years, I know right away it's Diane

Schermer. Even when I walk over to her and say my name she hardly knows I'm there, but when I say I heard what happened and that I'm sorry she turns and looks at me, her face an absolute mess, her eyes in the dim light huge, watery, and sad. She says she's sorry, should she know me, then realizes she does and wipes at the slick water on her cheeks and just under her eyes. "No note," she says, "no nothing. Just the goddamn phone call."

"I'm so sorry," I say.

"How could anyone be so cruel?" she says and turns back to the ocean, its blackness even in the warm wind ugly and mean. After a moment she composes herself, sets her forearms on the railing and joins her hands as if she were kneeling in church. "Goddamn control freak," she says, to which I stay silent. She turns and says she means her father, who last year had a diagnosis of prostate cancer and said *he'd* say when and where he died. I ask, in a voice as quiet as I can make it and still be heard, why her mother, too. A thin hard smile slides across her mouth and she turns slightly toward me. "What can I say? That they did everything together?" She shakes her head, her composure, for the moment, almost fully returned, the grief drained out of her. "She was a doormat," she says. "Couldn't have lived without him for ten minutes." Then she turns toward me and bitterly asks if I want to buy an apartment fully furnished and real cheap. I try a smile, the kind that comes with a soft closing of the eyes, and she says 'cause tomorrow morning there's going to be one on the market. I've never seen anyone so vulnerable. It's then she realizes it's strange to see me and asks if everything's all right with my parents, says did something happen to one of them, is that why I'm here? As briefly as I can, I tell her, and she says she hasn't seen either one in a long time. I answer nobody sees them, they stay pretty much in the apartment, that they go out for dinner occasionally. When I ask how long she's staying, she says she hopes she'll be gone tomorrow night, one of her kids is in a play at Georgetown. As if suddenly this is now a brief social event, and nothing's changed in either of our worlds, we trade what our kids are up to and where they are in school, even their majors. Then she breaks everything by saying, "Just long enough to box up the clothes for Goodwill and bag the jewelry." She turns and looks back out at the ocean, rests her arms on the railing as before, and drops her head, then shakes it slowly. "I just don't understand why she went along with it," she says. "There wasn't a thing wrong with her." When I ask how old they were, she says her father was early eighties, mother seventy-five. I say that's awfully young, especially your mother, and she nods, pushes off from the railing, and as she goes by me without a word she lays a hand on my arm. "Good-bye, Diane," I say.

In the morning Able is surprisingly fresh, a sliver of his old energy returned. He eats a breakfast of Cheerios, half an English muffin, and a banana. For the first time since the surgery there's true color to his skin. This, he announces, is the morning that Lillian usually goes to the hairdresser, and she looks blankly at him across the table and says, "It's Thursday?" I say right away that I'll take her, I've got to do some shopping at the Publix for dinner, and they both look at each other and smile. When I say I'm making pasta carbonara for tonight, Able says that sounds fine but he doesn't want any heavy cream sauce clogging up his arteries. What you need, I tell him, is better food than you've been having. "You're too thin," I say.

"Thin's all right," he answers. A glance at Lillian tells me she loves this kind of banter, that it makes her warm and reminds her of years ago.

While Lillian is at the hairdresser, I drive the five blocks south to Sunrise Home Health, a small office in a flamingo-pink one-story building in a shopping center. It's next to a Target store. I'm taken in to see Ms. Grossman, a tall dark-haired woman of about forty whose beauty is remarkable, who refers to herself as the president of the company, and as I sit across from her I'm the one interviewed, not she. Legal pad in front of her, she fires questions for nearly half an hour, everything about Able's and Lillian's medical history and current situation meticulously covered. When she asks what marriage this is for both and I say it's the only one, she pauses and, without looking up, says, "So, a real love affair?" I tell her it's certainly that. She seems moved by the fact that they've been married almost sixty-seven years. Then she lifts the phone and presses a button, says for Claudia to come in, and hangs up. Then she looks at me and smiles, slides her fingers together under her chin, and says Claudia's the case manager I'll be working with should I accept the terms of their contract as Claudia will explain them. I'm beginning to realize I shouldn't have left Lillian at the hairdresser. It's a five-minute drive back to the shopping center where she is and I've got only about twenty minutes left before I have to leave. Claudia is a pleasant, plump woman in her early fifties, her hand warm and fat, her mouth round and with a thick layer of lipstick. She sits as though she's a witness to the contract Ms. Grossman hands me and now reads. She *is* beautiful, I think, but as she highlights the contents of each paragraph and explains it in detail I'm drawn away from her and to the amounts of money for the agency, case manager, aides, mileage, billing dates, rights of termination, affirmative action and antidiscrimination clauses, nurse and manager visiting times, waivers, and on it goes until she hands me the contract and says that in order to have someone in the apartment with my parents, which she can do on two hours' notice, there will be an initial payment of $2,800, $500 of which is a one-time retainer fee never charged again. The daily charge will be $100 for round-the-clock care, billed weekly with two weeks in advance. Total, she says, is $4,200 to get started. Then she says they also take Visa and MasterCard and looks at me as though now I'll snatch my wallet from my back pocket and flip down a charge card. Instead, I fold the contract and ask for an envelope, put it in, and then tell her I'm going to explain it all to my father, that she'll hear from me soon. "It's usual," she says, "for the children to pay."

"I'll let you know," I answer, glance at my watch, and tell her I have to pick up my mother at the hairdresser. I don't make it in time. Through the huge glass windows of the shop I don't see her in any of the chairs nor under any dryers, and inside when I ask the manager when she left I'm told not more than ten minutes ago. She asks if she's my mother and I tell her yes. She lights up and says Mrs. Neel's so nice, so lovely. "Elegant," she adds and smiles even more broadly. I thank her and get back into the mall as fast as I can. The marquee lights of the stores float overhead, the shoppers waver, kids smoking in groups appear hideous as I look for Lillian. The direction I take is based solely on intuition, and I head for the T-section that's the center of the place, but when I get there I've got two other directions to choose from, and it's only seeing a security guard that makes me stop and reason. I tell him what's happened and describe Lillian and he says unless she does something weird like faint or make a commotion nobody's going to notice her. He abandons me as a teenage boy goes by, one roller blade on, one off, and gives him the finger. I look each of the ways I might go and try to see if there're shops she's spoken of, places that might be familiar, something that would attract her. I even try the ladies' room and ask two young mothers coming out with toddlers in strollers if they've seen an older lady with fresh, light orange hair, and give her Lillian's height. Nothing, and neither even acts like it's important. I then go down the east wing of the mall, which I soon see is mostly shoe stores and sporting goods shops, give the end a good look from halfway, and then hurry in the opposite direction. All the time I'm blaming Able for what's happening, saying to myself that if he weren't so cheap an aide could have been with her and everything right now would be under control. I catch myself and realize

I'm just angry at the situation, that probably it's really my fault for trying to do too damn much and I didn't get away with it.

I find Lillian at the end of the south wing sitting on a bench in front of a small fountain that has fake flowers and birds in it, her hands folded over her purse, her feet properly tucked under her. She looks as if she's patiently waiting for a bus, and when I approach she looks up as if I'm only a shape she can't really recognize. I sit next to her and ask what she's doing way down here. A little startled, she tells me she's waiting for Able, it's where they always meet after she gets her hair done and he goes to the bank. She says they're going to have lunch at The Pancake House. My patience has run dry and I tell her she isn't, Able had a kidney out and he's back at the apartment waiting for us and that we'd better get going. "Why, that's right," she says. "What was I thinking?" I help her up and take her arm firmly, then relax my grip and we walk at her pace. As we pass a bank of phones I guide her to them and tell her I'm calling Able to see if he's all right, to which she nods and says that's so good of me. Able picks up on the second ring and I tell him I'd like to take Lillian to The Pancake House for lunch and there's a long pause. His voice breaks a little as he says, "You do that. She'd love it."

Late in the afternoon, when Lillian goes to take a bath and the market has closed, with LLY up another quarter, I ask Able to come out to the kitchen so we can talk about Sunrise Home Health Care. With one finger rigid in the middle of the first page of the contract, he says, "They get this? Really?" When I say they do he stares straight at me, then I say it's not going to get any easier with mother because Alzheimer's is a progressive disease. "Where'd you get that from?" he says, and when I tell him Benny he shakes his head. At first I think he's dismissing Benny but then I realize it's the idea of Alzheimer's. "She's forgetful," he says. "Hell, I am, too. But this other business, no, no." He waves me off with the index finger.

"And her sight is marginal," I say, surprised that I sound so determined, so clinical. From the way he nods very slightly I understand this to be a negotiation. He'll admit to the vision problem if I'll back off on the Alzheimer's. "We just don't talk about it," he says and looks at me, his eyes watery. Then he says it's macular degeneration but that she doesn't really know she's got it. He tells me she'll slowly go blind, but nobody knows how long it takes from person to person. Then he looks away to a corner of the kitchen and says that as far as he's concerned Lillian does not have Alzheimer's, nor will she ever have it. "How do you know?" I ask, my heart rate rising with anger.

"That was just not meant to be," he says. In his blue cotton robe and light summer pajamas, he's more fragile than I've ever seen him. He looks down at his hands as if they belong to someone much older than he. I decide to confront him on grounds he understands: money. What I tell him is that I read their long-term health insurance policy and that if there's a doctor's diagnosis of Alzheimer's Aetna will pay fifty dollars a day for nursing care. I expect now for him to nod and concede, to tell me that, after all, her going to a doctor will be the best thing for the situation. Instead, he says, his reference to the policy, "I know." There is, then, nothing more for us to talk about, and I sit perfectly still, looking straight at him, determined not to leave the table until he's given me assurance that he's going to do what he damn well should. He stares outside at the golden afternoon light, then he says, "Hire someone." Relieved, but hardly disarmed, I turn over the second page of the contract and point to the figure at the bottom and say, "I'll need a check." He leans over and looks at it, then nods and says, "All right."

"The problem with self-made men," Able once told me, "is that they never quite believe they've arrived." I think he said that about either Harry Truman or Lyndon Johnson, which one doesn't matter, but it had to be a Democrat because he's never had a bad thing to say about a Republican. He was, of course, talking about himself, although probably he wasn't fully aware of it, and I bring this up now to explain his racial prejudice, to which he feels fully entitled. Able's social ladder is among the shortest there is, with only three rungs below his: Italians, blacks, and Hispanics. Which of course spells serious difficulties with Sunrise Home Health Care and Ms. Grossman when I go the next morning and tell her my father will hire a full-time aide but that he's requested that whoever is sent be white. "Tell your father," Ms. Grossman says, "to get a life."

"Take it easy on the messenger," I answer and she backs off a little. She says she couldn't get a white aide for a million bucks and that, even if she could, federal law prohibits her from talking about race in any hiring matter. She does say that she can guarantee a thorough background check on anyone she sends: motor vehicle bureau, criminal, immigration, and all medical records and vaccines, and so forth, plus references as long as your arm. "My people are quality," she concludes. I tell her I'll talk to my father and call her.

When I get back, Able is on the balcony and fully dressed for the first time since the operation. In his light green slacks and white short-sleeve shirt, he lies propped on the chaise, feet crossed, eyes closed. He looks up at me when I come out and opens with whatever strength he thinks he has. He raises a hand and says, "No jigs. I told you."

"Fine," I tell him. "Then no aide." Surprisingly, this stops him cold and I seize the moment by telling him that if he doesn't get a little more egalitarian in his worldview he's going to end up with no one. He looks away toward the ocean as if the answer he seeks is there, then turns back to me, his head already nodding in conclusion, and says they need it, no doubt about it, and, after all, I can't stay forever. Then, as if he's prepared a mental list over the last hours, he asks precisely what the aide will do, and I tell him my understanding is that she'll shop, cook, do the laundry, drive mother where she needs to go, look after her all the time. "Just about anything you want."

"And she has to live here with us?" Able asks, hesitant again.

"In my room," I say. My patience at a lower ebb than I can ever remember, I ask him what he would do in the night if mother fell on her way to the bathroom, if he's going to eat Stouffer's Salisbury steak for the rest of his life, and finish off by saying that her eyes are so bad she ought never to drive again, and, since he's too weak to do so, who's going to shop? In a gesture of pure self-pity, more from the fact that I've argued him into the ground than any acceptance of reality, Able turns his palms up in surrender. "It's good," he says quietly. "All right." As I turn to go in to call, he asks when the woman can come, and when I say this afternoon his eyes widen as though he thought this were something that might happen in a week or two.

At five to five there's such a light knocking on the door that it gives the impression that on the other side is a small child, but when I open the door, Able standing behind me leaning on his walker, Lillian a little behind him, what greets us is nearly the largest woman I've ever seen. Holding both a shopping bag of groceries and a small piece of yellow paper, she asks if this is the Neel residence. I nod and as she comes through the door almost all the light from the hallway by the elevator is eclipsed. I tell her who I am, she says she's Charity Williams from Sunrise, and then I step back for what I expect to be at best an unpleasant confrontation. But Able is all charm and lifts a hand in greeting, announces that he's *Mister* Neel and then indicates Lillian and says she's Mrs. Neel. Lillian's eyes search the area in front of her and from the way they move I can tell she's having trouble seeing anything more than a huge outline of someone.

Charity goes to work with a remarkable expertise, as though somehow all apartments are generic, what she needs for dinner found instinctively, how she moves in the kitchen as though she's a professional actress in a familiar play simply now on a different stage. Able and Lillian go back into the den while I sit in the kitchen with Charity. I find out she's married, has two grown children, and is already a thirty-eight-year-old grandmother. She also has a sense of humor. When I ask what it is that her husband does, she says, "Time." I leave it alone and ask who she worked for last and she tells me a ninety-year-old widow, the nicest lady the world's ever known, and only two buildings down so she knows the area, the supermarkets and pharmacies. Then to my surprise she asks about me and my family, and when I mention my two daughters she smiles, her teeth perfect, and then nearly in mid-sentence she changes the subject to Mr. and Mrs. Neel. It's as if she has me cornered in a voluntary way and can know right away who she's working for. This is not, I think, a time to be anything less than honest, and I tell her right away what the medical problems are with both of them. As she stirs a light cream sauce on the stove, she listens intently, then says the agency told her that, what she wants to know is do I love them. I tell her Lillian's like the woman she just got finished taking care of, to which she responds, "*And?*"

"Well," I say, "my father's pretty set in his ways."

"I understand," she says, stirring. "Thank you."

It's right then that Lillian appears in the doorway and politely, graciously, says to Charity that the smell of the food is marvelous. Charity thanks her and then Lillian tells me Able wants to see me in the den. As I pass Lillian she takes no notice of me, so intent is she on watching Charity's dinner preparations.

"What are you doing in there?" Able asks as I come through the door to the den. He gives me no chance to answer. "That woman is *help*," he says. "You don't chat." He snaps his head back to the market wrap-up show, his cheeks sucked in, his eyes large with anger. His right hand, curled over the end of the recliner, shakes as though in the last minute or two Parkinson's has struck. From where I'm standing I can just barely hear Lillian say, "It just looks so good."

"You're not doing this for yourself," I tell Able. "It's for mother."

"That's right," he answers.

The worst, however, is still ahead, and it comes just before dinner when Lillian, who's been in the kitchen talking the ears off Charity, comes into the den and asks Able not only if it's all right if Charity eats with us but also whether she may have his seat because she's so large and it's the only place at the table she'll fit. When Lillian says this she sounds nearly childlike and it's impossible for Able to show anger to her. But when she goes back to the kitchen it's as if Able's a whole new man, his demeanor alive with energy, his new calling that of a full-fledged racist. I remember right then that when Benny and I would let the lawn go when we were kids he'd come home from work on an early summer evening, call us out to stand on the small front porch, and declare that it was time for us to "get this place looking like white people live here." He's now beside himself and says that colored girls ought not to accept invitations from well-meaning white ladies like Lillian, they ought to know better, and then he looks at me and asks why the hell's she doing it. "What's she supposed to do?" I ask, hands on hips.

"Know her place," he says slowly.

He's the last to come in to dinner, his walker in front of him like a small, empty fortress, and the rearrangement of the seating confuses him for a moment. Charity's in his place, Lillian and I across from each other, and he's at the foot of the table where Lillian usually sits. In the middle of the table is a small soup tureen I haven't seen since White Plains, tiny wisps of steam from it carrying a smell that waters the mouth. With some difficulty Able disengages from the walker and manages to sit, then slide his legs under the table. Just as Charity reaches for the serving ladle, Able astonishes me by requesting grace, something I haven't said since I was a child. I glance at him and Lillian, my mind a white blank, and then I say I can't remember how it goes. Without so much as a skipped beat Charity slowly says, "Let us all thank the Lord for this food, for this day, for His eternal blessings and the promise of eternal life." During this Able raises his head and looks at her. On his face is an expression that says he simply cannot believe a black woman's not only eating dinner across from him but is saying his grace as well. Charity, of course, knows this, and in a way that clearly states Able's hardly the first bigot she's worked for she makes her own statement by serving Lillian first, then me, then herself, and, finally, she asks Able to pass his plate. Mouth slightly open, like a child who thinks he's been left out, he hands it to her. As it comes back he asks what it is and she says, "My chicken stew." Cautiously, Able spears a bite-sized chunk of chicken and starts to eat it. Lillian, who's been waiting for him, then goes ahead, too. Able's mouth evaluates the food, then he closes his eyes, and finally he says, very softly, "My God," and looks at Lillian as if she were the one who made it. Lillian, though, is more lost than he, Charity's just breaking into a smile, and I quickly take a bite. Without question, I have never tasted anything quite so good. I glance at Able, who's staring at Charity as if she is now his personal salvation. She could be green with two pointy heads and it would make no difference to him.

It's then I say I think I'll make plans to head home early next week, that with the four of us living here the apartment's going to be crowded. I volunteer to Charity that I'll sleep in the den on the sofa bed, that she's to be in the smaller bedroom off the living room, and she nods as if it's information she already knows. "Do you have a television in there?" she asks Able, as though he's the one carrying on the conversation with her. He looks down at his plate and then back at her and says, "Get a small color one." I say I'll go to Wal-Mart tonight and Charity nods emphatically and says that's very nice.

I'm back by eight-fifteen and have the television set up in Charity's room in ten minutes, the carton outside in the service hallway ready to be picked up. I find Charity at the kitchen table playing checkers with Lillian as if they were lifelong friends, Lillian's face a little flushed from the excitement, her eyes like special blue-and-white marbles. Charity has set a small lamp on the table next to the board so Lillian can see better. "Miz Neel," Charity says as I approach, "you missed this one." She points to a double jump Lillian overlooked and it confuses Lillian, her concentration on me suddenly gone. "How could I?" Lillian says and turns her full attention to the board. Through the small side window in the kitchen I glimpse Able standing on the balcony, his hands on the railing, his neck and chin illuminated by the lights from below. He looks like an apparition that has chosen this moment to appear. His robe blows slightly in the evening breeze and there's the sense about him of someone no longer human, as if I've been allowed a glimpse of what he'll someday become. I watch him drop his head slowly, as if some thought of huge importance has come to him, and let it hang. Then he raises it and, although I cannot be sure, it looks as if there are tears glistening along his cheeks. I touch Charity on the shoulder and tell her I'll be on the balcony if she needs me. "We're fine," she says without looking up. Lillian makes a move on the table and Charity says, "Very good, Miz Neel."

"Well," I say to Able as I step out on the balcony, "what'd you think of that chicken?"

"Just to have someone take care of her," he answers. He turns slightly and I see that indeed he has been crying. He turns and says, "We have to talk," and then with his hand indicates I should sit in one of the chairs. On the floor leaning next to a leg of the other chair is a large worn file folder tied shut with what looks like an old long shoelace. As he sits slowly and then with effort leans over to pick it up, I see that written in the upper right-hand corner is *In Case of Death*. He opens it, untying the bow ceremoniously, and folds back the top to reveal that inside are several sections, the headings of which I can't make out. What I think is that, after all these years, he's going to take me into his confidence, perhaps even share his will and financial status. What I get instead is a story about how he decided a couple of years ago to sell back his and Lillian's burial plots he'd bought in his early seventies. He tells me the reason is purely financial: he's found a place that will do cremations and supply twin urns for a little less than half the price of the plots. He takes a folder from the file and hands it to me. It contains the contract, the names and addresses and phone numbers of those to be contacted when, as he says, "the last of us goes." Before I have a chance to read it, he takes it back and replaces it, then pulls out another file. In it are the instructions for a memorial service. Although of no particular religion all his life, Able has made arrangements with a Presbyterian church two miles south on A1A to hold it. He shows me the canceled check for four hundred dollars, and tells me that if there's any trouble I should remind them of his donation. I ask why he chose that church, since he's never been there, and he says that of all the churches in the area it has the best parking. Next is a list of the hymns to be played, mostly old favorites of Lillian's, the final one to be "Rock of Ages." Next he removes a file that looks thicker than it really is because in it are legal-sized papers folded over. They hinge open on his lap and he studies them for a few seconds, as though unsure if I should hold them. He sits back in the chair to rest, then sets both hands on the papers to hold them down against the mild, warm breeze. Just touching the papers seems to give him strength and he looks over at me and asks if I've ever heard of a living trust. I answer I've had a couple of meetings with TIAA-CREF people about what to do with my retirement funds and, yes, I've heard of it but really don't know exactly what it is. "That's because you've never made any money," he says, his gaze off into the dark air just over the edge of the balcony. This is an old theme of his, what he says almost a refrain, and I am not hurt by it. In fact, I smile and tell him that that's certainly true, then add that an average two percent raise a year puts a blanket over our caviar selection. There's a faint smile but it's impossible to tell if he's amused or if the expression is one of derision. Knowing which doesn't really matter. He explains that ten years ago he and Lillian divided their property right down the middle, says that she owns the apartment and some stocks, he most of the stocks and a few bonds. He says when the first of them goes the other will get the income but not the principal from that trust, that when the last goes the trusts dissolve and the assets pass. He explains that these trusts exist in order to pay less estate taxes. His mouth tenses and his eyes squint as if he sees something threatening in the night. "I hate the government," he says. This is not really true. What he means, I know, is that he hates the IRS and paying even one cent in taxes. He's as loyal an American as ever climbed the Statue of Liberty or stood in front of Rushmore. He still believes we never should have ended the Vietnam War, that if we'd pressed on there'd now be McDonald's and Exxon stations on every corner of the land. I have learned to avoid politics with him, feigning being dumb and uninformed when he's brought up some topic like abortion or school prayer. Able's the kind of man who likes to take a stand on an issue just to pick a fight. He does this because always in his life he's needed someone—Benny, me, even Lillian at times, a secretary or boss at Carbide, doormen, maître 'ds, and so on, even a TV news anchor—to be mad at. More than once Lillian explained his behavior to Benny and me by saying your father's just looking for someone he can yell at, it doesn't have anything to do with you. But there's a special energy to how he now says he hates the government, as if it's what's made him old.

I get up and go to the small window that looks into the kitchen and see that Lillian and Charity have abandoned the game of checkers and that they are now talking to each other, each smiling, both with hands folded on the table in front of them, Lillian more animated than I've seen her in years. "Mother looks very happy," I tell Able. "Charity may just be the answer." Able nods once and looks at me over the top of his reading glasses. Then I come back to the chair and sit down again and watch him put the file back in the folder. "I've shown you this because you need to know," he says, and I tell him I understand and then ask if he's done the same with Benny. He grunts, then shrugs, both the sound and motion weak and nearly undetectable. "Why doesn't he come to see us?" he asks. "Is he punishing us?" Knowing it's futile when Able starts a round of self-pity, I remind him anyway that Benny's on the West Coast and how busy he is. Another grunt is followed by a slow nodding of his head. With great difficulty he gets up and takes slow baby steps to the window to look in on Lillian and Charity, then turns to me and says, "The jig sure can cook."

Two days later I tell Able and Lillian that I'm going to the Blue Marlin Motel right across A1A and stay there. At first they object, but I'm adamant that they and Charity get down a routine without my presence. Why I want to do this is because the communication between them and Charity, and sometimes vice versa, has since the first morning largely gone through me. Able started it and Lillian was quick to follow, although I don't think she knew exactly what she was doing. It was rather like she simply picked up a pattern from Able. It took no more than that first day for me to see that unless I got out they would not be forced to deal with each other. For instance: if Able wanted his walker out in the hall, he would ask me to ask Charity to bring it instead of simply raising his voice slightly to call Charity in the living room, where she's already taken up what feels like permanent residence in one of the large, overstuffed sea-green chairs. Able was quick to resent how she seemed so quickly to make herself at home, and his punishment was an aloofness hardly lost on Charity. "Tell Mr. Neel," she said to the walker request, "that I'll bring it right along." I have done what I can for them and if this relationship is to be long-term I can help it best by my absence. Reluctantly, Able agrees, although he knows I'm forcing him to confront the fact that he has to get along with Charity, at least for Lillian's sake. When I tell Lillian that I'm checking in after lunch she looks at me as though it's the last time she'll ever see me. There's a slight panic and she leans over and picks up her purse from the floor and sets it in her lap, both hands securely around it, as if someone might take that away from her, too. I tell her I want them to start meals on their own, and she calms down a good deal, relaxes and smiles, eyes wide with anticipation. Able follows me to the door barely using his walker, only his fingertips picking it up and setting it down. I realize that already he really doesn't need it. His back's so much straighter than just a week ago and some of his height's restored, his strength building. He looks like he's relieved that I'm leaving and, as though this were actually my departure for Pennsylvania in a few days, he shakes my hand and tells me to enjoy myself at the Blue Marlin and asks where I'm going to have dinner, says that if I want he'll call the club and I can eat free on them there. I say I'll probably go to Nick's down the street and have the sausage and pasta. "And a salad," he says, "get the Caesar." Amazingly, then, he gives me a twenty-dollar bill, as though I'm still a college kid and need to do the laundry. I thank him and put it in my pocket. Then he leans in and says he needs me to do an errand tomorrow, that he wants me to take some things to the safety deposit box down at Sun Trust. He asks if I can do that and I tell him of course. He looks very relieved, reaches out and pats me on the shoulder, and then I go.

It's not until I get back from Nick's that I realize an Italian tour group has taken over the Blue Marlin, with the single exception of my room, and I watch them from the third-floor balcony as if I'm high above a square in Venice or Bologna or Florence. The one thing I did not see when I got the room this afternoon was that between two long hedges about thirty feet from the pool there's a lighted bocce court. All around it now the people from the tour, mostly in their seventies, sit four, five, and six to a table, soda and wine and beer bottles in abundance, portable radios playing, some couples dancing, others playing bocce, but most simply sitting in the mild evening breeze, hands comfortably joined across their round middles, as though this is the same pleasant air of home. I watch them as if before me is a wondrous play, each person with a specific role, each a destiny nearly within reach. They seem so happy and they seem so young. I feel like a boy. Then one of those dancing, who's apparently been watching me, calls out to come down to the party. He lifts a bottle of beer from a table and holds it up to me. At first I wave a little to tell him no, but then the woman he's with wheels her arm in a large circle once, then twice, and as if it's just pure reflex I find myself up and heading for the stairs.

The group is made up of retired union workers from Milan and they come to the Blue Marlin every year in October. The youngest, I'm told, is sixty-eight, the oldest eighty-four, and the union's been doing this for twenty-eight years. They set two beers in front of me and ask where I'm from, what I do, and why I'm here. They say being a professor of literature is very important, that they, too, would like to visit Pennsylvania, and how sorry they are about my mama and papa. A man with two broken lower teeth, whose face glows with the warm night air and wine, says it's no good to live too long. Three others at the table nod in silent confirmation, then one of them touches her cheek under an eye and then moves her finger to her ear and shakes her head. "Everything use-a up," she says. "Wear out."

"The walking dead," the man next to her says. She slaps his hand and says something curt in Italian that makes him feel bad.

Then there's a long time when no one says anything. I watch the bocce game, where a small argument breaks out between two men but is resolved as quickly as it began. People dance, a few holding each other closely, some in stylized moves and pirouettes that each knows is meant to be funny, others with eyes closed while their bodies move as if buoyed by tiny unseen waves. Able and Lillian were like this, but it now seems so long ago.

I get back to my room just as the phone rings. Without carpet or draperies, its sound seems ten times louder than it really is. I expect something's happened, probably to Lillian—maybe she's fallen—and Able's calling and hysterical. Or it's Charity and Able's said something awful to her and she's going to quit. It's Benny, and I'm glad to hear his voice and be able to talk to him without either Able or Lillian there. I bring him up to date on Charity, who Benny calls a saint, and tell him that the only problem is Able being such a goddamn bigot. "He's a sweetheart," Benny says and laughs, then asks if Able got around to going through all that crap about the memorial service and the cremations and obituaries. "Oh, yes," I say and then out of the blue he asks how much I think Able's worth. "That apartment's close to two," he adds. When I tell him what I found out about Able's stocks, Benny says, "You devil, peeking around like that." I tell him it was accidental but admit I couldn't resist. "That much?" he asks, his voice distant as if he's dreaming suddenly about how much will be his and what he'll be able to do with it. I answer that Able's lived a long time and gotten rich on the economy, to which Benny says, "You got that right, pal. When it's all over we're going to have a nice chunk of change."

"A lot of money for a professor," I answer.

"You got a retirement fund?" he asks. I tell him of course, and he astonishes me by saying, "Well, I don't."

"Come on," I say.

"I'm serious," he answers.

"Why the hell not?" I ask.

"Two words," he says with a little laugh. "Casinos and babes."

"God almighty," I say, "you're sixty-two."

"That's right," he answers, the laugh lingering as if without it he would be unable to speak. "I screwed up." Then there's a long silence and he finally says, "I'm going to need that money; it's plain and simple." From time to time I've regretted that Benny and I are not closer, but right now isn't one of them. Melissa started referring to him a few years ago simply as *Loser*. I guess she saw something I didn't want to. Then he asks if I think maybe Able's money goes into another kind of trust and I say I don't know and there's a long "Hmmmm," and he says he wouldn't put it past him.

"How can you even be sure he's left it to us?" I ask.

"Come on," Benny says, "he's going to leave it to a cat hospital, I suppose?"

"People do some damn strange things with money," I say. This triggers a recollection of a patient of his whose family got none of their father's five million bucks. "Not a thin dime," Benny says, "because he suddenly decided he wanted his name on a flamingo preserve in the Keys." He laughs and then cuts himself off as if he realizes it could happen to him, too. "Listen," he says, "can you dig around there and see what the will says? Make sure we're in the chips?"

"No, of course I won't," I answer, then tell him again I found the stock book just by accident and feel guilty enough about that.

"You're talking your future, you know," he says.

"I'd like the money," I answer. "Who wouldn't? But it's his business." Then, as if he's all along been holding it back, he says he might be coming to a conference in Miami just after Thanksgiving and he'll drop in on them and see if he can snoop around. "Not on my account," I tell him, in my voice a distance I hadn't consciously intended, and it offends him.

"The guy did it to me," he says forthrightly, then launches into how twenty years ago on their last visit to Santa Barbara, he knows Able went through some of the files in his den. I ask how and he says he found that the files on his will and divorce settlements had been gone through, and that they hadn't been stuck back in properly, plus the lighthouse lamp on top of the files was turned sideways. "Helped himself," Benny concludes. "Why shouldn't I?" I ask if he ever confronted Able about it and he says he'd just deny it anyway. Able's always respected Benny for being a psychologist, but he doesn't like him much because his personal life's always a mess. Able knows he gambles; he's told me several times how much it pains him, but we've never been much of a family for directness. Benny asks when I'm leaving and I tell him, then he asks how my wife and children are. He has two daughters from his marriages that he never sees, and it's as if he's asking after them. Benny's just never been able to stay out of the fast lane. He says he'll call around Thanksgiving and let me know how things are with Able and Lillian, then we say good-bye.

I go out on the balcony that runs the length of the front of the building and see that it's empty, as is the large area below where the Italians were having such a good time. There's a gentle stillness to the night, the orange lights along A1A like a string of tiny, burned-out suns, and in Able's and Lillian's building only about a quarter of the lights are on, most of the snowbirds still north. When fall is over they'll be back like always, and the building will come alive again. Especially if the weather's good around Christmas, the place will be packed with young families with kids, the way Elaine and I did it several times. Now and then at dinner when we're all home over a holiday we talk about those times and how our daughters couldn't wait to tell their friends at school that they swam in the ocean on New Year's Day.

In bed in the morning I hear the faint melodies of an opera I cannot name, no doubt on one of the boom boxes down by the bocce court, and I smile, remembering that for some people, like Elaine, the first music of the day is as necessary as breakfast. Just as I realize that I've now been here two weeks, the fullness of the light in the room tells me that it's not so early after all, that I've overslept for the first time in years. It's just past nine o'clock, a time I'd ordinarily be in class, and it seems like the middle of the day. I wonder, as I shave, just what kind of effort this visit has taken. Generally, I don't need very much sleep, and often read until one or two, but now I realize I've slept more than eight hours without waking. While refreshed, in a way I'm still tired, as if sleep has been an escape.

Just as I start to cross A1A to the apartment building, I'm astonished to see Charity standing about fifty yards away at the southbound bus stop, the two bags she brought with her on the sidewalk. The double take I do is damn near theatrical, and it's certain from how she stares in my direction that she's seen me. I look at her in true disbelief, then walk down to her as fast as I can. I'm at least ten yards from her when she raises her voice and says, "Mr. Neel fired me, if that's what you're asking."

"He can't do that," I say stupidly.

"Then why am I standing here?" she says. Her eyes burn at me as though she's found a reliable substitute for her rage. Dumbly, I say again that he can't do that, then with a weight as heavy as I've ever felt I understand that indeed he can and did. She tells me she can't go someplace and get fired the third day and expect the agency to send her out again like nothing happened. "Your father," she says, "is

Beelzebub." She says the agency is going to blame her, that this kind of work is hard enough to get with *good* references. As I ask what happened, I suppress a desire to touch her on the shoulder or put a hand on her arm. She says that from the first second she walked in he was frightening, there was something about the way he looked at her that made her feel afraid. "Like he was trying to tell me to go away without using words," she says. She looks over my shoulder down A1A for the bus. "What did he do?" I ask. Her eyes come back to me and she says, "Came into my room right before breakfast and told me to clear out, I was all done here, then left." These are the same words Able used years ago when he told the story of firing one of Carbide's plant managers, Hugh Biggle. He always said how difficult it was for him to do that, but there was something in the telling of it that said some small part of him liked having that kind of control over someone else, however briefly. Then Charity looks at me and asks if she did something wrong. Was she not kind to Miz Neel? Was the food no good? I tell her of course none of that was the problem. Then I say, "Sometimes my father thinks only of himself."

"He can't take care of Miz Neel all alone," she says, pauses and looks away to the sidewalk. "She's so nice."

"She liked you, too," I say. "A lot."

It's then that she looks again over my shoulder and I know by her eyes that she sees the bus. I tell her that if she needs a letter or a phone call explaining why things here didn't work out I'd be happy to supply either. She says she'll have her case manager call me if there's any problem and then she shakes my hand and says again what a lovely mother I have.

I stay right there until she's on the bus and after it pulls away I start across A1A to the building. So absorbed am I in my feelings toward Able that I badly misjudge the speed of the oncoming traffic and have to sprint to the divider. Even so, a blue pickup nearly hits me, the driver's face a blur of anger and intolerance, and then I put one hand out against the prickly surface of a small palm to steady myself. I stand there for a few moments, heart pounding, thinking that this is really all about damn control, that it's Able and no one else who's in charge of everything. It's time, I think, that someone told him that he can do what he wants with his life but he's not going to hurt my mother.

In the apartment I find Lillian at the kitchen table and Able, dressed as if for a golf game, standing at the stove making scrambled eggs and sausage. It's absolutely as it was twenty years ago but with older actors on the same stage. Even how they are dressed is the same. And Able is as prepared for me as if he's been up all night studying for an exam. When, stirring the eggs, he says Charity's gone I answer I know, and tell him I saw her at the bus stop. He does not seem to hear me ask what happened until I ask it the second time, and then he slowly turns to me, his eyes watery with fatigue, and he announces that Charity's a thief. "Don't give me that," I say, to which he looks genuinely surprised. I glance at Lillian and see that she's staring straight ahead as though already Charity's only a swatch of a memory. Quietly, he explains that he found Charity on the balcony with Lillian's purse, where, apparently, Lillian had forgotten it, and that Charity was going through it. "Looking for money no doubt," he says. He takes three warm plates from the oven and sets them on the counter and then, carefully, with the spatula, slides the eggs onto each. "Do the sausages," he tells me and I pick two links for each of us and put them on the plates. He carries his and Lillian's to the table and I follow with mine. Just as I'm about to ask him what now, he bows his head and starts grace, his words a slow careful procession without inflection of any kind. Finished, he raises his head and looks at Lillian. "Eat, dear," he says. It's then that the tea kettle on the back of the stove starts its low whistle and Able looks at me and says, "Get that, will you?" The instant decaf has already been spooned into the cups beside each of the plates. I get the water and pour it into the cups, then sit down again. Able's looking at Lillian with an intensity of feeling that I have never seen before. Perhaps, I think, it's how he must have looked when he first fell in love with her.

We eat in silence for several minutes, Able's eyes going from his plate to Lillian, until I say in a voice as even as I can make it, "What're you going to do when I leave?"

"We got by before you came," he says, turning to me, his resolve plain.

"I'm not worried about you," I say.

He gestures toward Lillian with his fork and says, "You think I can't take care of her?" Before I can answer he turns back to Lillian and says, "Tell your son here if you've ever wanted for anything."

Lillian glances at me, her eyes wide even in the bright morning light, and smiles. Then she places a hand on my forearm. "We're going to be just fine," she says. "We've always been fine." Then she looks in Able's direction and says she's going to get ready to have her hair done, but first she's going to put the TV on for him to check the market. She sets her plate on the edge of the sink, where it sits so precariously that it rocks slightly in an almost perfect balance. I reach out a hand and steady it before it falls into the sink. As soon as she's cleared the room, I turn to Able, who's ready for me, a hand up to indicate he knows I'm angry. "I thought about all of this last night," he says, "pretty carefully. And what you don't understand in the slightest is privacy." The expression on his face seems to say, well, that's all there is to it, discussion ended, you may now go back to Pennsylvania.

"Listen," I answer, "if you want to stumble around here by yourself that's your business, but mother deserves care. And she needs it beyond what you can give her, regardless of your own sense of immortality." In a way, I can't believe I've said this, and I'm certain that Able sees surprise on my face and will take it as a weakness. Instead, he looks at me in a long appraisal, then says, "I'm serious about the privacy." He then says that as soon as I left last night Charity came into the den and sat right down next to Lillian. "Held her hand, for God's sake," he says, "and watched television for two and a half hours. I thought the woman was going to come in and sleep on the floor between our beds."

"That's her job," I answer.

"Not anymore," he says and looks away through the window toward the ocean. His eyes are red-rimmed and still watery, as if his hard determination is suddenly overcome by sweet memories.

"I'm not leaving until you agree to have someone in here to help," I tell him.

For the briefest moment the minute muscles of his face collapse, then tighten again, and he looks back at me. "Let's negotiate this," he says.

"It isn't a business deal," I answer.

He ignores this and goes right on. "If I can show you that I'm quite capable of running this household, that Lillian is taken care of to your satisfaction, then you let me do it my way."

This is, I think, utterly useless. He's going to do what he wants and I'm helpless to do anything about it except stay right here forever. "I don't think you can do that," I say.

"We'll see about that," he answers.

I go back across A1A and check out of the Blue Marlin.

It's Thursday again, the day Lillian goes to the hairdresser. This is, I think, how I'm starting to tell time. Able drives, Lillian rigid and anxious in the passenger seat. I'm in the back with the seat belt on as tight as I can get it, prayer not far from my lips. Curiously, though, Able's not tense at all, his hands on the wheel at ten and two, the center rearview mirror adjusted so he can see out the back window but also see me, too. Twice I swear he winks at me when we're stopped but it's so subtle I can't be sure if it's that or a fatigue twitch. He takes the speed bumps in the parking lot behind the Publix as smoothly as I could, and glides into a space at the end of a row with a right and proper two feet to spare on either side. As I get out to open Lillian's door, Able raises his hand over the roof of the car and says, "You stay there." I watch as he comes around, opens Lillian's door, and then helps her out. Together, her arm through his, they walk slowly across the parking lot, stop in front of the curb, and then, as if rehearsed, each raises one leg and they step up. In just a few more seconds they're gone inside the mall doors. By the car the morning sun is warm on my face.

When after about ten minutes Able comes out, he seems drained of every bit of energy rallied for the morning's effort. He sits in the car heavily, as if even the key is too weighty to lift to the ignition. When I ask if he's all right, if he wants me to drive around to the Publix, he shakes his head, starts the car, and drives off. "She'll be in there about an hour," he tells me as we turn down one of the parking lanes in front of the market. "She loves that someone does her hair." As we get out he takes Lillian's shopping list from his shirt pocket, the three index cards held tightly by the thin rubber band, and looks at it. "Damn it," he says softly, and when I ask what's wrong he hands me the list almost as if it's a gesture of defeat. The first four items are: vegetable soup, tomato soup, cream of chicken soup, and minestrone. "So?" I say, to which he asks if I've looked into the cupboard over the washer and dryer where the food's stored. I shake my head and he says, "Well, about all that's there is soup." He pauses as if what he's gotten himself into is suddenly too much and then says, "Maybe fifty cans." The next card is empty except for *Stouffer's*.

Inside, he needs some help yanking one of the shopping carts out from the long line it's in, and then he's off with the cart in front of him as though it's a new walker. I follow close behind, although a discreet distance away so he won't feel I'm about to pounce on him with help. Truly remarkable is his ability to remember, or at least take a calculated guess about, what's needed. He gets the soup, with a glance at me that says mind your own business, and nine or ten frozen dinners, and in between his eye seems flawless in what it spots and how quickly. One thing I know they need is margarine—the dish was empty after breakfast this morning and there was none in the refrigerator—and as we pass the dairy cases it's as if he reads my mind. But first he goes by the selection, then backs up as though a message has come to him and he's waiting to understand it fully. Finally, he leans over and takes two one-pound packages and drops them into the bottom of the cart. He gives me a quick look as if to say, "Take that." So thorough is he in what he gets that for a while I don't understand what he's really doing. Then it becomes clear that he's trying to get almost everything that he thinks of, as though, if he makes enough guesses, he'll get about everything right. When the cart's nearly half full, Able is suddenly very tired and asks if I'll push it for a minute or two. I take over right away and he walks beside it, one hand in a tight grip on its side edge. Still moving, I put in a fat six-roll package of toilet paper, which causes not more than another glance, and then he asks, his voice soft, if I can think of anything else. Where I was smug before in thinking that he was going to botch things up and make a fool of himself, I now look over what he's gotten and see that in his way he's been more thorough than I could have imagined. In the checkout line I ask him what he'll do if he's forgotten anything. "Get it next week," he says. He looks up then at the large clock on the wall over the front windows and says we'd better damn well hurry up 'cause Lillian's due out of the hairdresser's. The groceries bagged and back in the cart, we go out and toward the car, Able's pace now significantly slower. I see sweat on the back of his neck and along his collar, and the back of his hand is corpse-gray from how hard he holds the side of the cart. He takes his keys from his pocket and presses a button on the flat keyholder that flips up the trunk lid. I see him smile at this, as if the gadget satisfies some long-ago unfulfilled childhood wish. "Had it put in," he says. "Something, isn't it?" I don't tell him that most cars have this now, but instead ask if he'd like me to drive. He doesn't answer until I've put the last of the bags in the trunk, and I've taken his silence to mean no. Then as I close the trunk and turn, he's holding out the keys to me. I take them and get in the driver's side, hit the button that unlocks the doors, and Able slides in slowly. It takes great effort for him to reach out and pull the door closed.

At the curb in front of the mall entrance for the hairdresser's, he asks me to go in and get Lillian. I say sure, then remind him it's only been a little over two weeks since his surgery, that he ought not to try to do everything. As I open the door and get out I add, "Even though you think you can." There's no doubt about my tone, and as I pass in front of the car and glance at him through the windshield I expect a scowl or at least a shadow of anger across his face. Instead there's an expression of satisfaction in his slight smile, as if he's heard in my voice the first signs of his victory. Right then Lillian comes out through the huge glass doors looking as if she's actually seen us from inside and for a second or two it's as though nothing's wrong with her at all. But then I see that clearly she's confused and it's her anxiety that has driven her outside. She doesn't see us at all, her head going right and left like a confused child's. Even twenty feet from the car she has no idea we're there, but when I say, "Mother, right over here," she smiles and relaxes. I open the back door and as she gets in I notice that her hair is nearly as flat as it was this morning, and that there're still flakes on her scalp. She has not had her hair done. It's been fluffed a little and heavily sprayed, but it sure hasn't been washed or set. As I get in the driver's side Able asks how the hairdresser's was and Lillian says, "They're just so nice in there." Able smiles and turns to me and says she's been going there for over twenty years now. It's a fact that seems to give him great satisfaction. I keep my mouth shut, although it's difficult. Maybe next week, I think, they won't rip her off. Then I wonder what kind of holes her mind must have that she can be in a hairdresser's for an hour and not know, or remember, what they did to her. Did the woman tell Lillian five minutes after she was in the chair that she looked terrific and all that was left was the dryer, which ran on low for forty minutes? Then did she fluff her up and spray the air all around her and that was it, the woman giving a wink to the cashier as Lillian went to one of the straight-back chairs by the window and was handed a magazine? "You look beautiful," Able says to her as I drive off.

Sidney tells us that the repairman from A&E Electronics came by but he wouldn't let him up to the apartment because no one answered the intercom. "That's absolutely right," Able tells him and turns to me and says something about the crime rate going up in Fort Lauderdale. Then he looks at Lillian, who's staring out the huge windows of the lobby, and says, "Did you call anyone?"

"Don't think so," she says, preoccupied. Able looks at me for an instant and then knows that Lillian did indeed telephone. Able asks what happened and the doorman says the guy went away and he wasn't very happy. "I wouldn't be, either," Able says and we head for the elevator, Lillian holding his arm like we're all in a procession.

It's not more than twenty minutes after we're in the apartment, the TV in the den religiously on CNBC, that Lillian comes into the kitchen. She says she's looking for her purse, that she needs her magnifying glass. The purse is back in the den, and I get it for her. I watch as she takes the magnifying glass out, then reaches for the telephone book, and laboriously begins to look through it. I ask if I can help her find something and she says she can take care of it on her own, thank you very much. She finds the number, writes it down on one of the index cards in her purse, and then one by one pokes at the numbers on the front of the phone. There's a long pause and then I hear her say she's Mrs. Able Neel from 4900 North Ocean Boulevard, apartment 11J, and that there's a problem with her television. A pause and she goes on to say there's no color, there hasn't been for a while now. Then she becomes confused as, apparently, the man on the other end tells her that he sent someone out not more than an hour ago for an appointment and no one was home. Lillian denies this, says she never made any such arrangement, and politely suggests there's been some mistake. She's silent for a few seconds and then says, "Of course I want you to come. Tomorrow between ten and twelve will be fine." Another lull. "I will be here," she finally says, and then adds, "Good-bye," and hangs up. She looks at me with the pride of someone who's done something good, who's in charge. I don't even have to go to the den to know that there's nothing wrong with the television, it's her world that's gone gray. She gets up from the table and touches me on the shoulder as she passes, says why don't I come into the den and watch the market. I say I will in a minute and when she's gone I take the number she wrote down and call the electronics place, explain what happened, and cancel.

In the den Able's asleep in the recliner and Lillian's lying back on the couch, shoes off, one arm across her eyes as if she feels that since he's napping she ought to be, too. Right then I see through the floor-to-ceiling window that on the narrow service balcony that runs along the street side of the building two men in dark suits are wheeling out a body from some apartment on our floor. The gurney goes past slowly, so close to Able that if there were no glass he could touch it. In the sky beyond the men, even beyond the great flatness of the city, there are huge late-morning thunderclouds hanging in the light, washed-out blue. Some already have anvil tops and are nearly finished but others that are still rising seem like mushrooms and tumors and fists. It'll be late afternoon at the earliest before they get over here. I glance at each of my parents, Able in heavy sleep, mouth open, Lillian, her arm still across her eyes, and wonder at the power of living, how the desire for still more life hardly diminishes from moment to moment. They seem to take energy to live from each other, as if each says *if you're here so am I, because you're here so am I.*

I make lunch for them, two peanut-butter-and-jelly open-faced sandwiches on toast, with skim milk, a banana for him, a diced peach for her, and put eight or ten cookies on a plate in the middle of the table. Able's groggy from his nap, but Lillian is delighted with the sandwich and says I've got just the right combination of jelly and peanut butter, that it tastes so smooth. Able eats the sandwich in a familiar moody silence, the likes of which I've seen rarely in recent years, but I know it's a warning that in some small way he's going to pick a fight. And, just as he's peeling the banana, he begins to, but this is no quaint argument about politics or affirmative action. "Will you give me a kidney?" he says and then, right away, changes it to "*Would you?*"

"I beg your pardon?" I answer.

"You heard me," he says quietly.

I glance at Lillian, who long ago learned to turn her head away as though hearing private music. She stares out the window as if she's alone. Able takes no notice of her, his eyes hard on me. "Do you need one?" I ask. The question's direct enough that it disarms him and he stares at me in evaluation. I decide to push forward and ask if he's peed blood again, at which point Lillian rises silently from the table and heads out toward the den. His expression is gaunt, the mouth turned down, and I press him again. "So, this is theoretical?" I say.

"Would you?" he asks.

"Depends on the matching," I answer, then add, with a nod, that I'm O-negative.

"Assuming all that," he says.

"I'd try to talk Benny into it first," I say.

"I'm serious," he answers. "I want to know." There's a flash of panic on his face, water in his eyes, his lips tight.

"You'd do it for me, wouldn't you?" I ask. Clearly he hasn't thought about this. His eyes blink rapidly as he thinks.

"I would," he answers, "of course I would. However, not at the current moment." Then he smiles and adds, "And you would, too. I know you would." He gets up then and shuffles along the kitchen floor with steps tinier than I've ever seen him take. In our way, we have said we love each other.

At four in the afternoon Able tells me that when he went in for his two-hour nap he called the club and has reservations for dinner. Lillian is as happy as a child surprised by a circus ticket, and immediately she's animated and starts to get ready, even though she's got almost three hours. When she's in the bathtub I decide to be as direct with Able as I can. I remind him I'm leaving in two days and I say that in my considered opinion the two of them can't possibly get by without full-time help. He stares at the final market quotes as if I said nothing, as if I'm not even there. He's fresh after his nap, the effort of the morning obviously dim in his memory. "Will too," is all he says.

"It's not you I'm worried about," I tell him and gesture with a thumb over my shoulder in the direction of the sound of the running water. "It's her."

"I will take care of her," he says, as if it's a regal pronouncement.

I slap my hands on my knees and stand up. "Fine, fine," I tell him. "But why would you run the risk of hurting her?"

"I'm doing no such thing," he answers. He snaps his head at me and says, "This is our life. We'll live it as we choose."

"You're heading for disaster," I answer.

And it's not very far away. During dinner at the club, where Able has two glasses of burgundy, he seems to take little notice of Lillian rising to go to the bathroom. He raises one hand as if to dismiss her, his eyes on the band, the other hand lightly keeping time on the soft tablecloth. I watch her as long as I can—until she rounds the far corner by the maître d' station—and then check the time. At ten minutes, just after Able's said, "Isn't this place just great?" I ask what he thinks I should do. He waves me off and says she's often in there talking with this hen or that, then smiles as if the thought pleases him. At twenty minutes I tell him I don't like how long she's been gone and he looks at his watch and shrugs, then says for me not to be such a worrywart, she's all right, he knows she is. Five minutes later I'm standing in front of the ladies' room waiting for anyone to come out so I can ask if my mother's in there. When no one does, I finally shove open the door and call out for Lillian, get no answer, and then go right in to find the place empty. I'm suddenly hugely angry with Able and terribly frightened for Lillian because it's possible that she's had nearly a half-hour start on wherever it is she's gone. Outside, all around the club, are the small canals and boat slips that access the Intracoastal Waterway, which now, as I stare out the huge floor-to-ceiling windows of the dining room, look like asphalt streets. I ask myself what the hell is a nearly blind, half-daft woman going to make of *them?* It's on my way back to Able that I tell Eduardo that my mother has been missing for nearly a half hour and ask if he or any of the staff has seen her. Eduardo lifts the phone and presses two buttons, then asks the carhops if Mrs. Neel's been out that way. He shakes his head to me as he listens. I ask if he could have some of them—"anyone," I say—look around the grounds, just to check if she's out there. In response to his quizzical look, as though I've asked about a missing child, I tell him she's got Alzheimer's. "No," he says. "Not Mrs. Neel."

"*Yes,*" I answer. "Mrs. Neel."

"Who would have guessed?" he says. Then as I turn away I see him press two more buttons, the receiver hard to his ear.

From across the dance floor I see Able's turned his chair to sit cross-legged and relaxed. This is the position he used to assume after a holiday dinner at home when sometimes he'd have a stinky cigar and a glass of port and tell Benny and me what was right with our family and wrong with just about everyone else's. They were rare moments in which he felt—I think justifiably—pretty good about himself and what he was doing with his life. As I approach, the slight tilt of his head to the left reminds me of the times he had too much wine and his bland recollections somehow transformed themselves into lectures on what Benny and I should do with our lives, or on the virtues of how Richard Nixon was going to sell his family to America in 1960, or the criminal dealings of Joe Kennedy before he got to be a hoity-toity ambassador. All this rushes back within a few steps and I can feel my anger at his self-centeredness spring alive. I realize as I approach that quite possibly he will sacrifice Lillian in order to have his life absolutely the way he wants it to be—and I have to stop that right now if I can.

"Well, she's gone," I tell him, jacket open, hands on my hips. He slowly raises his head and looks up at me as if I've said something to him in Chinese.

"She's in the ladies' room," he answers. He has no understanding of my saying that she is *not* in the ladies' room, as if no fact or statement could possibly alter the picture in his head.

"She's gone," I say again. The certainty of my information makes me feel powerful, as though I'm in possession of the one piece of evidence that can now change him.

"Where?" he asks weakly, the truth of things slowly setting in.

"God knows," I answer. Then, after a second in which I hope he's feeling some degree of my own panic, I tell him that Eduardo has people looking for her and that I'm going outside, too.

I put out a hand like a traffic cop might in front of a child and tell him he's to stay where he is. He ignores me and starts to rise, both hands pushing up on the arms of the chair. "I'll find her," he says and I put a hand on his shoulder and gently push him down. He offers no resistance at all. "You stay here," I tell him. "You're too weak." This makes him angry and even more determined and stubbornly he rises again and I have to sit him down again. Nearly exhausted, all he can do is glare up at me, in his eyes a fire and energy that's all-consuming, as if his resentment goes far beyond me and even his own physical limitations, as though he's justified in being angry at time. Then his body, as if made of not much more than inflated paper, sags into the chair and he drops his head and nods. He dismisses me with one hand, saying, "Find her, find her." He's near tears and I want to stay with him. Instead I tell him I'll do my damndest and hurry across the dance floor toward Eduardo, who's signaling me with a raised hand. As I get to him I smile, thinking he knows where she is, that a carhop or one of the pool staff found her, it's all right now. "Nothing, Mr. Neel," he tells me, arms slightly out from his sides as if already he's given up, as if this is really just a pain in the ass for him. In a moment of what I recognize as pure irony I have a flash thought of my long-time friend Lou, who teaches at Dartmouth and whose parents moved to Hanover to be with him. I think of our e-mails about the lives of our parents and how we've naïvely talked of their growing old with grace, able to embrace one day the dignity of death. A few problems, sure, but if his mother wandered off in the night up there she'd be dead in an hour or so. "What do you mean, *nothing?*" I ask Eduardo. To this he shrugs and I want to slug him. "Call the police," I say, and the idea staggers him so that he backs away from the phone and at the same time gestures toward it. "Dial nine," is all he says. This is an easy decision because I know what else is just beyond the club grounds: narrow, dimly lighted streets, houses with tall, dense shrubbery. I tell the police what's happened and they respond more quickly than I could have imagined. As soon as I get out on the front steps, one car is pulling up, another just making the turn into the grounds. I repeat myself to them, giving her name, age, and condition, and one of the officers comforts me by saying this is the second call they've had this evening, everything will work out, I'll see. As they start out into the neighborhood, two on foot, two in their car, Able is suddenly right beside me, his eyes wide on the parked police car. "What'd you do this for?" he asks.

"Because I want to find her," I tell him.

"She's here somewhere," he says. "She never goes far." He realizes right away what he's said but there's no effort to cover himself. The words just plain hang in the air as I turn slowly to him and say, "How long's this been going on?"

"Six months," he answers softly.

"How many times?" I ask.

"A few," he says.

"Oh, really?" I say, expecting him to give some further explanation, but he doesn't. From where I'm standing by his side I see his eyes have watered, that tiny reflections from the distant streetlights are everywhere in them.

"She's right around here somewhere," he says. "She's got to be."

"I hope so," I say.

Then we both hear the police begin to call out Lillian's name, alternating it with, "Mrs. Neel?" in regular intervals. The words sound eerie and very distant, as if they come from a place between here and death I cannot get to. I turn my head almost fully to Able and say, "Somebody's got to be with her. Do you finally understand that?"

"I've been a fool," he says, then reaches up and takes my arm as though he's become her and I him. He holds it more tightly than I think he has strength for. We stand on the narrow steps of the club for a long time listening to Lillian's name being called and watching the long white lines of the police lights, both flashlights and car headlights, duel with the heavy vegetation. Softly, Able begins to cry. It's not anything hysterical, not even close to it; rather, there's a letting out of tears accompanied by soft throaty noises, as if he's trying to speak in a new, much simpler language. It's the kind of crying one does when there's sadness that cannot be comforted, as if inside one there's a howling wind only the slightest portion of which gets out. I pat his hand on my arm but there's no response, no acknowledgment at all that I'm even there beside him. I glance at his face to see him staring out into the night as if he alone might see through the dark to where Lillian is.

When one of the carhops asks if we'd like to sit down, it takes Able a few seconds to understand him, and then we both go and sit on the folding chairs by the side of the entrance. We watch people leave the club after dinner, but we're sufficiently back in the shadows that there's no interaction even with those who know Able and Lillian well. Able sits straight up, hands on his knees and rigid because it's what's best for his back. He looks like he's just taken in a huge freeing breath of air and has decided not to exhale. "What am I going to do if they don't find her?" he asks.

"They will," I say and put a hand on his. He recognizes instantly that I'm patronizing him and snaps his hand away.

"I asked a question," he says.

"I don't know," I answer.

"I could not imagine a day without her," he says, but this is not directed to me. It's as if he's uttered a spontaneous thought. Then, as though he's looking into the distance for an answer, he says, "Your marriage is good, isn't it?" I say it is and he goes right on with, "I idolize her." His face seems to glow with the thought, as if he sees her coming toward him through the dark.

Astonishingly, it's not more than a few seconds later that Lillian does appear—with a cop on either arm—just coming out of the shrubbery across the parking lot. In the dim lights from the front of the club they are like apparitions from eternity. I see them before

Able and spring out of the seat and go between the two police cars and straight across the small asphalt circle to them. At first I think that she's all right—she's actually smiling and looking from officer to officer as though in wonderment—but then I see the cuts on her face and the bruises, one above the right eye, one below it, and the way her lower lip is split about a quarter of an inch right on the center crease. I ask the officers if she's all right and it's Lillian who answers with, "Where's Able?"

"Right here," he says, just coming up behind me.

The officer on her right says that they should take her in to the emergency room at Broward General just to get her checked out, and almost before the sentence is completed Able says they're doing no such thing, he's perfectly capable of taking care of her. He steps next to Lillian and takes the officer's arm from hers, replaces it with his own, and then begins to lead Lillian to the car. The police look to me to stop him and as I turn to go to the car I tell them that if there's anything really wrong with her I'll take her myself. Then I ask if they know if she fell and they say from what they got out of her she just wandered around the yards of some houses until one of them caught her in his light not more than five feet from a pool. He smiles and says she was sitting on the rear of a diving board like it was a park bench. "Damn lucky is what I'd say," he tells me. Moving off further, I say thank you and reassure them that I'll look after her.

In the car, I drive and Able and Lillian sit in the back, he with an arm around her. She lightly touches the cuts and bruises on her face, as though their origins are already mysterious to her. When I tell her that she's going to be fine, that she may be sore and tender for a while, she nods. With a quick glance, I catch Able's eyes in the rearview mirror and see that he's crying silently. "When we get home," I tell him, "we have to talk."

He sits Lillian in a chair at the kitchen table, turns the hanging light on, and shoves the dimmer switch up as far as it'll go. She lifts her head in its direction as though she seeks warmth from the sun. Her face is not badly torn up, but it's clear it's going to take several weeks for it to be normal again. As if all along he's had a plan, Able goes to the bathroom and returns with hydrogen peroxide, Q-Tips, and a packet of small gauze pads. Like an artist at a crucial point in a painting, he starts in on her, a dab with the peroxide here, a stroke of a Q-Tip there, the small cuts along her cheeks and the one on her lip suddenly redder. Throughout, Lillian makes no objection, her voice curiously low and intimate. What she wants to know is what happened to her and if it was her fault. Able and I reassure her that it was only confusion that caused her to wander off, and Able makes a joke of her wanting to go for a swim. Even through the winces, she keeps her head turned up as though offering it to Able to do with whatever he wants. Finally done, Able steps back and says, "Well, there," and is quite pleased with how he's cleaned her up. It's only then that I see the knuckles on her right hand have been scraped severely enough that on the index and middle fingers some flesh is missing and that two tiny pools of blood have congealed in the first layers of scabs. So far as I can tell, she does not know it's happened. I show Able and he immediately gets Epsom salts from the bathroom and fills a salad bowl with very warm water, then lowers the hand into it. It stings Lillian a bit, but almost immediately the heat and salts combine to make her hand relax, the blood mixing slowly with the water. "I'm hungry," Lillian says, and instantly Able gets down the Ritz crackers from the cabinet and then the slab of Cracker Barrel cheese from the bottom of the refrigerator. He cuts the cheese squares precisely and places one on a cracker and hands it to her. Her mouth, though, is so dry that she is able to take in only the first half of the cracker, the other falling in a shower of small pieces down her front. Able gets half a glass of milk faster than he got the crackers and after she takes a large sip she's able to eat three crackers right away. Her watery eyes are so open and relaxed that it's as if a great joy has come to her. She flexes her hand in the water and then looks down at it as if it belongs to someone else. Slowly, Able takes it out and begins to pat it dry. He does not touch the scraped areas but, rather, bends his head and blows softly on them. Lillian looks down at her hand and studies it, then says, "How in the world did that happen?"

"You went to the ladies' room at the club and wandered outside," I answer, unable to keep the irritation I feel at Able out of my voice. "Probably through the pool doors." Slowly, Able helps her up and together they go out of the kitchen toward the bedroom. "Sleep well," I call to her, then say to him that I'll see him right here when he's put her to bed.

Fifteen minutes later he comes back into the kitchen, hands up as if already we are in the middle of an argument and he's asking me to be quiet so he can make a point. "I'm convinced," he says. "Tomorrow you get anyone you can in here."

"I'm staying until I know she's safe," I say, to which he nods, and then eases himself into the chair on the other side of the table. He puts his face in his hands and then slowly shakes his head. "It's all over," he says. I'm not buying into his pity, so angry am I at what he's damn nearly done to her. "Privacy and freedom," he adds, as if I've asked what's over.

"All you need is someone to stay with her," I tell him. "A companion."

"We've been here thirty years," he says. He raises his head, his eyes red and watery, hands shaking slightly, and looks around. "What joy," he says and then looks straight at me. "There's nothing wrong with my mind, is there?" he asks.

"In what area?" I say and fold my arms.

"I won't get like Lil, do you think?"

"No," I answer, "but you won't own up to your responsibility to take care of her." To this he nods slowly as if finally I've gotten through to him.

"Do you believe in heaven?" he asks, and I simply don't answer because I know it's a diversion. "Do you?" he pushes, and I know he's suddenly scared, that what he wants is for me to tell him his life and Lillian's will go on forever.

"It'll be all right," I tell him.

"But you don't believe that," he says. When I slowly shake my head he says, "Well, what then?" It's as if he's expecting me to throw at him a maze of abstract words in which I've buried some personal answer. His face is stern, he's still ready for combat. "I'd like to be remembered as somebody who didn't hurt a lot of people," I say.

"So you think that's what I'm doing?" he asks, then pushes back from the table and grips the end with the fingers of both hands, his back perfectly straight.

"It's what you did tonight," I say softly, as if he's asked nothing more than the time. Then I add, "By the way, I know about her fall. Joseph told me." This is more of a blow than I intend it to be. From his face it's not so much that I know what happened as it's the jolt of recollection. It's as if he sees her again rolling down the concrete steps of the building.

He turns his head to look out the window, although in the darkness there's nothing to see but a few dim lights across the way. He stares at them for a long time, his eyes going from one to another as though each might have an answer for him. Finally, he looks back at me and says, "You make a good point." I nod, feeling like maybe after all he's coming to his senses and is going to do what's right for Lillian. Then he startles me by saying that in addition to getting someone in to help out he's also been thinking about Fair Oaks—he says he saw Lighthaven a couple of years ago and didn't like it—and would I go with him tomorrow to have a look. I tell him as soon as an aide sets foot in the apartment. He stands and takes the two or three small steps to where I am and reaches out to shake my hand. I rise and suddenly he embraces me, both hands on my back, and we stand that way for a long time. Then he turns and leaves without a word.

I sit again, this time in the seat where he was, and reach up to turn out the light. The full moon hangs over the ocean like a postcard photographer has stuck it there. I remember Elaine and I once sneaked out of the hotel when our daughters were asleep and not fifty feet from the ocean made love under a moon like this. We were in our thirties and knew everything then. I want to call Elaine and remind her, but I sit still. My relief that Able will go to look at Fair Oaks tomorrow is nearly profound. I imagine the two of them sitting in rockers on a verandah holding hands, caretakers everywhere around them, she safe, his every need met. Soon, I think, I'll be going home.

At five past eight in the morning I call Sunrise Home Health Care and the reception is very cool. The episode with Charity, I know, has done Able some serious damage. When the case manager tells me that there's no one immediately available I remind her that I've read the contract carefully and the agency has two hours to supply an aide. More stony silence until I bring myself to apologize for Able and to explain that the care I want is not for him—"He can go jump in the Intracoastal," I say—and then she comes around and tells me that Charity thought Lillian was the nicest woman she's assisted in a very long time. I tell her I've had a long talk with my father and that he's promised to mend his ways, that things this time will be different. After some hemming and hawing and flipping through what sounds like a Rolodex, no doubt for effect, she tells me I can expect one Mayflower Jackson around ten o'clock. This time I'm smart enough not to ask the woman's race and thank her several times, my relief bubbling over. She says she'll be temporary, perhaps not more than a day or two, until one of the permanent staff comes free from a case. "Fine, fine," I tell her. "Whatever you can do."

When I call for an afternoon appointment at Fair Oaks, I get a woman practicing to be a Southern aristocrat who has an accent dripping in oleo. She's concerned that I want to come so soon, as though she thinks seeing Fair Oaks ought to be a social event made more appealing by the buildup of some days' anticipation. I tell her it's not for me but for my parents, ninety-two and ninety, and she says in that case how's one-thirty? Then she asks if I'm aware of their fees, and when I say no she tells me it's a one-time $50,000 nonrefundable charge, plus daily room tariffs depending on whether they'll be in independent care, assisted living, or the full-time nursing section, "Gateway." I ask what the cost is for assisted living and she says it's currently $91 a day each, which of course includes everything, even once-a-week gourmet meals. In my mind I can just see Lillian trying to dig a snail out of its shell. "Fine," I tell her, "one-thirty." I ask her name and she says it's Miss Golly and she's in Room One on the first floor.

At quarter to eleven Mayflower shows up and I'm surprised but delighted that Able apparently doesn't want much to do with her. He stays in the den watching the market while I show her around. Lillian at first is confused as to who she is and several times calls her Charity. But after about half an hour she's got Mayflower's name in her mind and the two of them are sitting out on the balcony while Mayflower's talking about her five grown kids. Mayflower says she might be temporary or permanent, depending on what the office wants, but I know that she's gotten it all from Charity and is here to do some interviewing of her own. By the time Able and I leave, great calm has come over Lillian. I think that if Able will permit it, the two might become inseparable. But in the car I sense a mood in him that I plain don't like, as though Mayflower is a rival of some sort, as if at a high school dance Mayflower has just rudely cut in. To my saying that maybe Mayflower might work out really well, he answers that Fair Oaks could be just the thing they've been looking for. It's not until we get out of the car in the great semicircle in front of Fair Oaks' main building that I realize that during the night the weather's changed for the first time since I've been here. The sky's a stunning blue, the tropical air suddenly gone elsewhere, in its place the vague feel of home and fall. Able seems to sense it, too, and he looks around as though there's something about everything that makes him uneasy.

Being politically correct, as my profession demands, I address Miss Golly as *Ms.*, and, boy, is it a mistake. Her glance says I'm one of those liberal Northerners whose ancestors raped and pillaged her people and I belong in chains. She is remarkably good-looking, probably in her early thirties, and has an accent that's a work of art. She also has a gift for dealing with people like Able. In her office we sit in two low soft chairs in front of her desk, Able uneasy and anxious. Although I've told Able what the fees are for the place, he plays dumb, and Miss Golly has to start from the beginning. But she does so with an ease and demeanor that is just short of flirtatious, and within five minutes of her going through the brochure she's got him right in the palm of her hand. It's then that she asks what his and Lillian's medical situation is and Able stiffens, says he's just fine except for having had a kidney out. "And Mrs. Neel?" Miss Golly says.

Able takes a deep breath and slowly lets it out in what I know is pure defeat. "She's got Alzheimer's," he says.

"My grandmother, too," Miss Golly tells him, smiling, her tone as if she were giving him an item from the Sunday menu.

Able looks straight at her and then says, "How is she doing?"

Miss Golly glances away toward the floor and the lines of light the venetian blinds let in, then back at Able. "She doesn't know me anymore," she says, "and barely my parents." She seems like she might cry but then she steels herself and tells Able, without ever looking at me, that it's the cruelest disease she knows and certainly Mrs. Neel would probably be better off if she started out in assisted living, given, of course, that she still has "hygienic parameters." She adds that, on intake, the staff physician would evaluate what's appropriate.

"What about me?" Able asks.

"Why, you'd have your own place," she says, "and could visit any old time you wanted." As if this is a cue she rises and goes to the window, raises the blinds about three-quarters of the way up, and then points out as she names the buildings. "It's just a hop, skip, and a jump," she says. For the first time, then, she looks at me and asks if we'd like to have a tour of the facilities. Able is slow to get up but his determination is very strong. "Let's see what you've got," he says.

We take an oversized golf cart around the circle, Able in the front with a seat belt on, I in the back, Miss Golly at the wheel. The lawns are as well manicured as I've ever seen, the shrubs and flowers, even the dirt they're in, as though recently arrived by truck. I think Miss Golly is even prettier in the sun than she was inside, her complexion smooth and perfectly clear like my daughters'. There seems a vitality to her that even she is not aware of, something, I think, that not even age will dilute. In front of me Able seems frail, as if Miss Golly's presence somehow subtly drains what small amount of strength still remains.

My expectation is that Able will want to see the independent-living apartments first, and he does. The model they show is as elegant as a first-class hotel. He asks if the furniture comes with it and when Miss Golly says indeed it does he looks at me and asks what he should do with what they've got. Miss Golly answers for me: "Why, everybody sells furnished these days. Goodness, how long have you been here?" I tell her thirty years and she says, "Oh, I see."

"Furnished?" Able says. "I never thought of that." He reaches out and runs his hand over the back of an off-white French Provincial chair as though he's never touched such ornamentation. His fingers dwell for a moment in the grooves, hesitant and thoughtful, and then he grips the top of the chair hard, as if he's suddenly been given an answer. "More," he says, raising an arm toward the bedroom across the room. It's still luxury, the twin beds wide and extra long, the vanity-bureau combination with a mirror trimmed in gold leaf, the lamps full and tall, the sitting area by the window with inviting shafts of sunlight. It's as if he sees Lillian sitting there peacefully. Even the bathroom is to his liking, but it takes him a moment to understand the support bars next to the toilet and the two inside the tub. The side-by-side sinks in the Corian counter, however, are apparently something he's seen only rarely, if ever, and he stands in front of one and looks in the mirror as if he expects to see Lillian beside him. Able seems very vulnerable, as if what's suddenly occurring to him is that one of them must die first. He gazes into the mirror as though in it he sees a true glimpse of the future. I can just see the way his shoulders slump almost imperceptibly and how his eyes blink more slowly.

Miss Golly senses something's not quite right, too, and to distract him she asks him in her bubbly innocence what he did in his business career. There are a few questions which, when put to Able, he cannot answer within the boundaries of normal conversation, and right at the top of that list is what he did in his business life. In the bathroom doorway I close my eyes and lean back against the doorjamb, thinking, Miss Golly, you've probably made a sale here but it'll cost you a couple of very long hours. He says he worked for Union Carbide and Miss Golly smiles politely, clearly not having ever heard of it. "A chemical company," Able says patiently, for this is hardly the first time he's run into this problem. To locate her in the spectrum of corporations, he says, "Eveready batteries, GLAD wrap, Prestone."

"Isn't that nice," Miss Golly says.

"That's just the consumer division," Able goes on with a little wave of his hand. "Not more than five percent of the corporation. We make over five hundred products."

What holds Miss Golly's attention is the way Able's talking, as if he's still working there and still filled with the need and desire to get the company name around. "And you did what for them?" she asks.

"Finance," Able says, modestly. He says this in a way that indicates he expects her to draw him out, as if he's met someone newly retired at the club and they're playing a game of how far up in the corporate world each got. He was, actually, an assistant treasurer of the corporation but, as he once told me, he never got past that, never got to be a vice-president with the pay that came with it. Miss Golly takes this small downturn in the conversation to ease herself out of the bathroom with a statement that he must see the generous closet space. "And all the kitchens," she adds, "look out on the lake." As we pass the kitchen, I look in to see that in fact Miss Golly means a pond, a perfectly circular man-made saucer of water that has a light green and yellow scum over it. Able takes no notice of it as we leave.

We take the golf cart around the pond to the assisted-living units, which, we soon find out, are nowhere near as nice as what we've just seen. Although furnished in the same way, they are cut-down versions of the residential apartments: instead of a second bedroom, there's an alcove with a small window; instead of a full-size kitchen, a stove-sink-refrigerator combination sits just off the dining area; instead of an ample living room, there's only a sitting room with a couple of chairs—no deep sofa, we're told, because they're too hard to get up from—and a small coffee table between them. When we look into the bedroom, though, it's clear where the space has gone. It's much larger than the one in residential living, made to be the place where the most time is spent, the bathroom off it larger, too, as if in moving here one commits to a living area greatly reduced, even purposely shrunk. Able's reaction is to look it over quickly and then head for the door, the significance of the place clear to him more quickly than to me.

The other end of the building, which is separated from where we are by an atrium with a huge lovely skylight in it, the sun pouring down on a garden of plants and small trees, is "Gateway." Its stark purpose cannot be covered up either by the fine furniture or the elegant wall paneling or the smooth, indirect lighting. It's got three long corridors that go off from a central nurses' station, each with single rooms, doors open; bed, chair, and small bathroom in each; no different at all from a small, efficient hospital. Able walks a ways down one corridor, then turns and glances at me and snaps up his eyebrows as though to say he fully understands that this is not only how, but where, his life will end. As he looks around the nurses' station he becomes even more uncomfortable, and Miss Golly senses it, too. I'm thinking I'd bet this is where you lose a lot of sales when she moves the few steps to Able's side and takes his arm. He looks at her as though he's never seen her before and then says, "Quite a place, really," and together they head for the door.

In the golf cart on the way back to the administration offices, Miss Golly starts her final sales pitch by asking Able what his overall impression of Fair Oaks was. He thinks for a moment, then says, "Where are the people?" Miss Golly accommodates him immediately by saying that's just where they're going. Able turns to look at me, his lips tight, his eyes determined, as if to say nobody's putting one over on him.

It's just the end of lunch in the dining room, and Able's sold on the place completely when he sees it. There's really not much difference between it and the club, and the white tablecloths and napkins, high-backed chairs, and fine cutlery make a positive impression on him. One thing does catch his eye, however, and that's how many of the tables have only one person at them lingering over an iced tea or coffee or having the final spoonfuls of ice cream or pudding. He looks very lonely, his body tight and skeptical, sensing a message in what he sees that he will not permit himself to fully receive.

When Miss Golly says she'll next show us the recreation rooms—says we'll love the arboretum because of its Jacuzzi—Able tells her that he's seen quite enough and would like to go back to the office to talk about a contract. It's then Miss Golly tells him that a five-thousand-dollar deposit is required. "Refundable, of course," she says, but that at the current moment there's a two-month waiting period. She'll be glad, she says, to put him on the list and give a tentative date for moving. Able's remarkably quiet as Miss Golly takes him through the contract, and only twice does he look at me and ask if I think this or that point is all right. In the car on the way back I tell him I think for what he and Lillian will be getting the arrangement is quite fair, but he doesn't respond. When I ask him what's wrong, he says, "I don't like it."

"Fair Oaks?" I ask in disbelief.

"I don't like any of it," he answers. "No, not Fair Oaks."

"What are your alternatives?" I ask, holding my voice even, as though in preparation for a drawn-out exchange.

"Be quiet," he says.

Just as we enter the apartment building, Joseph holding the door for us, we see Lillian and Mayflower walking toward us, Mayflower very close to her. It takes Lillian until we're almost right in front of her to notice us and her hands come up in surprise. Able asks Mayflower if everything's all right and Lillian answers that it's so much fun to get out and walk a little. Able says to Mayflower, almost defensively, that before his operation they took walks all the time. "We did," Lillian says, turning to Mayflower. It's then that Mayflower looks at me and says my wife called from Pennsylvania and wants me to call back as soon as I can. I ask if something's wrong and she shrugs and says again as soon as I can. Lillian puts in that she doesn't know, she didn't talk to Elaine, but I know Elaine and she wouldn't stress a return call knowing what I'm doing here unless something was going on. Able tells me to go on up, he wants to walk a while with Lillian, but I know he senses something, too, and wants to give me privacy. In the elevator, my worst fears are that something has happened to one of our daughters, and my heart is mess as I come into the kitchen and go across to the phone. The tips of my fingers are moist as I press off the numbers, but when I hear Elaine's voice say, "You're not going to believe this," I calm down instantly. Several things have happened all at once: a chimney fire in our woodburner that Elaine says did no damage to the house but that we're going to need a new lining for the flue and the damn estimate's close to twelve hundred bucks; our old yellow Lab has had another pretty serious bout of colitis and she's had to keep him in the kitchen the last two nights ("You remember how that used to look in the morning," she says); Melissa has declared that she absolutely hates her job as an alcohol and drug counselor in Rochester ("'All day, all day talking to sociopaths,' were precisely her words," she says, then adds that she thinks maybe she wants out to go to law school); and Rebecca has declared a change of majors from chemistry to philosophy that will require either an extra semester or two summers and, hence, more tuition. When I say we can get the twelve hundred from the credit union she says we get everything there and she's getting damn tired of having no money. This is nothing new for either of us, one or the other boiling over about every three months with the frustrations of mediocre salaries, a kid in college, and the other one on long-term loans. "I'm sorry," she says, her composure back fast. "It's just that you've been there for nearly three weeks." When I tell her I'll come home tomorrow she feels guilty and says I don't have to, she can handle things by herself.

"I've done all I can here," I say.

Just then Able, Lillian, and Mayflower come in the kitchen door, and the look I get from Able is intense enough that I think somehow he's heard what I've just said. His expression is a mixture of panic and anger, as though he knows he's now stuck with Mayflower and the contract to move in two months and there isn't a thing he can do about it. Lillian speaks first, her concern for me as if she, too, knows something's not right at home. Standing in the middle of the kitchen, Mayflower holding her left elbow, she says, "Is everybody all right?" She looks around as if she simply cannot locate me. I assure her that things are okay. "Just the usual middle-class family crises," I answer.

"But everybody's all right?" she presses.

"Just fine," I say and she smiles in relief.

"You have a wonderful family," she says.

Then, as the three of them leave in single file heading for the den and the interminable market quotes, I hear her ask Able if something happened to the Schermers. "It's all right, dear," he says.

"Oh, good," fades away into the living room.

Later, just as I hang up, Able comes back into the kitchen as though he's been right outside the door waiting. He stands looking at me, then walks slowly to where I am and sits down at the table. "What is it?" he asks. When I shake my head and shrug to dismiss any conversation he puts an arm out on the table as though to reach over to me and says, "Tell me." As I repeat what Elaine said, he nods slowly and thoughtfully, then turns to look out the window. The light is orange and full of angles, weak and already at four o'clock starting to fail. For the briefest moment I catch it in his eyes. Although his tan face looks exactly like the shell of a brown egg with a hundred cracks, his hands that way, too, there's a quality to his eyes I've never seen before. At first I think it's resignation, that he's given up this stubborn struggle for independence and is on the brink of some important relief now that things are decided, but then there's a nearly imperceptible narrowing of the eyes, as though all at once the muscles around them have gotten the signal that right now is the time to be ever more vigilant. He shifts his line of sight and his eyes come back to me. "I want to pay for your trip," he says, then reaches into his shirt pocket for a check he's already written. I'm more astonished than relieved about the money, for the simple reason that, except for fifty dollars for Elaine and me at Christmas—and our daughters, too—he's never given me anything. I say I'd be grateful for that and then he hands me the check and I see it's for five thousand. I tell him he's way off, it couldn't have come to half that, and start to hand it back. He puts a palm out to stop me, his head shaking in a quick rejection, and says, "I don't know what I'd have done without you." This is the first time I have ever heard him admit to a situation in which he did not have control. When I was a kid I used to think he *did* have control, but as I grew older I came to understand that even when he didn't he thought it best to look as though he did. I tell him I was glad to do it, and then right away change the subject to ask what he really thought of Fair Oaks. He thinks for a few seconds, then nods slowly and says, "It'll be good for your mother."

"And you?" I ask.

"I suppose," he says. He turns again to look out on the pool area, the great shadow of the building now more than halfway across it, the beach and ocean still shimmering in what's left of the sad yellow light.

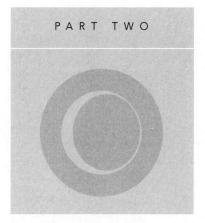

PART TWO

For the next month and a half, I telephone at least twice a week—sometimes, if I'm worried about how they sound, three times. There are two weeks, when first Lillian has the flu, then Able, that I call four times. Usually, both are on the telephone, Lillian in the den, Able in the bedroom after some moments of slowly walking there, but during those two weeks only the well one talks to me. It's clear that they are very sick, Lillian unable to eat anything for four days, and then when Able gets it she is beside herself with anxiety because he can hardly get up to walk to the bathroom. The real disappointment during this time is Mayflower, who, I'm told by both of them, spends most of her time in her room, fearful that she, too, will get sick. Her role is babysitter, not caregiver. But very slowly these two weeks pass and, finally, about a month after it's over I hear in their voices that everything is again normal, that on Tuesdays they go to the club for lunch, and, of course, Lillian gets her hair done on Thursday. In response to my questions about Mayflower and how she's helping them, especially when it comes to settling the apartment for their move to Fair Oaks, I'm told all is well. Able says he's even gotten the locker in the basement cleaned out, the old stuff from White Plains off to Goodwill. To this Lillian says, "You did?"

"It's all right," Able answers.

"Oh, yes," Lillian says.

It goes like this until Thanksgiving, when Benny comes to see them, and on the second night he's there he calls to tell me that from what he's observed it's quite amazing they're still alive. I tell him they've sounded good on the phone and he says he's talked to them a few times and he thought so, too. He tells me that Able looks a lot different from when he last saw him, he's slower and more stooped, and that Lillian's a flat basket case, she can't remember anything from one minute to the next. "But she looks fine," Benny says with some bewilderment. When I ask how Mayflower's doing he says he hasn't met her, she's apparently been off for a few days and there's another sub in, someone named Hertie who keeps to herself and her Bible. I ask, too, about how preparations for the move to Fair Oaks are proceeding, and Benny says Able told him just last night that it's been delayed until after the first of the year because Fair Oaks had an electrical fire in one of the main units and repainting and so forth will take that long. I then ask if he's on the kitchen phone and when he says he is I say, "Look in the freezer for me." As he steps across to it he asks if I've lost it, or what, and I say, "Just tell me what's in there." I hear the short whoosh of the door opening and then there's a pause and finally Benny says, "It looks like about fourteen thousand Stouffer's frozen dinners." I swear softly and Benny asks what the hell's the matter with me. I explain that from what I can tell Hertie's just been called in for the couple of days he's there and that the Fair Oaks fire is crap, Able's decided they're not going anywhere. Benny strongly disagrees and says that just last night after dinner Able showed him the brochures, complained about the price of the place, but assured him they were going. "And what preparations do you see?" I ask. After a moment, he says none, the place looks exactly the same. I tell Benny Able's had a month and a half to start getting ready, that he's been telling me all along about packing up, getting rid of the stuff in storage, even bringing in boxes one at a time from the Publix when he shops. "I don't see a thing," Benny says. I swear again and then there's a pause between us, one in which it feels like Benny's about to shut the whole thing down, and then I ask for an honest appraisal of how Lillian's doing. For a moment Benny doesn't respond, then he says she's okay physically, he'd guess, but she's much worse in the mentation department than what I'd last described to him. "How the hell does Able get her past their doctor?" I ask. Without so much as a second's consideration, Benny says it's real easy to do if you've got a doctor who doesn't want anything to do with it and a husband who probably answers all the questions in the office. In response to my asking if he'll call Gandhi sometime, he says sure but it probably won't do any good. "If you don't want to be treated," he says, "nobody's going to treat you."

"Do you think she knows something's wrong with her?" I ask.

"Sure," he says, "but she doesn't know what."

"Why doesn't Able tell her?" I ask.

"What would it accomplish?" he says. Then, after a moment, "Why can't you leave well enough alone?"

"You could do something," I tell him.

"Like what?" he asks. When I don't answer because I don't know what to say, he adds, "This is Able's business."

I understand this to be Benny bailing out, and I expect that within a few moments he's going to tell me he's leaving a day or so early, that something pressing has come up back in Santa Barbara. Instead, he takes a moment and then says there's one thing about Able he doesn't like seeing. I ask if he thinks maybe they didn't get all of Able's cancer and he says, "No, it's the way he sometimes glares at her." I tell him I never saw anything like that, that the whole time I was there he was attentive, really overly so. "And in conversation when she gets something wrong he snaps and tells her she's got bats in the belfry and like that."

"But *why?*" I ask.

"Because slowly she's leaving him," Benny says. "And he doesn't like it." I ask if he thinks things'll be better when they've finally moved to Fair Oaks and he says of course they will, she'll have all the care and attention she needs and he'll have people to talk to who don't forget what he's said in five seconds. "I don't think they're going," I tell Benny. "I think Able's just made it all up."

"Well," Benny says, exhaling like he's bored and wants to hang up, "then that'll be their problem." I ask if he'll push Able a little for me to find out if I'm right and he says, "Look, if the guy wants to die with his boots on that's his business. You did what you could."

"Do you think she's being abused?" I ask. "Do you think he might hurt her?"

"I don't see that," Benny says. "Most of the time he's looking at her, his eyes all watery, like he just doesn't believe life's about over." He pauses then and finally says that, well, maybe it's not. I ask what he means and he says it could be they'll live a lot longer, one of them maybe to a hundred. For some reason this amuses him and he laughs as though to himself and says he heard that if you live to a hundred you get a card from the President. "Imagine," he says.

"I'd rather not," I answer.

"Listen," he says, his voice falling off, "I don't know if this is right, but I think maybe he's doing her makeup." I ask how he knows and he tells me that her lipstick's a lot heavier than he's ever seen it, that her powder's just laid on. "But I could be wrong," he says. "It might be her vision."

It doesn't matter which it is, the picture makes me want to scream, and when a moment later Benny says good-bye and hangs up it's just fine with me. Before he does he says he's done what he can and tells me that I ought to come back down after Christmas and check things out for myself. I tell him I certainly will, and when I say I'll let him know how things are he says, "I bet they'll be grim."

Other evidence about their condition is mixed. Elaine starts to call once a week on her own, feigning I'm not home, and gets nothing from either of them except what we already know, and it nearly drives Elaine crazy that she has to talk to both of them at once. After the third time, she says it's impossible to ask Able a direct question about

Lillian's Alzheimer's with her right there on the line, then stops and looks at me and says he's using her as a shield. But on Christmas afternoon, when Able calls to talk to my daughters, a long-standing tradition, and with Lillian again in bed with the twenty-four-hour flu, he flat unloads on them. Mostly, he talks about how hard life is on him, how his strength hasn't really come back after the surgery, that they hardly go out at all anymore—having groceries delivered and some meals sent in, he says, is damned expensive—but that Lillian is doing okay in her way. Then Melissa tells me that she just casually asked when they were moving to their new retirement home and, she said, there was a long pause and Able said, "Oh, that," and right away covered it with, "Soon, honey. You bet, soon." Rebecca looks at me and says, "They aren't going, are they?"

"And there isn't any Mayflower," I say. "Nothing's changed." Then Melissa asks what's going to happen to them and Rebecca, after a short silence, looks at me and says, "Why's he like that?"

That evening I make a list and decide to call Able to confront him. I want to know exactly how Lillian is—if, in fact, she's really just got the flu or if it's more serious—and to ask him point-blank why they're not going to Fair Oaks, and, perhaps most important, what happened to Mayflower. When I call, I'm surprised that I get Lillian in the den, Able now suddenly laid low with the flu—it came on this afternoon, she tells me, and he's quite sick, she's never seen him so sick. When I say it must have been right after he talked to the kids, she says she didn't know they called and I tell her he called them, it's Christmas, after all. "Why, yes, it is," she says and then asks if we all had a good Christmas and I tell her we did, and then she asks how classes are and if I still like it at the university and I say yes, except the new department head's a jerk, the same exact conversation we have each time I've called and it's taken Able a few moments to get to the extension in the bedroom. Stock questions, stock answers, but we talk. "And everybody's all right?" she asks. "Your family's fine?" I assure her all is well and then she says it's been so long since she's seen us all and when might we be coming down. I tell her I was there in October and she says, "Why, yes, that's right." Then I say that she just saw Benny and there's a long pause and finally, in sad, wandering language, she confirms that she did. As if I can no longer tolerate her condition, and can wish it away with directness alone, I ask her the questions I should have put to Able. "Are you okay?" I ask. "Are you over the flu?"

"Weak," she answers. "And Able said it wasn't the flu, just a bad cold."

"And how's Mayflower?" I ask. She doesn't remember who Mayflower was and when I say it was the woman who cooked and stayed with them it finally registers.

"Well, we found out we really didn't need her," she says. "We get along just fine."

"Are you eating all right?" I ask.

"Why, of course," she says. I make the mistake of asking what she had for dinner and when I hear her struggle I realize it's a cruel question. She tells me it was the creamed chipped beef for her and a Salisbury steak for Able. Before I can stop myself, I say but I thought he had the flu. "Why, that's right," she says.

"Do you get anything from Nick's?" I ask.

"I think so," she answers. "I do love their food." There's a long pause and she says that the weather's been terrible there, lots of dark, cloudy days, that things seem so chilly she and Able hardly go out. Suddenly I hear the extension phone—and I know it's in the kitchen because the dishwasher's going in the background—rock off its cradle and Able says hello and asks how I am. "It's how *you* are that's important," I say. He answers he's just fine, he wasn't feeling so hot a little while ago and took a nap. When I say mother told me he had the flu he says, "I'm fine." Then, as if he's actually taken the time I've been talking to prepare himself, he asks why I've called. "Because I think you've been less than truthful about things," I say. I tell him I've talked to Benny and neither of us is buying the fire at Fair Oaks, to which he says there really was one, but not in the unit they'd reserved. "I see," I answer, and right away, now that he's opened up, I say, "And what about Mayflower?" Lillian answers with the same thing she said about Charity: "Why, the woman was a thief," she says.

"Dear," Able says, his voice suddenly so soft it's as if someone else has said the word, "please hang up and let me talk to Ted."

"Love you, Teddy," Lillian says with a little giggle, then hangs up.

"You have got to stop trying to tell me what to do," Able says right away. There's not a shred of anger in his voice, not an emotional syllable. It's as if I'm his secretary back at Carbide—it's the same exact voice I heard him use with her—flat with self-assured authority, the relationship from speaker to hearer utterly clear. It disarms me totally. I say I'm not trying to tell him what to do, it's that I'm worried about Lillian. "Well, she's fine," he says in the same cool way.

"Why aren't you going to Fair Oaks?" I ask. "Tell me what's wrong with it."

"To be honest," he says, "nothing. We're just not up to it."

"It's a beautiful place," I say.

"Here's fine," he answers. His tone is killing me, his stance on everything impenetrable. On instinct, I come back to Lillian and ask if she's the same as when I was there or is she worse. "No change," he says, and this makes me angry because he's doing the judging, and when I shoot back how can he tell, he flattens me with the statement that he's had her to Dr. Gandhi, who sent her to a neurologist. Still a step ahead of me. "And?" I say in a way that signals he's once more in full control. "I told him what it was over the phone, even before we walked in there," he says.

"Fine," I say, "but what'd he say? What'd he do?"

"Pills," he tells me. "It's what they do now. I found out." Before I can even ask what they are, he says he's contacted a place in Atlanta, or near Atlanta, that does mail-order medicines, that all he's got to do is call an 800 number and the prescription's filled in a flash, they get it two days later. "Billing's all through Medicare," he says. "It's practically free." He seems so pleased with the arrangement.

"But how is she?" I ask again.

"No change," he tells me. "Like I said."

"Who's the neurologist?" I ask. There's a long pause while he makes two slow sounds in his throat that make me even more impatient, then he says he's got it written down in the kitchen somewhere, it's a name that sounds like Colin Powell. I think he knows perfectly well the name of the neurologist, he just won't tell me so I can't call him up and go behind his back.

"Just a second," he says and puts down the phone hard on the counter. "Don't *do* that," I hear him say in the distance. Then, "Damn it. See what you've done."

"What's wrong?" I call out. "Dad, what's wrong?" In my mind I'm suddenly in their kitchen and hear my voice across the room coming from the phone in a way tiny and hopelessly weak. What I'm saying doesn't mean a thing. It takes a long time but finally Able picks up the phone again and, out of breath, tries to downplay Lillian having put a tray full of Ritz crackers, about eight of them, on high in the toaster oven. When I ask if everything's okay, Able says, "Under control," then pauses as if waiting for me to yell at him for having let something like that happen. "She's all right?" I ask.

"Sure," he says. "It's the third—fourth—time she's done it."

"She's worse," I say flatly. "She's getting so she doesn't know what things are for."

"She's all right," he says, then adds that she went back to watch TV. "And I'm all right, too, thank you."

"One question," I say. "What happens to her if something happens to you?"

"You think maybe they didn't get all the cancer?" he says with a light arrogance. Before I can answer, he says, "Erg's a fine surgeon, the best. He got it, all right. He told me."

"I'm talking about a fall, a stroke, a heart attack," I say. "What about Lillian then?"

"It's not going to happen," he says.

"No?" I say, my voice rising.

"Not in the cards," he says.

"I see," I answer. "Did you ever do anything about moving?" I ask, shaking my head. "Clean out stuff, pack boxes, get to the basement locker."

"Nothing," he answers.

"Why?"

"No strength," he says.

I imagine him in the chair by the dark window, elbows on the table, holding the phone with both hands, eyes out toward the ocean looking for something. "Would you move if I came down and did it for you?" I ask.

"Now that's a tough question," he says after a moment. "I'd have to think about that."

"You wouldn't, would you?" I say.

"I don't think so," he tells me.

"Why?"

"Because we're getting along all right," he answers. "Tomorrow's our day at the club." I tell him they could still go to the club if they lived at Fair Oaks, and he answers, "I know," and then there's silence. Then he says this: "Your mother and I have decided that if something happens to either one of us the other will have someone come in full-time." His voice is flat and distant, as if he's rehearsed the sentence. "So," he says, his tone much lighter, "we're going to be fine."

"She's only going to get worse," I tell him.

"She's holding her own," he says proudly.

"And it's your intention to take care of her?" I ask.

"That's the picture," he says.

All I can say to him then is that I hope things go well and that if he wants me to do anything, all he has to do is ask. He says he appreciates that and that he'll let me know, "in the eventuality that should arise." Just before I hang up he says, "And you'll call? Your mother likes that."

"Of course," I answer and put the phone down.

It's several weeks before I understand the significance of his saying that, and it's only slowly that it dawns on me that he's decided to avoid me. I wait a week and call again as usual, but Lillian tells me Able's in the shower and can't come to the phone. This doesn't even register with me and she and I have a nice talk about how well she thought I did in high school, how proud she was that I was salutatorian. Her recollection of graduation day is unbearably clear, as though it plays in her mind like yesterday's events. She also wants to be reassured that I and my family are well and asks at least a handful of times how we are. "Your lovely daughters," she says, for the first time not using their names, "and that wonderful wife of yours," followed by a long pause, as if she's waiting for me to supply *Elaine.* Even when I say everyone's just fine, she says, "You're sure now? You're sure?" and I have to tell again.

I call again about ten days later, this time on a Sunday afternoon, and, as usual, because she sits right next to the phone in the den, she answers. I have no trouble hearing an NFL playoff game in the background on the television, and I assume when we start to talk that Able's on his way to the bedroom extension. But when he doesn't pick up in the usual thirty seconds—I ask if he's getting on. "He's in the shower," Lillian answers, her voice as flat as if she were reading the words.

"And I take it you've become a Dolphins fan?" I say, then instantly regret both the statement and my tone. Before she can say anything, I cover it by asking if they've been to the club, if their weekly routine is the same as always.

"I think so," she says, her voice light with relief.

"And the Nicelys?" I ask, trying for her same amount of lightness, "do you see them?"

"Not so much anymore," she says. "They're so sweet, you know." There's a pause and she lowers her voice and says Bill's not so well, but that when she talks to Margaret she can't get a word out of her about what's wrong. "Able and I think," she says, "that Bill's got dementia. I don't think they even go to the club anymore." This frustrates me so that I'm right on the edge of asking why Able's avoiding me but I control myself, say I'm sorry to hear that, and change the subject to whether or not they've heard from Benny. Lillian pauses for just a moment, as if she's sorting out who he is, and then says he came to see them Thanksgiving, or was it *last* Thanksgiving, then adds that here in Florida the weather makes all the months run together. Then she downright giggles like a schoolgirl, the sound a slow emptying of some peace-filled place in her soul that, no matter what, will never change. A second or two later, when I hear the channel change to one of the NBA games, I tell her I love her, that my daughters and Elaine all send love, and that I'll call again soon. On purpose I don't mention Able. "It's so good to hear your voice," she says, and then I say good-bye.

Although for the two weeks I throw myself into my work, actually getting to the end of the third chapter—doing at least a thousand words a day—my concentration is unexpectedly broken by things I think I ought to be doing. At first, I make small notes here and there on Post-its that then lie around in yellow and green squares on my desk: 1) New will (long overdue since kids now both +21); 2) e-mail TIAA-CREF for long-term health insurance information; 3) total amounts on term policies and riders; 4) plan to do *something* about what's collected in the attic over the last 22 years; 5) inform our daughters of our financial situation in case something happens to Elaine and me; 6) call Social Security office for a printout of estimated annual income when I retire; 7) discuss with Elaine when we might take tours of the two retirement homes here in town. It feels good to organize these things, but when I mention them to Elaine at dinner one evening she says, "Aren't you a bit premature?" I answer I'm not going to be like Able, I'm not screwing over a loved one just because I haven't—or won't—prepare. When she tries to make light of it and says I'm only just sixty, that I've probably got one or two good years left, I say don't trivialize my efforts, that there's already one serious jerk in the Neel family who's doing plenty of harm by not taking on his responsibilities. Elaine tries to lead me away from a discussion of when we might make appointments with the long-term care facilities by asking why Benny hasn't taken more of an interest in Able and Lillian. "Benny cares about Benny," I answer, then the edge in my voice goes as I tell her that I remember Lillian telling me years ago that Benny was such a difficult baby, especially at night and in the early morning, that Able got a roll of chicken wire and fastened a removable section over the top of his crib so he couldn't get out until Able let him. Elaine stares at me, shakes her head, and asks if Benny knows that. "I don't know," I answer. Then, in the same sentence that she says that's a pretty horrible thing to do, she says she's not going to look at any kind of a home or village or whatever, nor buy that expensive long-term hospitalization insurance until she's sixty-five and/or the kids' loans are paid off.

"What I really want to do," I say, "is go back down there."

"He's sealed you off," she says.

"I know."

Within the hour I get a call from Margaret Nicely, who gets right to the point by asking what Able's done with her Lillian. When I tell her I don't know what she's talking about, Margaret says that in the last two weeks she's called a bunch of times and Able's always told her that Lillian's in the shower, that he'll have her call back, but she never does. Then she says that she saw her just this afternoon in the lobby getting the mail and Lillian ran smack into the glass door of the mail room, that when she helped Lillian find the elevator she barely knew her. "He is not taking care of her," Margaret says flatly. When I challenge her by saying that they're still going to the club, that they both told me only a week or so ago that they're still doing everything just the same, Margaret, laughing, says so far as she knows the last time they were at the club was Thanksgiving with Benny. "Not since," she adds, "or we probably would have seen them." I ask how her husband is and when she says what do I mean I tell her I was told he wasn't well. She says he had walking pneumonia for about two weeks back in early December but other than that he's just fine.

"We're having a ball," she says and then asks how my family is and says to give her love to Elaine and the girls. I say I will and then there's a long pause in which it seems she's forgotten why she called, then she says, "Well, bye-bye for now," and hangs up. I put my head down, hands over my ears, and Elaine finds me that way at my desk and softly, with great concern, asks what the call was. I tell her and then at the end say, "Are we all going to end up just nuts?"

Almost exactly an hour later the phone rings and both Able and Lillian are on, saying hello as though we've spoken yesterday, and then Lillian asks for Elaine. Dumbly, I hand the phone over to her, at the same time saying, "They want to talk to you." Elaine's eyes widen in astonishment as she takes the phone, says a tentative hello, and then falls utterly silent. I find out what's going on when, after a moment, she turns the receiver away from her ear toward me so that I can hear Lillian and Able singing "Happy birthday to you, happy birthday, dear Elaine, happy birthday to you." As they finish, she puts her hand over the mouthpiece and asks, "Do I tell them?" It takes me not more than a second before I nod, hoping Able will see that he's set up Lillian and himself to look like fools. I know what's happened: somehow, from somewhere—maybe, I think, a direct communiqué from Mars—Lillian's gotten it into her head that it's Elaine's birthday and has marched into the den and told Able that they've got to call, they've never missed a family birthday and they're not going to now. I go into the kitchen and quietly pick up the extension. Elaine is kinder and gentler than I would have been, and she says very slowly, as though talking to small children, that it was so nice of them to think of her but her birthday's in May. Lillian says of course it is, and that's why they're calling. There's a short pause and Lillian says, "Did I get the day wrong, honey?"

"It's all right, dear," Able says, and then easily dismisses everything by saying, while chuckling, "You know how all of us old people get." Elaine slides over the moment by laughing along with them, and then, still loving and generous, says we'll be talking to them soon, they answer of course we will, and then they all hang up. The phone in my hands feels like I'm holding a very heavy dumbbell and haven't got the faintest idea what to do with it. For a long time I look at it as if it's all I've got left of my mother and father.

This is what makes me decide to go back to Fort Lauderdale: two more weeks pass without talking to them, although I try to call twice, both times leaving a message on the answering machine. When I call at the end of the second week I get Lillian right away and ask her where they've been. She thinks for a moment and says, "Why, right here. We don't go anywhere that I know of." Her own irony escapes her and I tell her about calling and ask if she got my messages. "Not that I know of," she says again. I imagine her staring the five feet or so across to where Able's watching television, waiting for a cue, asking with her large empty pupils what to say. Then, to my astonishment, I realize that he can't possibly be in the room—perhaps he's napping or has sought relief from her alone on the balcony—because she's suddenly animated with the news that a state policeman came to the apartment this morning. It's as if she's got that one picture in her mind and that's all that's allowed to be there. To prod her along I ask if he wanted a donation, or was he taking a survey or what. "I know, I know," she says, excited both by the event and, for the moment, her ability to recall it. "They took Able's driver's license." I think that surely this is a fabrication, that she's probably seen something on television that's lodged in her mind like a child's fantasy and she can't distinguish between it and what reality she's got left. "He was a big man," she says and pauses, then adds, "in uniform." Wholly without meaning to, I quietly laugh, and that, I realize instantly, is the wrong thing to do. "Well," Lillian says indignantly, "I don't think it's so funny. Neither does Able." Then we are talking as though there's never been anything wrong with her. She is lucid and coherent in responding to my asking if she's really serious. "Never more so," she says.

"What happened?" I ask quietly, even apologetically.

It's Able who answers, who's been on the line all along. "My damn eyes," he says very softly. When I tell him I didn't know anything was wrong with them, he says, "Cataracts," and goes dead silent. Twenty years ago he had both eyes done down in Miami at some institute and said his sight would be just fine for the rest of his life. Finally, after a pause, he says, "They're coming back is all." Then he goes on to tell me that just before Christmas he was up for his three-year license renewal and that's how they nabbed him.

"What are you going to do?" I say slowly.

"I'll be all right," he answers. "We'll be all right." Way too quickly I jump in with the information that the aides at Sunrise Health all have cars, that driving people to see the doctor and to shop and so forth is part of what they do. "Like I said," is all the response I get. Then I hear, "Good talking to you, and love to the family," and then the rattle of the receiver finding the cradle. "Mother," I say, "what the hell is he going to do now?" Before she can answer I say, "He's going to drive anyway, isn't he?"

"Without his license?" she answers, now bewildered. "Oh, I don't think so. I don't think he'd do that."

"Well," I say, "then how're you going to get groceries and get to the club?"

"Oh," she says, "I'll drive. I've been driving for sixty years. Did you know that?" I say yes, I did, and before I can get in another word she further informs me that those were sixty accident-free years. I answer I knew that, too, my patience now nearly at an end. "You simply can't drive," I say.

"We'll see about that," she answers. "Able always said mine was a tight ship."

I understand then what Able's plan is: he'll give the incident a few days and when Lillian forgets about it he'll go on driving like nothing happened. What I want to say to her but don't is that it's probably only a matter of time until Able gets you both killed. What I do say is that she *did* run a tight ship, that when it came to organization and running a household there was no one like her. Her voice changes instantly, the flash of hostility gone, and it's as though we've been talking about the weather. Right away her mind flashes back to White Plains like it was yesterday and Benny and I were just coming home from school to chocolate chip cookies and a glass of milk, a stew already on the burner or a roast in the oven. "You boys never wanted for a thing," she says. "You were *cared* for." How much, I wonder, of their lives do they now, at this time, choose to reinvent? Do they sit at their kitchen table by the window looking out at the ocean reshaping family history, each soothing the other with medals for parenthood, each saying he or she couldn't have done things any better? Has she, I wonder, forgotten the thirteen years Able drank and how every single dinner was an hour from hell for Benny and me, or is that period erased from their memories along with Able's unpredictability, like a disease in the house, when one moment on a Saturday morning he'd be calm and resolute with the *New York Times*, the next a marine drill sergeant with a list of things to be done that would cancel city-league baseball and Pop Warner games and take from us our entire weekend. Does *cared for* mean her silence the morning after a drunken tantrum from Able because he came home without the long-sought Carbide promotion, the day at forty-three he knew he probably wouldn't ever get any higher in the corporation? Does it mean her having to say of Judith Katzman, the first girl I fell in love with, that I couldn't go to the movies with her because her people had killed Jesus and I'd be a Jew-lover? Is this what awaits Elaine and me—one day having re-constructed our lives?

"He's going to drive anyway," I tell Lillian.

"We've decided to go to the club now just for lunch," she says. "His eyes are fine in the daytime."

"Suppose he hits somebody," I say. "Suppose there's an accident."

"Teddy," she says, "you're always looking on the dark side, aren't you?"

"You could take taxis," I tell her. "You could be safe."

"And just where are we going to get the money to be taxiing all around Fort Lauderdale?" she says.

"You have plenty of money," I answer.

"What we have has to last a long, long time," she tells me. "You know people in this building have run out of money and have had to leave?" I answer I do, she told me that. "Able says you worry about us too much," she says.

Then I tell her that I'm thinking of coming down for a visit when I get back from England at the end of next month and her tone changes abruptly to conciliatory, as if she thinks that if she stays stubborn I might change my mind. "Let me tell Able," she says and relays the information to him in a rising voice. In a few moments Able's back on the extension in the bedroom and he says, "What for?"

"To see you," I answer. "To see how things are."

"They're just fine," he says, as if that's all he needs to get across that my coming isn't the highest thing on his list. Lillian picks up on his reluctance more quickly than I would have thought possible and intercedes for herself by saying that she hasn't seen me in she doesn't know how long and wouldn't it be wonderful to have me come. Able, sounding like a king granting a special favor, says that, well, if it means so much, sure, come ahead, Ted. "How long will you stay?" he asks. When I answer only about three or four days, he says fine, let him know when and he'll pick me up at the airport. My answer is to say that I'll rent a car like before and just come to the apartment.

"No, no, honey," Lillian says, "we'll be there like always."

"We'll work it out," I answer, exhausted and feeling close to despair. Then there's no more to talk about, an emptiness on the line that feels as if they now recede at the speed of light. I say I'll let them know and then I wait as each hangs up without another word.

I end up going *before* my England trip because within three days Able runs the Cadillac into one of the concrete support columns in the basement garage. He's not hurt but Lillian is because she didn't have her seat belt on. I suspect right away that probably both her eyes and mind failed together, and that she *thought* she had it on. I've never known her not to, but I remember when Able was in the hospital in October and I drove her there I always had to do her seat belt. When the call comes from Margaret—and then one about an hour later from Dr. Gandhi—the reports are mixed, and when I tell Elaine what Margaret told me, most of it has to be revised after Gandhi's call. Margaret says that Able's okay but has some bruises and is pretty shaken up, but that Lillian's got a bad gash on her head and no memory of what happened. "She has no memory anyway," I tell Margaret, relieved after knowing nothing's critical about either of their conditions, and she pauses and then says, "That's right, isn't it?" Gandhi, however, is much more cautious about their conditions, and has admitted them to the hospital straight from the emergency room. I double-check with him that they aren't in any danger and he immediately clears Able but he says he's not so certain about Mrs. Neel. It's possible, he says, that she's got a concussion, perhaps even some brain damage, perhaps even a subdural hematoma, only tests scheduled within the hour will confirm or rule out such possibilities. I tell him I'll be there sometime this evening, assuming I can get a flight out of here to Pittsburgh or Philly and then one on to Fort Lauderdale. Remarkably, he gives me his home number and tells me that Dr. Asham will be on call since it's Thursday evening, but that if I have questions I should call him direct. I tell him I appreciate that and that in any case I'll see him tomorrow.

While I pack, Elaine has no trouble getting me on a flight to Pittsburgh, but from there to Fort Lauderdale is a scheduling mess. Freezing rain and fog in Pittsburgh delays everything for nearly three hours, and several flights to the West Coast are canceled outright. The activity around the nearby gates where I'm waiting is like a tiny revolution in search of a leader. With it comes the unexpected informality of strangers talking to each other with their frustrations and guesses as to just how long we're all actually going to be there. It's like a little leftover Christmas spirit has come into the place, as though we all know each other from somewhere but not a name will come. I listen to all of what's going on, but see the activity only in the reflection of the huge semi-dark windows directly in front of me. Now and again, way in the distance, the headlights from a ground vehicle snap on in the growing dusk. Relentlessly, the rain slides down the window in random streaks, nothing but gravity making any sense. I look to the side along the row of seats to see a very old couple—not quite the ages of Able and Lillian—both with canes, sitting side by side, two fat cloth bags in front of them as close as pets. Weather not permitting, I think, they are in for a long night, too. I wonder about their health and their relationship, if one already takes care of the other or if they're not quite there yet. They are very erect, almost on guard for something unseen but expected, as if each moment has a brittleness beyond my comprehension. Her eyes are closed, but from how her hands are joined over the top of the cane she must only be resting. His cane lies along the edge of the chair, his arms tightly folded across his chest, as if in rejection of an unpleasant thought just arrived. I wonder if he's as self-centered as Able, as stubborn and defiant. Suddenly, he throws a glance at me as if to ask what it is I think I'm looking at. His right hand goes down to his cane and rests there. I turn my head away enough to look at them in the reflection of the window, and I see the man relax and bring his hands back to his lap. Beyond them the late afternoon is dark, the rain and sleet on the window like stars in a winter sky gone haywire with motion. Maybe, I think, I should be more like Benny and wash my hands of Able, let him do what he wants, play the game of telephone chitchat and then one day fake surprise when Margaret or Gandhi calls and says there's been a fire or accident or Able's died and what do I want done with my mother.

Another couple, each with a duffel bag, who must be mid-eighties, comes into the waiting area and sits down so awkwardly and heavily that I wonder if they'll ever get up. They look confused, jaws a little slack, mouths open, as if compelled to work for air. The man drops his head to his chest and closes his eyes, asleep, it seems, almost instantly. But the woman, who is round and has heavy legs, stares ahead, eyes wide and determined, her back rigid and full of alert tension. I watch as she reaches in her bag and takes out a bagel folded in two napkins, and then nudges the man and hands it to him. From his shirt pocket he takes out his dentures and, upper plate first, puts them in, adjusts the lower with his thumb and index finger like a clamp, and then takes a small bite. He eats like Able when he's truly hungry, the taste of the food less important than the comfort it supplies.

Finally boarded, the plane taxis several hundred yards for de-icing, the two lighted trucks around the wings, the men in yellow rainsuits in the hydraulic buckets instantly at work. Finished, we taxi for what feels like an interminable length of time, then sit, lights out, for nearly a half hour. In the rotating light on the top of the plane I have no trouble seeing the ice begin once again to build on the wings— first in a thin layer, then a mottled crust, and sure enough within the next few minutes we're taxiing back for another round of de-icing. That accomplished, we go back in line and within five minutes we're at full throttle heading down the runway. My sense of relief that finally we're nearly off is eaten away at by how long we stay on the runway, the wheels seemingly unable to give up contact with the tarmac. Then, just before we lift into the air, there's a sideways wiggle to the left, then one to the right, a clear skid, and then the modest tipping back of the head. I glance to the side to see the second older couple from the waiting area, and they are remarkably calm. He's eating the second half of the bagel, she's holding a pear with one bite out of its fattest part, neither with the slightest regard for what has been a very dangerous moment.

A few minutes later, when one of the flight attendants slowly makes her way to the back to start around the drink cart, she glances at me and smiles. "That felt like a close one," I say, to which she simply raises her eyebrows and moves on by. By the time the cart gets to me the older couple is sound asleep, heads touching.

Astonishingly, Able meets me at the gate in Fort Lauderdale, with him a man about his age, only taller and straighter, who Able introduces as Jeremy Bright, a friend of his from the building who he's known for years. I recognize the name—he and Able have been exchanging books and videotapes from clubs for years. I assume that Jeremy's driven Able out to get me, but on the way down the escalator to baggage claim Able tells me, pointing, to go pick up my luggage, that he and Jeremy are going to get the Cadillac. Right then I realize he's brought Jeremy along so that I won't immediately yell at him for driving without his license. Outside, Able gets out of the car, pops the trunk electronically, and I put my suitcase in. Then I turn to him, hand extended, for the keys. For just a second or two he's reluctant to hand them over, then he does. Without a word, he turns and gets into the backseat. In the car, when Jeremy twice in five minutes asks me my name, I discover he's worse off than Lillian.

I sit in the north lobby of the building while Able takes Jeremy back to his apartment, and when he comes through the glass doors and toward the elevator I rise and go to him. "You simply can't drive without a license," I tell him.

"I did, though, didn't I?" he says, nodding his own approval.

"I forbid you," I answer.

He reaches out and presses the call button, then turns to me. "Who do you think is in control here?" he asks. So direct is the question that it disarms me completely. I have a flash of my last visit when, if he'd asked me then, I'd have said I was. This is not true now. I look at him with his cloudy pupils, his stoop, the wrinkles, his weight loss, and I say, "You are."

"What're they going to do," he asks, "put me in jail?"

On the way up in the elevator, he says that we'll get something to eat and then go to Broward General to see Lillian. When I ask how she is he tells me she's all right. We get out of the elevator and he hands me the door key without explanation, and I insert it and then open the door and we go on in. Following me, he says, "Except there's something wrong with her heart." I turn sharply and look at him. "They've put in a pacemaker and she'll be home in a few days," he says. I stare at him as he tells me her heart rate was under thirty. "She should have more energy now," he adds. He opens the freezer door of the refrigerator and asks what I'd like tonight, chipped beef or a Salisbury steak.

"You choose," I tell him and go sit at the table by the window. He says he's low on the Salisbury steaks and will the chipped beef be all right. It takes a few seconds to respond because I've picked up a packet of photographs fresh from Wal-Mart that have been leaning against the salt and pepper shakers. "Anything's okay," I answer as I open the packet. He sees what I'm doing and says he and Lillian had those made up for Benny and me. *Duplicate Prints* on the outside of the inner envelope verifies this. It takes a moment to understand what the photographs are, but as I shuffle through them I realize that it is a brief history of them, ten or eleven pictures spaced more or less evenly throughout their married lives. Some of the early ones even have Benny and me in them at different ages. I lay them out on the table in chronological order and what I see are two long lives that have progressed gently and properly without particular illnesses or setbacks or disappointments, but also with no distinguishing moments, either. Before me are ordinary, satisfying lives, as if Able and Lillian have prevailed over an invisible force I can neither name nor even get a sense of. The whine of the microwave makes me turn to look at Able standing in front of the counter staring through the tinted window at the turning plate with both the dinners. "You want a salad or something?" he asks without looking at me.

"I'm okay," I answer.

"Gandhi's kicking himself, you know," he goes on.

"Did you know about her pulse at the physicals last year?" I ask.

He nods and says once when she didn't feel so good he took it and it was very slow. I ask if he thought it might be serious. He nods again and then says, "I just wanted it to go away." He pushes a palm out in my direction as if to stop what I might say. "I don't need a lecture," he tells me.

"And what about Gandhi?" I ask.

"He asked if we had any problems and I told him no," he answers. "We were both there."

"And she just nodded, I suppose, just agreed."

"He had a busy day," he says. "He was backed up."

"He did nothing?" I ask.

"The nurse took some blood samples," he tells me. "They called in a couple of weeks to say we were fine."

"Jesus Christ," I say softly.

"Don't blame him," Able says. He turns to me, arms loosely folded, and adds, "We got there late, he was rushed, you know how it goes." I'm right on the edge of telling him that he did it on purpose, that he knew how to play the system and get in and out without Gandhi finding out a thing. But I don't. His stare is one that tells me he knows what I'm thinking and he says, "She'll be all right. She'll be okay." He brings the dinners over to the table and sets them down on the place mats, I turn and take silverware from the drawer behind me, and then we begin to eat directly from the Stouffer's containers. "Actually," he says without looking at me, "she ought to have more pep." The remark seems directed to the middle of the table. "Maybe it'll help her overall. Who knows?"

Then, Lillian gone from his mind, he asks for the first time in a great while how my life is, the progress of my book, and how Elaine and the girls are. As I answer, I get the feeling that he's testing out what it might be like for him if Lillian should die, realizing that he might have to begin to make extra efforts with me, and even Benny and others, so he would have people to rely on. Such has hardly ever been the case, with Lillian always his social shield, the one who planned the small parties at the club, who accepted or regretted all the invitations. It occurs to me that almost never when I've telephoned over the years has he ever answered. Always he waited to see who it was and then, if it was important to him, he got on an extension. Just as I finish with the fact that Melissa is thinking of changing jobs, he asks, "What do you think of Benny?" He holds my eyes with his, the question not one intended casually. When I answer that Benny's Benny and try to let it slide, he shakes his head a little and says, "I want your opinion." Able's never been this direct with me and I'm wary of saying what I think. He senses this and raises his chin slightly for me to speak. Talking family with family is usually a bad idea, but there's something in Able's eyes I don't quite understand, as if even at his age there is plenty to discover.

"I think he's wasted his life," I answer. If I'd said something like that twenty years ago Able would have thrown me out of this place, but now he nods very slowly, then says Benny told him about a year ago that he hasn't had a new patient in two years, that all he's treating now are returns from his early and middle years. I say Benny makes a fortune, though, and Able, looking away, says, "He's a playboy." That out, Able then really lets go on Benny, the pain from his two broken marriages and the daughters he more or less abandoned, grandchildren Able hasn't seen since they were toddlers, right at the top of the list. "And his education," Able says. "Just the best, even now." He looks at me again and says, "Something happened to him in college, something went wrong with his values, his way of thinking." He talks on, the gravy in the bottom of the Stouffer's container in the first stages of congealing, about Benny's first wife and how sweet, even naïve, he thought she was, and then his eyes water when he mentions the bright vivaciousness of Benny's second. Then his wandering is abruptly cut short by a thought. "Know what he told me about you?" he asks. I remain very still as he says, "That you were such an idealist that he and I were going to have to take care of you, that your head was so far in the clouds with this poetry business that ever earning a decent living was probably out of the question." He smiles and I do, too. "And now you're a professor with a Ph.D., for God's sake," he says. I know he's on shaky ground because he really doesn't know much about my professional life, but he wants to say something important to me and I know he doesn't know how to do it. "I'm happy," I say and he points a finger at chest level and makes two weak stabs in the air with it, as if in punctuation.

"And you've got a family," he says. He pauses, then adds, "And that's everything." For a moment he seems satisfied with this small proclamation. Then he says, "Benny's shifty, if you know what I mean." When I say he likes the babes, all right, Able, his face hard and solid, tells me Benny gambles, as though it were news. "On everything," I say and Able realizes I know.

"Why?" Able asks, his eyes now off me and fixed somewhere in the middle of the floor. When I tell Able I asked Benny once about it and the answer was that Benny liked the action, plain and simple, Able slowly shakes his head and says, "I'm going to leave you my money."

"I hope you won't," I say. For just a couple of seconds this makes Able mad as hell. His eyes flash like I've slapped his face. Slowly, Able asks why the hell should he give a cent to Benny when it'd be gone in a twinkle. "Maybe not," I tell him, then reconsider and say, "It's possible, yes."

"Then what's wrong with you getting it?" he asks.

"It's not fair that Benny should end up hating me," I answer. Eyes back in the middle of the floor, he stares again. "You can't show Benny what you think of him through me," I say. This causes him to raise his eyebrows and hold them that way a couple of seconds, then his mouth turns down, and he nods. "Never thought about it that way," he says. Then he looks at me and asks, "If you were me, what would you do?" I tell him that our will says fifty-fifty to our daughters, no frills. "Suppose one of them marries a jerk," he says. "A Benny."

"We can't control that," I answer.

"I can do anything I want, you know," he says. I let this go and he seems to hear his own words as hollow, as though they make him feel uncomfortable. He clenches his fist on the table and says something under his breath that sounds like, "Jesus Christ," but I can't be sure. "Know how much I've got?" he asks. It takes me a moment to decide if I'm going to lie, and he fills it with, "Do you?" I shake my head slowly. "About a million," he says. Apparently, the flat expression on my face isn't the response he was looking for, or expected, and he adds, "That's pretty good, don't you think?" As I nod he says, "For a guy whose father was a night watchman." This is only the second time I can ever remember Able mentioning his father, the first being years ago when I was a kid and even then I had had to ask. "It is," I answer. "You bet it is." There's a tone to my voice that I hear as if someone else, quite sincere, has spoken, and I'm glad it's come out that way. His eyes wander over my face, then my shoulders and chest, in an open appraisal, as if he's really seeing me for the first time. "So, you and Benny, right down the middle?" he says.

"It'd make it easier on me," I answer.

"You'd get more money," he says, eyes narrowing as part of the test.

"Benny's a jerk," I say, "but he's not a criminal."

"We'll see," he says, eyes still on me. Then, as if some silent bell has gone off in his mind, he looks at his watch, then brings it closer to his face, head bent, the fingers of his right hand moving it to catch better light. "You drive," he says.

Lillian doesn't know right away who's come into her room. Her head moves from the center of the pillow to the side where our sounds comes from, and she stares right through us until Able says it's us. The bandage on Lillian's forehead is about four inches long and narrow, just enough to cover the suture line. The brown and yellow from the bruise spreads out to either side in a way that is remarkably symmetrical. Able goes directly to her, spreading his arms as though to make himself larger in her line of vision, and says, "How's m'darlin'?" Lillian's eyes fix directly on the sound but in how wide and soft they are she does not see him well, if at all. With some difficulty Able leans over and kisses her, then drops his head on her pillow next to hers. "Teddy, Teddy," Lillian says, her arms coming up toward me. Able moves back and I lean down to hug her. Right away she wants to know if everyone's all right at home, and I tell her Elaine's just fine, then what our daughters are doing. "I'm so glad," she says as though she's just felt a weight removed. She glances in Able's direction and then back at me. "Isn't he handsome?" she says of Able.

"I've had my day," Able answers, actually a little proud.

It's right then that the sheet slides down a few inches and I see the outline of the pacemaker under the skin on Lillian's upper left chest, the fine sutures on the top like a tiny crown. It looks like it's balanced perfectly on two ribs. I can also make out a faint pulse nearly lost among the thin cords of her neck. It seems perfect. I turn to look at Able and he's watching her, his face alight, eyes watery. He tells her he drove with Jeremy to the airport to pick me up, then what we had for dinner, and then adds that it was a beautiful day with perfect weather. She turns her head so that it's straight on the pillow and looks up at the ceiling as though she sees a blue, cloudless sky. Able, arms folded, says, "You're going to be all right, you know." Then to me, "Other than this, she's in excellent health." One hand flops out toward Lillian in emphasis. As he turns to look back at her, there's a stillness the likes of which I've never known. Absolutely no sound comes from the hall nor is there a rustle of a breath in the room. It feels as if time's been inverted and we are in this instant starting backward to what we were.

Then, surprisingly, Dr. Gandhi comes into the room, shakes hands with Able, says hello to me while he's doing it, and then steps over to Lillian's bed and reaches out to take her hand. This catches Able off guard, and as he moves to the side of the bed it's as if he feels shut out, as though he's lost control of things. Right away he's asking questions about how Dr. Gandhi thinks she's doing, and when she might be coming home, will it be tomorrow or the next day, are there special things about the pacer that he should know, all of which Gandhi ignores as he looks at Lillian. Finally, he says, "How do you feel, Lillian?" Slightly startled, she rolls her head a bit more toward him and smiles, then Able says, "She's doing fine, don't you think? Those cheeks, that color." Still Gandhi ignores him, and says, "Feeling a bit weak?" Able turns to me and says who wouldn't, what with the food here. His agitation is visible now, and I think that what he'd like to do is push in front of Gandhi and say ask me all the questions and leave her alone. Lillian then turns her head enough so that her eyes find Gandhi and she nods. Her voice is like a whisper as she says, "Very weak." Gandhi pats her hand and tells her she's had a rough time, that the head blow and the pacemaker procedure have taken a toll.

"They have," Able says, leaning around Gandhi so Lillian can see him. He puts a hand out and lets it rest on her shin just below the knee. This makes her smile, too, but at the same time, as if it's a signal, she also closes her eyes. It's as if we're at the bedside of someone whose death is but seconds away. We stand like acolytes watching her long, slow breathing and the pinpoints of sweat that give her face the sheen of new makeup. Then Lillian sleeps, her face so perfectly still and relaxed that it's like she's a young woman again, her breathing unchanged. Gandhi says she'll be fine, and turns to leave, says goodbye to Able and me, then says he'll see Mrs. Neel during rounds tomorrow morning and will advise on going home. I reach out to shake hands but just before I do he turns away and heads toward the door.

Able looks at Lillian as if he's falling in love with her for the first time. So intensely private and open is the look on his face that I know it's something I have no right either to share or intrude on, and I silently turn and go into the hall. Visiting hours are just ending, and I watch the relatives and friends leave the rooms along the hall, some quickly, as if they can't stand the place or the patient, some more slowly, lingering in the doorways with hands up, two even blowing kisses back into the room. Nurses with med carts have already started down the hall, each working one side, the pills lying in the small, fluted cups like tiny pieces from a rainbow. It takes less than ten minutes for the hall to empty of visitors and for the nurse to work her way down to the room next to us. Then I turn and go back in to tell Able the nurse is coming. He's on the edge of the chair next to the bed, forearms on the mattress, hands joined, like someone in a pew having trouble kneeling. I want to say something to him that will help him, but in a flash I know there's nothing, not a damn thing, what I am is only a witness. Slowly he gets up and leans over and kisses her, but there's no response, so dead asleep is she. He seems quite content to stand by the bed and watch her, all calm and smooth, as if he considers it a privilege.

When the nurse comes in, Able steps back to stand beside me and he takes my arm. For a second it feels like Lillian's there. He says we ought to go now because he doesn't want to see them wake her up to give her a sleeping pill, and then he puts pressure on my arm to turn me and we go on out.

When we get home, the faint red light on the answering machine's blinking steadily across the dark kitchen. In the moment just before I can get to the wall switch, it reminds me of seeing Mars at the Hayden Planetarium when Able took Benny and me and two neighbor kids one Saturday. God, I think, that was a wonderful time, and then I turn on the ceiling lights. "Who the hell could that be?" Able says, then turns right and goes into the living room, his dismissal of the message complete. The woman on the tape says hello, and is this the Neel residence, her voice so slow that I almost laugh. I do when she identifies herself only as Eulie Jean, a not-too-close friend of Benjamin Neel. There's a long pause and just as I think this is one of Benny's bimbos, someone who's probably in the area looking to mooch a place to stay, she says Benny wanted her to call this number and tell whoever was there that he was in the hospital in Vegas with a heart attack. She follows that with the number and then pauses again. "Well," she says, kind of twangy, "thank you so much," and hangs up. Able appears in the doorway, his eyes wide. "The number," he says. "Get it." The tape goes back to the beginning of the message and Eulie Jean oils through it again, I at the ready with pencil and a Post-it. As I write, I glance across at Able. His head's down, one arm dangling, the other on the doorjamb for support. Slowly, he brings his head up and then without a word points to the phone and moves his index finger up and down to tell me to call. I do, and when I get the hospital operator and ask for Benny I'm put right through. His voice sounds no different, and if I hadn't known I'd called a hospital I wouldn't know a thing's wrong with him. At first he's very upbeat, even jovial, and says, "How you doin', bro?" and then tells me he was on a roulette roll to end them all, played the thirties for seven hours and was heading for the stars. Right then I realize he's on medicine— not a narcotic for pain but something heavy-duty for anxiety. "Had seventy-five big ones tucked in Eulie Jean's cleavage," he says, then laughs more deeply and juicier than I've ever heard. It's as though the smoke from every cigarette he's ever had is still in his chest. "Hey, I'm going to be all right," he says. "Just checking in with the fam." I ask who the doctor is because, of course, I want to call to find out how he really is, and he says he doesn't know, the guy came and went, but that they told him he was going to be fine. "Just take a few weeks is all," he says. "How's everybody there?" he asks, his voice lower and more concerned, as though he feels nostalgia. I tell him Lillian's in the hospital and what happened and he asks to talk to Able. I turn and hand over the phone. Able sits down at the table, then takes the phone in both hands and puts it to his ear. For several moments he simply listens, staring into the middle of the room, now and then a nod. Finally, he says, "I'll tell her. Count on it." Then there's another nod and from nowhere Able's eyes are all filled up and the skin around them has turned red. He can barely speak when he says thank you and good-bye. He hands me the phone, his eyes way across the room, and I hang it up. Then Able puts his hands on his knees and shoves himself into a standing position. "Do you think he'll be all right?" he asks. I answer I'll try to get hold of someone out there. "It's possible," Able says, carefully considering his words and hardly talking to me, "that I have lived too long." As he turns and heads for the bedroom, his steps are shorter and back to how they were just after his surgery, as if all the progress he's made has been suddenly snatched away.

Right away I call the hospital and explain to the operator what information I want. I'm immediately disconnected and call back again, same tone, same request. This time I'm put straight through to Benny's floor and a male nurse named O'Brien tells me Benny's critical but stable, and the resident, Dr. Goodly, is with him now. He gives me the number to call in a couple of hours if I wish to speak to him directly. I answer I certainly do and write it down and hang up.

Then I go back to check on Able and I'm surprised to find that the bedroom door is closed almost all the way, that the room is dark. I push the door open a few inches to see if perhaps he's in the bathroom, but that's dark, too. Then in the pale light from the small hallway where I'm standing I see his outline in the bed, the sheet and blanket already up around his shoulders. He's on his side, his face away from me and toward Lillian's bed. When I softly call his name, the only response is his raising of one hand, palm toward me, to say *stop*. I say his name again and the hand stays exactly where it was as he answers, "Not *now*." His voice is suddenly as strong as when Benny and I were kids and had done something to get on the wrong side of him, and when we heard that tone we knew he was starting to boil. It's more that reflex than what he's said that makes me back away and pull the door closed. I can't help but think what an ugly tyrant of a father he sometimes was, and this is like that in miniature. Here I want to bring him the news of Benny and he's pulled away and become self-absorbed, his feelings and needs first in his mind. It seems then that for the first time ever I notice that there's an odor of age in the apartment, something faint and very distant to be sure, but nonetheless present. It's as though time has managed to get inside everything—the curtains, the wall-to-wall, the appliances, even the furniture—and has embedded itself like a sleeping disease. As I walk slowly through the living room toward the balcony, the facing couches and the huge square coffee table between them seem so hollowed out by time that a puff of air could collapse them all. The matching straight chairs are as fragile as drawings, and the built-in bookcase on the wall, which contains only a decorator's arrangement of a few books and pieces of Spode and plants, has no more strength than cardboard. The heavy double curtains along the windows by the balcony hang as if in immense fatigue.

It's different now with Able here who doesn't need looking after, and it's a relief to go out on the balcony and not have to worry that Lillian's going to get in the bath with her hair dryer or while my back's turned put the *TV Guide* in the toaster oven. As I sit down on Able's long chaise, the wind off the ocean is like a sweet hand that goes all through my hair and over my face. I close my eyes and receive it. Then I see that the lights in the two other parts of the building are almost all on, the snowbirds here in full force. Why is it, I think, that one second we're not old, the next we are, and then I let that go as a surprising shot of anger at Benny flies through me. He's brought this on himself, I think, and if he died he'd have no one to blame but himself. He's always denied his own mortality. The one time I brought it up to him a few years ago he laughed and said that one should never underestimate the body's ability to accept punishment. Well, I think, your body's finally getting *its* say. After that thought I just feel sad, the undulations of the wind going by my ears like tiny pieces of a lost chorus, the strong ocean smells cool and sexual, the darkness at the horizon line broken now and then by the dim reflected light from thunderstorms so far away they must be near the Bahamas. Above them the stars are like the lights from lost black ships.

Turns out when I talk to the doctor around midnight that Benny's heart attack has been downgraded to angina, and he says that in the morning they're going to cath him to see if he's got coronary artery problems and, if so, whether or not they'll settle for angioplasty or have to go ahead with a bypass. I ask what's a good time to call Benny before they do it, and he says they'll be taking him in about six-thirty. I thank him and hang up, and just as I do, everything about Able falls slowly and gracefully into place: he's dying. It explains everything so clearly that no reasoning needs to be called upon, each decision since his surgery a clear and direct result of what he's known but won't tell anyone. So sure am I that there's absolutely no necessity to think back over these past months. If I had figured it out I would have probably made fools of both of us trying to save him. Making no sound at all, I go back to his bedroom door and open it a crack. The weak lamplight from the hall table just behind me bores in on his face, now turned toward me, like a narrow flashlight beam. His sunken jaw hangs slack, his mouth is open like a fish's, and it seems impossible that I will ever be as old as he, that one day my kidneys will shut down or, like Benny, chest pains will strike without warning.

I try to sleep for a while on the couch in the den, the television on very softly, but there's a low-level panic that moves through me as though I've had a strong, unexpected dose of caffeine: heart rate's up, eyes feel stretched a little in their sockets, I'm aware of my breathing and the exact location of my diaphragm, but most of all there are two circles of smooth warm sweat in the middle of my palms. I spread my hands on my shirt and press down, then relax them into loose curls, but within a few seconds they're as wet as before. I know right then that within a year, perhaps two, my parents will be dead, and I know that Able knows, too.

As if someone else suddenly occupies my body, I get up and go to my suitcase, open it, and take out the swimming trunks Elaine packed at the last minute with, "You'll be in Florida, you never know." The cool air from the AC vents high on the wall is like a settling blanket as I change, and when I leave the apartment, my shirt open and a towel over my shoulder, I feel like it's twenty years ago and my kids and Elaine are down by the pool waiting. The night doorman is dozing on the stool at his station, the lobby is dazzlingly lighted, the great chandeliers and mirrors a Versailles knockoff. I go quietly out the side door toward the pool, and instantly the ocean air billows my shirt and I'm alone and free. The pool is so smooth and still in the night air that it looks purely ornamental, as though no one has ever swum in it. It seems at once inviolate and artificial, as though if I were to go in it I would be transformed into glass.

I leave my shoes and shirt on a chaise and go down the wide concrete steps, then through the gate and onto the beach. By the seawall the sand, an inch or so down, is still warm from the day, but where the tide has come in the sand is cool, flat, and hard. To my left, the fishing pier down at the end of Commercial is lighted, as is the restaurant on it where Elaine and I used to eat hot dogs with the kids years ago. To the right, the great sweep of the coastline is marked by the lights of the tall, rich buildings for as far as I'm able to see. The storms over the horizon are still there, but they've lost strength and have moved off to the north. All that's left of them are small crescents of orange on the horizon against the night sky. The southeast wind is warm and very light, the weak waves long and even, their tops blue, black, and white in the strange, fake light from the building. I make a square of my towel and put it on the dry sand, my glasses right in the middle, and then enter the water slowly, feeling for the first dropoff, only a few yards out. Even though I know it's there its abruptness surprises, and I'm waist deep in a blink. Then there's a plateau that goes for thirty yards or so, a safe place where Able and Lillian used to swim and talk every morning with their friends years ago. The second dropoff comes as unexpectedly as the first, and even though I think I'm ready for it I go under so fast it's as if I've stepped off a building. Within a few seconds, though, the feeling of deep submersion is among the most pleasant I can remember. It feels as though the temperature of the water and my skin are exactly the same, as in an impossible equilibrium. Eyes closed, for a moment I don't know where the surface is, and there's a seductive feeling, very powerful for just a second or two, that asks if that matters. Then I slowly surface, hardly out of breath, and lie back among the small waves as though I believe the salt water can support me forever. In this moment it's like I am an offering to the stars or, possibly, what is beyond them. I rock up and over one small wave and down into the trough of the next, and on and on, the feeling like morphine just before sleep. I have no idea how long I do this, but it's over far too soon, a small upwelling of colder water suddenly around me like a coat. It's when I come upright and start to tread water that I realize how far out I've drifted with the tide. The buildings along the beach are half their size, the expanse of water between them and me like a black slab of time. What I've done is to give myself a test—not to see if I can swim back, because I know I can, but to see if I want to. What surprises me most is that this is not a simple decision but an act of will, probably the first I've known of such magnitude. Thoughts of family flash in one part of my mind, but in another, deeper place that seems now to be awakening only for the first time, there comes a powerful, benevolent calm, the message of which is that even in death I am undiminished, that there is a wholeness of experience from which there cannot be separation. As I start back toward shore, breaststroking so as to keep the buildings dead ahead, every movement is effortless. As I swim, each stroke measured like a small step, the vision of death

I had when I was young comes back: everything in life finally accomplished just the week before, a large family in a semicircle around a perfectly white bed, a grief-stricken wife of many years closest to me, children and grandchildren in abundance, even, I once let myself think, some nice music. As I inhale at the end of a small, unconscious laugh, about a cup of water is suddenly in the back of my throat and then half way down the windpipe. For several moments I cough so hard that I'm close to the dry heaves, all the time trying to keep my head up and back so as not to suck in more. The distant lights from the buildings blur, the small waves feel suddenly higher, the heart races, in my mind only the one hard thought that what I'm learning from Able is that we do our dying on our own.

I don't know how long it takes to finally get back to the beach, but the effort expended is much more than I counted on. When my foot finally goes down and touches bottom I stop, the buildings rising high and close in front of me, and stand, my breathing and the pulse in my neck that of a long-distance runner's. I know I'm exhausted, but also finally safe, and I stand with the frail waves sloshing warmly around my shoulders, glad to be supported. It's only a short moment before I realize that somehow I'm in the middle of a school of fish — what kind I can't imagine — and that I am certainly a major attraction. So gently that they feel like testing kisses, tiny mouths are all over my legs, back, and belly, a bump here and there from something larger. I don't move for a few seconds, the sensation humbling, one species inspecting another, and then I swish my arms in the water and in an instant they're gone. As I walk slowly out of the water, I feel my weight increase, the legs ever slower, as if my human form is being forced to return.

I go straight to where I left my glasses on the towel and find that the towel's been stolen, the glasses flipped over and half buried. As I wipe the water from my arms with my hands, I see through the bits of sand on the glasses that two cigarettes glow in the dark up by the seawall. My towel, no doubt, I think, and start up the small incline. Just before a young male voice says, "Get your ass out of here, man," I see in the shadowy light that the two of them are naked, except for my towel, which is a white swatch across their middles. "That's my towel," I say, hands on hips.

"Was," the young man says slowly.

"I want it," I tell him, and take a small step closer. Neither is at all large, the young woman has the same slight frame as my daughters'. I suddenly feel an adrenal surge that seems way beyond what the situation really calls for, as if these two in front of me represent something else I can't explain. "Let's have it," I say and take another small step. This time I square myself at their feet and cross my arms. "Jesus Christ," he says, but hardly in an offensive way and certainly it's not directed at me. Rather, it actually sounds as if he's just discovered he's tired. He stretches his right arm over his head and slides the hand under his clothes. Then, in a movement that's so quick I can hardly track it, he's sitting up with a gun pointing straight at me. "Don't kill him," the young woman says. She rises on an elbow, her breasts very small, nipples hard.

"Why not?" he answers. Perfect white teeth, a little blue in the darkness, shine at me. He turns to look at her. She seems unaware of her nakedness.

"Mister," she says, "get out of here." The adrenaline makes me feel as though I've got armor on.

"I want my towel," I say.

"Look," she says, "he'll do it. He *will*."

As though some higher, saner force takes me over, I feel myself moving several steps backward, my eyes still on him and the gun, which doesn't move at all, doesn't even waver a little.

"Say something," the young man tells me. Another two steps. "Something nice," he says.

"Enjoy," comes out before I even think about it. "And have a nice night."

"That's right," he says slowly. "Very good." I watch as he raises the gun more and fully straightens his arm. Then he says, *"Pow, mother,"* and the arm recoils upward as though he's really pulled the trigger. I'm at the gate to the pool and through it and heading up the stairs before I know it, everything a blur. I imagine that even with the light wind and the low sounds from the surf I can hear him laughing.

My call to Benny goes straight through, and I'm relieved that he's not nearly as high as earlier but, rather, coherent and scared. He takes some pleasure in telling me what the doctor already has, and, typically Benny, he throws in a few medical terms along with their explanations, like I'm a dunce. Under stress, and even sometimes when not, Benny always has to tell the world how things really are. When there's a pause, I ask him what happened to the seventy-five grand and Eulie Jean. "Guess, pal," he says, and I answer I don't have to. "The thirties just kept coming," he adds. "Almost didn't matter what I played." Then I ask if Able called about the accident and Lillian's pacemaker and there's a long pause and finally he says he's been in Vegas a week, says it was a real blowout, if you know what I mean. Just as I think he could be the new poster boy for dysfunctional psychologists, he asks, his voice lower, all the b.s. gone, if she's really okay. She isn't fine, I tell him, but she'll probably come home in a day or two. "I don't have anybody here," he says, as though he's just discovered he's really alone. Another pause and he adds, covering, "Where are all the Eulie Jeans when you need them?" I wish him good luck and end by telling him I'll check in later in the day to find out how it went. Then he makes a sound as though he's starting to say something but suddenly can't get it out, then a faint, whispered, "Goodbye," and the line's dead. I go out on the balcony and lie down on the chaise, the very first light of dawn easing over the edge of the ocean like the start of faint organ music in a great church.

Four hours later I wake up when Able opens the door and sticks his head out. He's fresh and clean-shaven, his sports shirt and slacks like new. He asks if I'm all right, and as I pull myself into a sitting position he asks what's wrong with the bed in the guest room and smiles. It seems like months since I've seen him do that. He says he's already eaten but left out some cereal and juice. Then he asks about Benny and I tell him what I found out. As I pass him on the way to the bathroom, I say I wouldn't want to be Benny right now for anything because of what he's going through alone. Able says nothing, which surprises me until I glance back and see him smile slightly and then nod. "We'll call," he says.

As I eat a bowl of Cheerios, Able sits across from me. He suddenly seems to have lost a little more weight and height. I look out the window and down at the beach, the couple with the gun like an impossible dream. For a few seconds, it's as though the last of the adrenaline will never go away. Then Able asks when I'd like to go see Lillian, and I tell him I can be ready in a few minutes. "She sure won't know if we're late," he says. While at first this sounds mean, when I glance at him I see that that was hardly his intention. He's looking out the window seeing nothing, gone away in his mind for the moment, his face relaxed and full of resignation. He looks like he just might stay that way forever. Then he says, "The woods decay, the woods decay and fall, / The vapors weep their burthen to the ground, / Man comes and tills the field and lies beneath, / And after many a summer dies the swan." These are the first lines from Tennyson's "Tithonus," one of the poems I wrote about in the last chapter of my second book. He has said them quietly, almost privately, as if for pleasure. Then he looks at me and smiles slightly, his head down. I know I'm staring at him but I can't help it. Over the years I sent Lillian and him copies of my books—and even some of my articles—but there's never been any indication that he's ever read them. I know from questions about certain poems and people in the letters that Lillian has read everything I've published. But not Able. The only thing I can ever remember him asking me was if I knew the average unit cost in the publishing business. When I told him I hadn't a clue he nodded as if that's exactly what he expected and that was that. "Your Tennyson," he says, "writes some nice poems." My only answer is to chew more slowly and nod. In the same quiet tone, he says, "I *have* read all your books. I wanted you to know."

"I appreciate that," I answer. Our voices stay flat and quiet.

"Some things I didn't understand," he goes on.

"Like what?" I ask. I take the napkin and touch the corners of my mouth, a little excited, ready to explain.

"Just some things," he says. I notice how bright the morning light is as it pours into the room. "Reading and writing were always hard for me," he says and glances in my direction but makes no eye contact. "Always a numbers guy," he adds. Then he does look at me directly and says, "Where'd you learn to do that? How'd you learn to weave words?" I suddenly remember the books he brought home, how he worked through *Thirty Days to a More Powerful Vocabulary*, *Speed Reading Made Easy*, and all the others. When I answer it's just the way I am, he smiles a little to himself, as if now, right in this moment, it's all okay. He starts in on a story, one I've heard before many times, about how in a one-page memo the CEO of AT&T split off the Baby Bells. "You should have seen the writing," he says, then catches himself abruptly, the space right between his eyes tense, as though somewhere in his body he feels a sharp, small pain. Then he gets up and stands looking at me. Before he leaves, he says, "I wanted you to know." It's direct, with no ceremony, equal parts business and love.

I call Benny and find out that he's not only passed the catheterization with flying colors but he'll be checking out and heading back sometime early afternoon. He sounds a little weak, but it's the same old Benny. He tells me the docs said it must have been anxiety and excitement, that they told him he's got coronaries like the Lincoln Tunnel, just he should cut way down on the smokes and get out for some exercise. "Got to shed some flab," he tells me, and then, as though it were in the same sentence, "Guess who's back?" Obviously, he's made a face or done something like wink lasciviously because I hear Eulie Jean's distinctive voice slowly say, "You devil." They both laugh like children for a moment and then Benny asks her if his ten gallon's on the way she likes it and she answers that people are likely to figure them for Roy and Dale. Another laugh and then Benny asks how things are at my end and I tell him that in a few minutes Able and I are going down to Broward General. "You give everybody my best," he says. It's like he can't remember any names.

"Will you take care of yourself?" I ask.

"From now on," he says, "just blackjack." Then he adds that he'll give a call next week sometime to check on Lillian and before I can answer he hangs up.

I turn to see Able standing in the doorway. Right away I tell him Benny's fine, that there's nothing to worry about, he's flying home this afternoon. Able makes little, if any, response, his eyes going from me to the middle of the floor and then back again. So unusual is this that I repeat that Benny's fine, he's had a scare is all, and is going to have to take better care of himself. "It's about time," Able says and turns toward the kitchen door that leads into the hall and the elevator. Cracks like that are not unusual where Benny's concerned, and as I follow Able out I expect one or two more going down in the elevator. Nothing, not even a light comment indicating relief that he's okay. From how Able's eyes move slowly all over the inside of the elevator it's as though Benny's dropped off the face of the earth. "He says he's got to quit smoking," I say, "and lose some weight." After a moment in which Able seems to search out the subject matter he grunts very lightly, as though he's reached a private, not-too-important conclusion.

In the garage, Able points to the driver's side as if he's giving me both permission to drive and an order to do it at the same time. It's then I see the damage to the front end of the Cadillac for the first time, and I'm very surprised at how little it is. The bumper has a deep vertical crease and the grille just above it has a series of small wrinkles in the metal. It reminds me of Lillian's forehead. As we go west on Oakland Park, I try to bring up Benny one more time, and from Able's response it's as though he's been thinking about him, too. "I think he's going to be all right," I say, like we're in the middle of a conversation.

Able, looking out the window, says, "He thinks he's immortal."

Lillian is much better physically—sitting up eating an early lunch, a round, kind nurse's aide helping her find the various foods on her tray—but, mentally, right away there's no doubt that the accident has taken her down a notch. She recognizes Able when he says, "How's my darlin'?" and leans over a bit to kiss her on the forehead, but when I do the same and ask how she is, there's a slight recoil in her, as if my voice and shadowy form are only passingly familiar. "It's Ted," I say, her head rigid, eyes straight at the wall. "Teddy."

"Why, yes," she finally says. One hand lifts off the tray in feeble acknowledgment, and then whatever shards of her memory are left pull together and she says, "What're you doing here?" She turns her head in Able's direction, as if it is he who will give her the answer. I tell her I just came down to see how you and Able were doing. "I was in yesterday," I say.

"You *were*?" she says, her glance again toward Able.

Just as I start to silently reprimand myself for confusing her, Able says, "We both were."

"Why, I must have been asleep," she says.

"You were," Able tells her. Surprised, I look directly at him, but we make no eye contact at all. Instead, he's watching her intently. This is the first time I've ever heard him lie to her. Then, as if he hears my thoughts, he turns to look at me, the truth clear in his expression that it doesn't matter what he says to Lillian. Proof of this is immediate:

Lillian looks at me near the end of the bed as though I'm an apparition just off the ceiling, and says to Able, "Who's that?"

"I'm Teddy," I tell her again and, after a moment, she accepts it. Her mind sails among the stars. Then I tell her I've got a message from Benny and she smiles and asks what it is. I tell her what happened and she listens carefully when I say that he wanted me to tell her he's fine, that everything's going to be all right. "I'm glad," she says, her face so vacant that I expect her to ask who Benny is. Instead, she tells me that Benny's her older son, that he's a doctor, which is how she's always thought of him, then asks if I'm a doctor.

"Ted got a Ph.D.," Able tells her.

"And we were there, weren't we?" she asks him.

"Absolutely," I say before Able can speak.

"I remember a rainy day," she says. There really isn't any need for Able and me to keep exchanging glances. It was a blistering hot Iowa day and I went by myself. "Did you see Benny?" she asks, to which Able reminds her that he lives in California.

"Of course he does," she answers, smiling to signal the end of the subject. It's right then that for the first time she notices the pacemaker, and it startles her. Looking down, she makes a small sad noise in her throat, then with one finger she touches it right in the middle. The area beneath it is a little sore and the light pressure surprises her. Able tells her what it is and she nods and looks up at him, eyes wide. He says it's going to give her more "get-up-and-go." Her eyes wander in my general direction, but I don't think she can actually see me.

"What do I do with it?" she asks. She lays a hand flat on it, like she's giving a pledge. Able tells her she's going to have more energy and she thinks about that, then says, "That'll be nice." Just as Able glances at me, Lillian says, "For what?" Lillian's mind may be doughy in places, and her eyes awful, but something's still there, all right. Able senses it, too, and looks back at her and smiles. She seems to see it, and it's almost like nothing's ever happened to either of them.

The doctor who comes into the room is a stranger to all of us. He introduces himself as Dr. Asham, which Able immediately mispronounces as *ashcan*. He says he's Dr. Gandhi's partner and he's come to see Mrs. Neel. Able asks where Dr. Gandhi is and Asham tells him that he's okay, but he's been in a motorcycle accident and sprained an ankle. Able stares at Dr. Asham like a child who's just been told his first wondrous fable. Dr. Asham takes the opportunity to step by Able and stand at Lillian's bedside. He pulls a stethoscope from his right-hand pocket and snaps the ends into his ears. For a long time he listens to Lillian's heart, first one place, then another, then back again. Satisfied, he asks Lillian to sit up, which she does with some difficulty, and then he listens again all over her back. When he's finished, he helps Lillian lie down and then tells her that she has some fluid in the lungs, nothing serious, he thinks, and that it should clear up in a day or two and then she can go home. "Headache gone?" he asks, to which Lillian nods. "Very good," he says, and then as though it were an important ceremony to him he shakes hands with me and then Able and, with a little bow, leaves. "Hear that?" Able says to Lillian.

She responds with nothing more than a visceral cough, the fluids having moved around when she sat up. From how it sounds I'll be surprised if she's home in a day or two. It's right then that for the first time the thought that maybe it would be better if she didn't arrives in my mind. Guilt follows it nearly instantly, silent reprimands going off one after another. I even glance at Able to see if maybe, as he could sometimes when I was very young, read my face for the thoughts I have. Eyes watery, mouth open and lips wet, he looks like somebody's punched him. My eyes go back to Lillian and I see only the shell of my mother, as if over these last months I've assigned old familiar things to her so I could keep seeing what I wanted to. For several brittle seconds nothing's there but the simple hard evidence of time, what was really my mother almost gone. But then she raises a hand from the bed and moves her fingers in a small familiar wave, a gesture she's used all her life to say either hello or good-bye. Now, sadly, it's hello, as if she's seeing me only for the first time this morning. "Do I know you?" she asks.

Able looks at me as I answer, "For a long time now."

"It's Ted," Able says. In his voice his remarkable patience has returned. What follows is a silence among the three of us so empty that the message it carries feels like a great deep bell in the soul, as if aloneness, even sadness, can make a sound. Able looks at Lillian for a long time, her eyes first in my direction, then swinging over to his, then wandering on the ceiling tiles as if she sees a road map. She takes a deep breath and lets it out in a single, long sigh, like she's suddenly bored, and then shuts her eyes as though no one's in the room. Able watches her chest rise and fall in a rhythm so slow it seems perilous to me, but then, satisfied, he turns to me and says, "Can I take you to lunch?" I assume, as with Lillian when he was in the hospital, that he means McDonald's, but when we come out of the elevator and I start toward the glass doors he takes my arm and says, "Hardly." Tuesdays, he says when we get in the car, it's the Captain's Table at the club. I've heard about this over the years but have never been to a meeting, which is only for the male members of the club—the women who come with them play bridge and eat light lunches in their own group called "Anchors." Able tells me that we'll have a fine meal, probably something like lobster thermidor with a couple of good wines, and then listen to the speaker. He adds that since he's been sick he hasn't been to the Captain's Table in a long time. His eyes are bright.

What I realize when we drive up to the main door of the club is that in all the years I've come here it's never been in the daylight. As the attendant drives the car away, I see lush tropical foliage everywhere, plants so well tended that they look to have only recently been brought in and set down on new, perfectly raked soil. The beige stucco of the building is bright in the high sun, a shimmering along it as though it's giving off its own energy. But most impressive, and what I've not seen before, are the yachts moored along the Intracoastal right at the back of the building. They're so close to each other in their slips that it looks as though a giant hand has carefully set them side by side. They seem so grand and so still, as if the club has its own peculiar navy. Able sees me looking at them and with a small snap of his head we immediately start along the walkway that goes past the pool and around the side of the building. I know nothing of boats like these, their size, gleam, and cost outside any experience I've had. Able tells me there's more than the usual number because the Battle of the Boats is soon, some kind of competition with another club up in Boca in which the owners theme-decorate their yachts and parade them past each other. He tells me this year it's here. He wanders back in time to several of the years he and Lillian were guests on some of the yachts, what the trip was like up the Intracoastal, how they came back overnight on the open water. He remembers it as a grand experience, as though the invitation to join these very rich people had been gratifying, and he now tells about it with a reverence and appreciation. Standing, arms folded in front of a forty-footer that says, "*The Witch*—Salem, Mass.," he remembers minute details of drinks and food and where he and Lillian slept and the fireworks and which boat won in which category. Then, abruptly, as if the memories suddenly become harsh, he shakes his head a little, smiles, and looks at me. "Out of my league," he says. I nod to tell him I understand, but he doesn't quite yet want to leave it alone. We watch as a large boat moves silently by in the center of the waterway, a lovely-looking thin woman standing in the bow in white top and shorts. The soft breeze tosses her pageboy gray hair. Then Able asks if I know how much one of those big ones down there costs. I answer I haven't got the faintest idea but I'd bet in the hundreds of thousands. He says the one he and Lillian were on went for a million five. "And that," he adds, "was fifteen years ago." He gives one last look down the line of boats, and just as he does the wake from the center of the waterway rolls under the line of yachts and it's as if, as they slightly rise and fall, each bows a small good-bye.

As we walk back over the long dock, Able takes my hand. At first he holds it in a way that makes me think he needs to steady himself for the moment—his grip is around the top near the wrist—but then as his hand slides down it's clear that he simply wants to hold it in affection. He neither looks at me nor says anything, and it's as if his gesture's the most natural thing in the world, a refined, silent form of saying something. He holds my hand all the way back past the carhops' station and down the long flagstone walkway to the club's two wide front doors. Then he turns to me and says, "Just one more time I'd like to take a ride on one of those babies."

Inside, Able's all business, the Captain's Table an event made for men who're mostly like he is, who've spent their working lives at various levels of the corporate world and who've come in their retirements to miss it badly. In one of the small dining rooms there are about ten large round tables each set nicely for six, about half of the seats already filled with men I judge to be from seventy to ninety, some dressed as I imagine the captain of one of those larger yachts would be, others, the younger ones, still in business suits. Able, I discover as we walk across to one of the tables in the rear, is a very popular man. While he doesn't know everyone there, it's obvious he's on more than hello terms with a good number of them. Our path to our table zigzags as Able takes me first to meet this person and then that one. Some of the men I know casually from dinners over the years, but most of them I meet for the first time. Each has an expectation as we shake hands and Able introduces me that I, like Able, am in industry: a quick raising of the eyebrows at my name, a flash of true interest across the face. But when Able uses the word *professor*, interest other than superficial is instantly gone. I get all the nice-to-meet-yous and hope-you're-having-a-good-stay comments, but their expressions say we've little in common. Even at the table, where we sit with three men Able knows, there's no conversation beyond the weather when they discover what I do. If it were the fall, I think, we could probably talk Miami football. But it is a pleasant and easy time, Able in his element, relaxed and, although clearly tired, as though he's found a peaceful place in the rush of the last several days. "Your father," the tall man across the table says to me, "is quite a stock picker." Able raises his right hand a couple of inches off the table and then, embarrassed but loving it, he nods, his eyes down. "Me," the man says, "I'm in munis. But him . . . "—he nods at Able—"nothing but growth, growth, right?" Another man, this one with a thin, gray mustache, slides his eyes onto Able and says, "Always observes the obvious." Then he smiles broadly and nods, his eyes still on Able in an almost adoring way. The man turns to me and says he asked Able two years ago for a hot tip on the market and Able thought for a moment and said, "Exxon." The man tells me he laughed for two days, then bought a thousand shares. "You know what it's done," he says to me. Of course I haven't got the faintest idea and Able saves the moment by interrupting with, "Doubled."

"Got another one?" the man asks, half kidding.

"Exxon," Able tells him.

"Munis are okay," the first man puts in. "Really, just right." Able nods at him, then holds his eyes for a long second, his expression one not unlike a proud child's after a fine move in Monopoly. "I know, I know," the man says, a hand up in defense, "you're in the market for the long haul."

The second man then changes the subject by asking when I'm going to retire and move on down here. In his tone the two are inextricably linked and for a moment I don't know how to separate them. My first thought is that the nearest library of any consequence is probably forty-five miles south and why would I ever live in such a place. Apparently, he sees the confusion on my face and asks if I'm going to be a snowbird, then. "I like the winter," I answer.

"Wait'll you hit eighty," he says as the first bowls of shrimp bisque arrive. He gives a small grunt, as if he knows everything.

When the shortest man at the table, who's having avocado salad instead of the soup, asks Able how his other son is, Able looks up and beyond him and stares for a moment as if Benny's picture hangs on the wall behind the man's head. "Good," Able answers, "heard from him just yesterday." He turns to me and says, "Didn't we?" I nod and taste the soup, which is exquisite, and then as I'm taking a second spoonful I glance up to see that none of the men is even looking at Able any longer. They're eating in a way heavily self-absorbed, the soup like a gentle drug drawing them ever more into themselves, as if the sensation of taste has for the moment closed down every other area of perception.

The second course is a choice between the lobster, as Able predicted, and crab cakes, which I have with a garden salad. After some small talk among the men about their wives—the short man is a widower now for eleven years but has a fifty-five-year-old girlfriend about whom one of the others remarks, "How do you do it?" (without looking up, he answers, "Do what?")—talk turns to matters of health. This starts with the short man asking Able if he's finally up to snuff after his operation. Able says the doctor gave him as clean a bill as there is, and then in the same breath asks how his skin cancer surgery went. "Piece of cake," the man answers. With his right hand he touches the left arm just above the elbow, then leaves the hand there for a moment. "Except I'm staying out of the sun now," he says. The other two nod as if they understand, as if perhaps they, too, have had similar scares. Remarkably, then, this small exchange leads into their medical histories, each in turn saying what his more serious problems have been, the treatment, who the doctor was with testimony to his being the best in the area, and a final statement that, thank God or keep your fingers crossed, it's behind me now. Each listens with the same kind of interest I'd have for a colleague telling me about a new book: attentive, thoughtful, even evaluative, but this, I understand, is much more important because each now gauges himself against the others in a quiet, testing way. The questions they ask about this or that difficulty more than suggest an apprehension that one day such an affliction might come their way, too. Only Able doesn't give long answers, not even to some searching questions from the short man. When the man across the table in the red bow tie declares with some pride that every single one of his coronary arteries has been bypassed, Able says, "Really, George, we know," and that brings the conversation to a halt. It feels as if they've been talking about serious world affairs and have suddenly come to the conclusion that, in spite of all their opinions, they can't do anything about a single one of them. Then the short man says to the table: "You hear Phil Bracken died?" This stuns everyone, even Able, who then quietly asks when and how. The short man says it was the day before yesterday, but he doesn't know the cause, only the obit was in the *Sentinel*. The short man then asks Able if he knew Phil well and Able says no and slowly shakes his head, then adds, "We were just on his yacht once." Then some new expression crosses Able's face, as if he understands only for the very first time that he's not going to live much longer. His face has a steady rigidity to it, his eyes across the table and on the floor maybe twenty feet away. He looks like he's listening hard for something. The short man mentions a few things about Phil Bracken's life, that he'd been an executive at Alcoa, where he'd lived, gone to college, and how long he'd been in Fort Lauderdale, wife, children, and so forth. It's as if in this short summary of the obituary Able really hears what a life finally boils down to and with his eyes still on the floor his eyebrows go up very slightly as though he's reached a conclusion about himself and finds it to be all right, even acceptable. It's then I notice that each man there has the same degree of tan on his face, as if a light makeup has been applied, but that just underneath the color there seems to lurk an unbearable whiteness.

The speaker starts just as the dessert tray arrives, and Able, so absorbed is he in the amazing selection of pastries, pies, and cakes, has to ask in a whisper of the man next to him who the hell's giving the talk. When told, Able looks up to the small rostrum, studies the man, and then shrugs, glances at me, and says, "Never heard of him." Then the short man across the table leans forward and says it's got to do with the United Way. That makes Able nod several times and start to pay attention. But that doesn't last long. The speaker is, essentially, giving a meeting-like report about where last year's money went, and what he has to say is cactus-dry and, for two of the men at the table, damned near snooze material. Within minutes of finishing a piece of chocolate cake and a slice of custard pie, respectively, each looks ragdoll tired, face slack, eyes going fast to half mast. It's only through what must be years of such a reaction that they know precisely when to prevent sleep, head up, eyes too wide, awake but a little disoriented. After about twenty minutes of numbers, both raw and percentages, how past projections shape future ones, board suggestions for new inclusions in the coming fiscal year—and some exclusions, too—it's my feeling that if he goes on longer than another ten minutes I will not be able to see a reason for living. Able glances at his watch, then leans a little toward me and says, "He'll shut up soon." As if on cue, the man signs off with a thank you very much and are there any questions. The response is an almost imperceptible uneasiness in the room, a moment in which the men snap sideways glances at each other, the statement clear that if one of them raises a hand he runs the risk of losing the arm. When a tall man in an off-white suit and red tie rises across the room, the low groans at our table are audible. He opens and reads from what he identifies as last year's United Way annual report, and, he says, he has some questions about the footnoted material in the back. Just as heads around the room slump first this way then that, the speaker suggests the tall man see him for coffee afterward and he'll be glad to accommodate him. Just as the tall man starts to reply, applause drowns him out and he sits down.

I lean toward Able and ask if they get many speakers like this guy and he nods deeply and says, "Last time I was here it was the regional director of the IRS." He pauses as if to consider the event, then quietly says, "Oh, boy." Then he tells me that, before him, it was some wig from the Lauderdale Rotary. "Nice guy," he says. "But had a lisp." With a nod to the short man at our table, he says he thought Herman over there could have had a stroke he nearly laughed so damn hard. I look around the table at these men and I can make no connection with ever becoming like them, ever being truly old. This will not happen to me, I think, and then I understand that they, too, one day had the same thought. Then it occurs to me that probably none of them thinks of himself like this, that it is I who now make them old.

When we're back in the car and I drive out to Sunrise, I assume we'll head west and to the hospital, but with a simple gesture, his left arm out, the index finger pointing, we go the other way toward the beach and A1A. All Able says is that Lillian'll never know if we've been there or not. I glance over at him as he looks out toward the beach, his face tired and gentle, but in his eyes there's a snatch of fire, as though it's only everything around them that's aged. When I drive into the garage, he directs me toward one of the parking spaces by the door that leads to the beach. Without a word he gets out and goes to the door, opens it, and then holds it for me until I catch up to him. It seems that although he knows I'm there it really matters very little to him. When I say that I think we look pretty ridiculous walking the beach in coats and ties, and I take off both, he doesn't even notice. He's a little bent against the soft breeze, his stride slow but very sure, his gaze up the beach and slightly toward the water. Then he nearly stops me dead in my tracks when he says, "Groucho Marx once said he'd give a million dollars for an erection." I look at him, wondering what the hell he's talking about, when he follows that with, "What would you give a million dollars for?" When right away I say my family, of course, he waves that off in the same way he gave directions in the car and says, "Personally." Three women in floral one-piece suits, who look to be in their seventies, pass us on the water side without so much as a glance. I fold the necktie and slide it into the pocket of my blazer. "To be able to sing," I finally answer. A small private smile floats across his mouth and his eyebrows rise slightly as we both remember my bitter disappointment as a kid trying for this church choir or that one, in high school being turned down for every singing group every year.

"One of the few things you can't buy," he says.

"I haven't thought about it for a long time," I tell him. "And you?"

"Absolutely nothing," he says, then turns his head to look out over the water. It is smooth and very calm, and looks as though any stirring up or turbulence would be impossible. "Your mother," he says, "Know what's it been like?" When I don't answer because the question's too vague, he turns slightly toward me and in a monotone says that what I've seen is just the tip of the iceberg, that last year's been like standing in a room with a hundred doors and having them close one right after another. His eyes are a little red and watery, but not from sentimentality nor even regret. It feels like he's holding back— and is completely in control of—an almost monumental anger, only a small piece of which is available to me. He tells me that Lillian's— situation, he calls it—has been going on for several years, that he's known for a long time something wasn't right. "But I was here during that time," I say, and he smiles and nods and answers that she always managed to rally for dinner at the club, too. "Just her way," he adds. He tells me that every time an old friend approached their table he'd lean over and under his breath tell Lillian his or her name, and when they met friends unexpectedly in the bar he'd learned how to say their names as they shook hands. "You covered for her even when we talked on the phone," I say.

"I did," he answers. A small gust of wind off the water lifts a few grains of sand that for just a moment sting the skin on our faces. "It's not been a happy time," he says, his eyes narrowed, waiting for more.

"Why didn't you say something?" I ask. "Go to a doctor?"

"Because I knew what it was," he says slowly.

"And all the housework, the meals?" I ask, to which he nods, then smiles again a little, as if now they have become fond times. "I didn't want any help," he goes on, "because I didn't want anyone to know." He senses my stiffening at this and shakes his head just a bit, then mutters, "No, no, hardly like that." He glances at me and then away. "If you bring in other people," he says, "then you share." He shrugs and puts his hands in his pockets, his coat jacket still buttoned so properly, and looks up ahead at the long fishing pier. "I'm going to have to now," he says.

Abruptly, he stops and turns around and starts back toward the building, as if all along he's been counting steps, parceling out his strength. I notice right away that there's been a wind shift, the breeze now out of the southeast and freshening. Far out over the Bahamas I see the bare beginnings of a fierce dark line that, along with the wind change, says bad weather. Able looks out in that direction, his eyes more sensing than seeing, as if he feels what I can see. "What galls me," he suddenly says, "is that Benny's going to blow whatever I leave him." There's something in the quality of his voice that says he isn't talking to me and so I don't say anything. After we take perhaps five steps, he says, "Okay, what would you do?" I tell him again that I don't want all of his money. I say Benny wouldn't leave me alone, that he'd start living in my garage or something. "Half of what I've made will go to the crooks in Las Vegas," he says. He hunches his shoulders as if there's a sudden chill from the warm, heavy wind. When I offer that Benny could change, maybe even *from* the money, Able says, "That ivory tower's pretty high." I tell him what I mean is that I don't think it's right to control from the grave, you can't predict anything about the future. "I can if I want," he says, his face hardening for a moment.

"Benny's Benny," I say. "Why punish him?"

"Why not?" he answers.

"It's not fair to me," I tell him. "Or to his daughters." From the expression on his face it looks as if this is the first time he's thought about Benny's kids. As though we've only just started the conversation, he asks sarcastically if I think those girls will ever see a damn dime. "I can't guarantee it," I say. "You know that."

"I'll leave his share to them," he says, his mouth turning down in defiance.

"And obligate them to look after him?" I ask.

"Big deal psychologist," Able says. "He's loaded."

I notice a thin coating of salt on my lips from the rising wind, lick at it, and then decide to tell Able what I know about Benny having no money at all except what he earns each month. As I finish with the fact that at sixty-two he hasn't anything, Able drops his head in something like a personal sadness that neither I, nor anyone else, can ever fix. After a moment I ask if he's all right and he nods, then looks up and says, "Which means he wouldn't understand anything about what I've done with my life."

"That's not an obligation," I tell him.

"It is, however, an option," he says. "I made something out of nothing," he adds slowly, then looks out over the water, straight into the wind, and says, "Hell, you know that." We're nearly back to the building and as we pass in front of it he stops and looks up at it, its existence something that clearly gives him pleasure. "I never made the big bucks," he says, "never got vice-president." He says this as he did a long time ago, utterly without tone, as cool in his assessment as it's possible to be. Then he adds in the same way, "But that's all right." He turns to me as though I've just appeared by his side and says, "I kicked some ass, you know?" As I nod he follows with, "And sometimes got mine kicked, too." The hopelessly tense, aggressive man of my childhood and adolescence is finally gone. The great building in front of us with its endless views of the beautiful ocean is where he's come to, and it is a good and fair place. "Drive me to the bank," he says.

When we get out in the small parking lot of the Sun Trust on Oakland Park, Able's unsteady on his feet and has to rest a hand on the roof of the car. He looks up at the bank just like he did at the apartment building and then shoves off from the car. He takes my arm to cross the parking lot. Inside, the bank is plush and quiet as we pass though its main area toward the elevator at the far end that takes us down to the vault and the safety deposit boxes. A woman about my age, dressed perfectly, sits behind a long desk, the open vault some twenty feet behind her. She's working on a stack of computer print-outs that are all rows of numbers. She looks up as we approach and says, "Hello, Mr. Neel," and then her eyes go over me in a way that feels untrusting. Able calls her Greta and says he wants into his box. Still for the most part looking at me, she hands Able the sign-in card and as he bends over I swear Greta flutters her eyelids at him. As they go back into the vault, Greta asks Able if he'll need a room and he nods and says, "Did you meet my son?" Greta turns around, raises a hand, and wiggles her fingers at me.

As they turn and disappear into the vault, what registers is the re-markable quiet of the place, not a sound from any of the devices and systems for constant temperature and perfect air circulation, not even the tiniest hum from the recessed fluorescent lights, as if the slightest noise or stray waft of outside air would be rude in this place. Able and Greta come back, she pushing a small wooden table on wheels, the safety deposit box in the middle, Able behind her as if in a small pro-cession. The box, I see, is certainly not like Elaine's and mine, which houses not much more than birth certificates and passports and a dead aunt's gold brooch. Able's erect, looks twenty years younger, and he's smiling.

Greta, one hand squeezing a key ring so that her knuckles are white, shows us to a small windowless room about thirty feet down the hall, then closes the door without so much as looking at either of us. For a moment Able acts like he's alone. He looks at the safety deposit box as though it's only he and it in the room right now, then opens it. The lid gone, the stack of stock certificates rises up and a few spill over onto the table. Able then carefully takes out more certificates until the box is about half empty. "I wanted you to see," he finally says, then takes out the rest of them and sets them in a disorganized pile to the right of the box. Then he digs down into the bottom of the box and lifts out two legal documents folded like they're ready for envelopes. He tells me these are their wills, and then offers one to me to read. As he's said, I'm the sole beneficiary. "You've got to change this," I tell him and set the will back near the box. He stares at the paper for a long moment, then nods and finally says, "If it's what you want." I don't say a word because I can see in his face that I don't have to. Then from nowhere I hear myself say, "You can't play God." He doesn't take this as a criticism but, rather, as an objective appraisal. "Oh, sure you can," he says, nodding. A small smile crosses his lips and then he tells me that he's had five or six wills, he can't remember exactly how many, and each has been entirely different. He says one, years ago, left everything to my older daughter, then three; one about ten years ago, when Elaine and I didn't come to see them, wrote us out completely; and one—he pauses and sighs—gave everything to cancer research. "It's just something I did," he says. He shakes his head and looks down at the certificates. "I don't know why." He looks up at me and says, "You can play God. Oh, sure." Then he shuffles the certificates into a loose pile, jogging the edges first this way, then that, his fingers as nimble as a teller's. Quietly, almost so I can't hear, he says that we'd better get over to the lawyer's. But I can see in his face that he's not going to make it, so empty of strength is he right now, and I tell him that I think it'd be a good idea if we both went back and took a rest, then maybe later go see Lillian. He nods and says he'll call for an appointment tomorrow. As he puts the pile of certificates back into the box, he says, as if he's actually counted it, that it could be as high as a million two, then adds that with their separate living trusts—he moves a hand in the air in front of him and adds, "Bla, bla,"—there shouldn't be any taxes to speak of.

"I know," I answer, then get up and open the door to signal to Greta that we're done. The two of them, the box squarely in the middle of the cart, make the small journey back to the vault. When Able comes out in a few minutes he's holding his keys tightly in his right hand, the one for the deposit box protruding from his leather key holder. He makes a small gesture with it toward me as if he wishes me to take note of where he keeps it.

Outside, the sun is gone behind great towering clouds, and toward the southeast, way out over the water, silent lightning pours down again and again from a long line of hard black clouds. In the car Able looks out that way, but I don't think he can see the lightning. Rather, it's as though in some special way he senses it, and all along A1A he keeps his head turned that way.

In the apartment he goes straight to his chair in the den, eases off his shoes with his toes, and hits the remote for the stock quotes. He stays awake just long enough to see that the market's flat for the day, turns to me and says he thinks what we have right now is a trading range, then puts his head back and falls asleep like he's been smacked on the back of the skull. His head tilted to the side, mouth open, he is corpselike except for two small pulses, one in his neck, the other just over the left temple, that gently play out in rhythms not quite in sync with each other. I watch him for a long time, and then go into the kitchen to make a drink. When I see the blinking red light on the answering machine I just plain don't want to know what the message is because I think it can only be bad news. It is. There are four messages from Lillian, each more incoherent than the one before it. They're all for Able and the first says she can come home tomorrow and call her back soon. The second and third repeat the same information but are filled with increasing anxiety, and the fourth is Lillian just crying, saying Able's name and where are you. I start to make the drink and then reach over and replay the tape, listen to it carefully for I don't know what, finish making the drink, and then do it again. Finally, I sit at the kitchen table in Able's chair and look out at the ocean. It appears stripped of its magnificence, all flabby water and disorganization, even the horizon line vague and dull now that the storms have slid off to the north. Nothing makes any sense, not a goddamn thing, the purpose of my mother and father living this way be-yond comprehension. None of us has anything close to a religion and we have no answers, easy or otherwise. Just believe in heaven, I think, and everything falls nicely into place. Easy beliefs, easy answers. Where, exactly, do reasonably moral lives lead? To this, a purposeless state that at this moment demonstrates no value at all? Hourly, Able summons a miraculous energy to make more war against his dying body, Lillian drifts ever deeper into the midnight of her own brain, and I am their guard, that someone who has to sit by the door. What comes to me then is that this is not the most important time of their lives, but of mine. I was sent here to learn, even to be tested. This is my journey, too.

Able sleeps in the chair without moving for almost two hours, his breathing mostly upper chest in short snatches, as if there's not much room in his lungs for air. I look in on him from time to time, but I cannot bear to sit in the room. When he awakens, it's not with the same kind of energy he's gotten from naps before. It seems that the sleep has not refreshed him, only prevented him from becoming weaker. The fourth time I look in, he opens his eyes and smiles as if he's sensed my coming, his face drawn and even thinner than this af-ternoon. His first words are that we have to see Lillian this evening and when I nod he says but first he'd like to buy me dinner at Nick's, then on the way to the hospital stop by the cemetery. He reads in my face that I don't want much to do with that and he says, "You should know where it is." When I tell him I remember the address is in the stuff he showed me last fall, he simply says, "You should know where it is." He eases forward in the chair and little by little manages to rise almost all the way, then stops as if he can no longer fully straighten his knees. I go to him and he reaches out to take my hand and steady himself. He looks across the five feet or so to the door as if the distance is huge, something that he cannot possibly traverse. Then he takes a moment, brings his free hand to his forehead and rubs it, says his pins aren't what they used to be, and shoves off. For an instant I'm certain he's going to fall, but as if he's supported by a group of unseen hands he moves across to the door, touches the jamb like it's a safe, familiar signpost, and goes on into the bedroom. Why is it, I think, that there is no name for this time of life, this fifth season?

In the car he says he thinks Nick's is out, it'll take too long and he's very tired, and could we just pick up something at a drive-thru and eat it in the car. We get a couple of burgers at McDonald's, with two medium iced teas, and head out Commercial to State Road 7, take a right, and just inside the city line to Pompano we go through the huge bronze gates of Heavenly Rest Cemetery. Able tells me to slow down as we come to the first left turn that, I can see, will eventually lead to the imposing main building about two hundred yards away. As the car nearly comes to a stop, he leans over and points to a small grove of trees not more than twenty yards away and says that when he first bought their plots that was where they were. In the lovely evening light the tombstones cast long narrow shadows along the short, perfect grass. Able motions with a hand for me to move along now and says that when they cut the rates on cremation and urn space in the main building he right away got his money back for the plots.

As we approach the main building, which is about three stories tall, and then park, I see that it's actually two separate structures joined in the middle like an *H* by a tinted-glass enclosed walkway. Walking toward the entrance, Able says on the right side are the chapel and offices, the left side all mausoleum. We go in and turn left and immediately I'm struck by how cool and still the place is, as though the air had been brought in from some other part of the country. The lighting is pale and so recessed that I cannot figure out where it comes from. Long leather benches are set every thirty feet or so along the walls. Able says, "Some very rich guys are buried here," and almost immediately what I see bears him out. The walls are actually crypts with surnames cut prominently into the marble, underneath them the first names of those already there and the years in which they were born and died. Able points first to one wall, then the other and tells me these go for well up into the thousands, lots more than being in just a simple plot outside.

Going down the long wide corridor, we suddenly hear quiet, piped-in organ music, then a choir softly starts a hymn that's familiar but I can't name it. At the end, a couple in their fifties sits close together on one of the benches, his back straight, hers curved in sorrow and contemplation. It's like being in a church that has neither an altar nor pews. We turn right at the end and Able picks up the pace, even gets a little ahead of me, as though anxious to meet a friend. Right as we turn at the next corner he stops and looks up. When I get to his side I see that we've left the section for vaults and are now in the one for urns. He raises a hand and points up to a tinted glass window about a foot square that's close to eight feet off the floor. "Me," he says, then drops his finger slightly to indicate the one under it. "Lil," he says. The urns are already in place. With his eyes up on them, he tells me that there's a brass date plate for each, the birth years already inscribed, all that's needed is for me to get the year of death put on. He says a Mr. Carmine Grandoli, whose office is in the other wing of the building, has them for safekeeping. "Anything you want to know?" he asks. I look at him, then up to the urns, then back at him and shake my head.

In the car on the way to the hospital, he puts the seat back about halfway and sleeps deeply, his head turned to my side. The first speed bump in the parking lot awakens him and for a second, as though he's been lost in a wonderful dream, he's disoriented. He looks at me like I'm a stranger, the location threatening. The high lights bordering the huge lot hang in the dark like dim forgotten ornaments. Then, just as quickly, he's alert and knows precisely where he is. He even points me into a parking space and has his door open before the car stops. The evening air is cool and moist as we go across the lot toward the building. Most of the time Able's looking up, his eyes as though in search of Lillian's room, perhaps even with the expectation that he might see her at a window. Just as we go through the automatic doors, and from nowhere, Able's talking—lecturing—about how if he and Lillian came to Florida now they certainly wouldn't come to Fort Lauderdale, it'd be Boca and north, that in the time they've been here everything's changed because of the Cubans. "They run Miami," he says as we get in the elevator. "It's us next." Of course, as we wait for the doors to close, two Cubans get on, one a male nurse, the other an X-ray technician, judging from what's scrolled into his white coat over the breast pocket. Both smile at us and nod, their conversation in Spanish uninterrupted. I catch a glimpse of Able giving them the once-over, his small eyes with a sudden tiny fire that makes me take a half step forward to block his view. When they get out at four and the doors close, he raises a hand in a slight, defensive way and says, "Nothing personal, you know, it just has to do with property values." We're silent until the next floor, but when we get out and start down toward Lillian's room he tells me that when I retire down here I ought to think seriously about somewhere north of Boca. I just let it go.

Surprisingly, Lillian's sitting up in the chair, a blanket around her shoulders, her hands folded so perfectly in her lap it's as if someone's done it for her, her feet in paper slippers, her head slightly cocked to the side like she's listening for something very far off. Instantly, Able's animated and really quite full of joy. He says her name as he approaches and Lillian's response is to look up and smile, then open her arms for what embrace they can manage. He bends over as far as he can, she rises up, but they're only able to have his cheek touch her temple, their arms in an awkward tangle. Then he goes down on one knee and truly embraces her, their heads firmly side by side, her arms around his shoulders as though she hasn't seen him in months. It's with difficulty that he gets up and steps back, taking her hands as he does. For a moment it looks as though he's just asked her to dance and will now playfully tug her to her feet. Instead, he stops and looks at her, then nods and quietly says, "Yes, yes." It's Lillian who, smiling, breaks it off by looking at me and then back to Able with the question "Who's this?" Able, lost in his moment, doesn't quite understand her question and I answer for him that it's me, I'm Ted, Teddy. Her stare stays blank and I add, "Your son."

Lillian answers confidently, with a small firm shake of her head, "Oh, no. My son's much younger." Able now catches on and tells her that indeed I am Ted, that the two of us were here this morning.

"No," Lillian says, drawing out the word, the denial utterly genuine.

"And Doctor Gandhi was here, too," Able says, nodding.

"Who's that?" Lillian asks.

I suddenly feel a strange desperation, as though if I could ask just the right question I could break through to her. "You have two sons, right?" I say.

"I do," she instantly confirms.

"And if I'm Ted who's the other?"

"You can say you're Teddy," she answers, her face now stern in rejection.

"Who?" I press.

"Benny," she says.

"What year is it?" Able interrupts.

"Nineteen fifty-two," she says as quickly as she's answered everything else.

"That's right," Able tells her, then looks at me. He holds his eyes on me long enough for me to read the message that we should go along with all this. "Of course," I say more to him than her. My mother is not dead, but she is.

Able then sits on the wide arm of the chair, one arm around Lillian, and holds her hand as if readying for an old-fashioned photograph. Both are looking straight at the door when one of the nurses comes in with Lillian's evening meds in a small cup. I get to see that two of the pills are exactly the same ones she took when I came down almost a year ago, and then there's another one I've never seen before. I follow the nurse into the hall and ask her what it is and she tells me it's something new for Alzheimer's. Right away I'm excited that there's suddenly medicine for what's wrong with her, and I ask what it does, what its effects are, and the nurse says, "Slows it down." She wads the cup and puts it in the plastic bag along with the others. "Sometimes," she adds and moves off.

While I'm standing there wondering exactly what she meant, Able comes out and takes me by the arm and without speaking walks me down to the balcony door. He waits for me to open it, as if he knows full well he hasn't the strength to do it, and we go out into a gentle evening breeze. At the far end two nurses stand side by side, backs to the railing, smoking. Able glances in their direction and then says, "No matter what, she's not to be in a home." He looks hard at me, as though I've suggested that as a possibility. "You hear me?" he asks. His eyes are watery and very stern, but in them there's more life than I've seen in years.

"Will that be best?" I ask, more wonder than argument in my voice.

"It'll be expensive," he answers. "But there's enough." He turns away and looks at the door that says in huge bold letters, *Level Five*. He stares at it as though it has absolutely no meaning. "She could have a long time," he says to the door. He turns away and steps past me and goes to the railing. Just then the two nurses go by and one says good evening while the other observes that it's a lovely night. "It is," Able says without looking in their direction. He puts both hands on the railing and stares out toward the ocean as if he can not only see it in the dark but all the things that are in it, too.

In the morning Able's his old self, at least in his dislike of lawyers. In the same way he's always liked banks but not bankers, Able has great respect for the law but hardly for, as he once said, "the eels who practice it." As I shave in the guest bathroom I know that Able's readying himself mentally to see Gil Gilbert, a man I've heard of but never met. "Nice fellow," Able once said of him, "but a bean for a brain." When I asked why then did he go to him for advice, Able said because he was one of two lawyers he'd ever met—the other was already dead ten or twelve years—who listened to him. "Never mind that he gets work done a year or two later," Able adds. While amusing when I heard it, this now worries me because there's nowhere near that kind of time left for Able. As we eat some cereal, Able still in his pajamas, and then Able has a cup of decaf, notes on his will on a small white tablet next to the table, he's withdrawn and barely notices me. Most of the time he looks out the window at the ocean as though he knows just exactly how many more mornings he'll be able to do this. Then he astonishes me by saying, without taking his eyes from the ocean, that he wants the number for the agency so he can get someone in here when Lillian comes home. When I tell him I'd be happy to do that, he says, "No, my job." Then he turns and looks at me and says, "If you'll help me get her home today or tomorrow, then that's all I need."

"I'll stay longer," I tell him. What I realize is how uncomfortable I suddenly am with the blunt knowledge that my time here with them is very close to being over. *He's* sending *me* away. "It'll take a while to get someone in," I say. "Someone good."

"A couple of days," he answers, then looks away again toward the water. "We'll be all right."

Right then the phone rings, and it startles me but not Able. As I turn slightly to get it on the counter, I cannot imagine because of how early it is that it can be anything but bad news. I can feel Able's eyes on me as I pick it up and say hello. It's the nurse on Lillian's floor, who says that Dr. Gandhi's already made rounds and has written an order for her discharge. Able knows instantly by the smile on my face exactly what the call is. His right hand makes a small fist on the table. The nurse tells me that it would be helpful if she could be picked up by eleven, and when I ask Able if this is all right he nods and says Gilbert won't take ten minutes, we'll be there. I tell this to the nurse and after I hang up Able asks me to set the phone in front of him, says thanks, and then with great care dials. As it's ringing, he asks if I'll find the number for the agency and without a word I open the cabinet under the counter and get out the phone book. He leaves a message for Gil Gilbert to the effect that he and I are stopping by in about an hour, that it's important that he sees him briefly to add a beneficiary to their trusts, and then hangs up, his entire concentration on the number I've written on my napkin. As he slowly presses off each number, I get up and leave the room, my signal that I respect what he said about this being his job.

I step out on the balcony and look to the left through the small kitchen window that's just behind Able and, one hand on the railing, watch him. He holds the phone with both hands, the mouthpiece very close to his lips, and nods as he talks. I turn away and lean on the railing and look down at the remarkable geometry of the positions of the planters and walkways below. There is an order, even a symmetry, that I have not seen before, the perfect sense it all makes dry and empty, the visual pleasure it's supposed to give too well thought out. I realize I'm only just in control of my feelings, that within a few days

I'll be leaving, and when I come back it'll be with Elaine and my daughters for Able's funeral. Lillian won't know anyone, will probably have an aide with her like a guard, and Benny will want to talk about how long she's got before he gets his money. I know in my heart that no one can know *why* some end up like this and others don't. As I look down, two women about my age come out of the building in one-piece swimsuits and short white terry cloth robes. They walk in step toward the pool and the chaises under the large cabana. They are full-hipped women with very large breasts and their thighs wobble with layers of cellulite. I wonder if either of them has an illness or may even be dying, and then I think the same about myself. Could it be that at this very moment one rogue cell deep in my gut or brain or pancreas has suddenly started to divide like crazy? A glance to the window shows Able still on the phone, but now he's more bent over than when he started. Even though I don't want to, I stay where I am. Oh, I think, who are we, really, and where is it that we are going? Of course, I expect no answer for this, no revelation, not even some small, soothing epiphany. I expect nothing but what I see—the ongoings of the ocean and the way the clouds move, the people walking the beach, the women breaststroking the widths of the pool. What I do experience, though, and it is profound enough to register fully, is a suddenly gentle calm, as if my blood has been whispered to.

When Able's off the phone, I go back inside and he's all business. He tells me that the case manager said that a permanent aide will be here this afternoon. He takes a deep breath as though he's talked too fast and then gets up and shuffles past me, the heels of his bedroom slippers clicking on the linoleum. "Come on," he says when he's just at the door, "help me shave."

What's clear right away is that he doesn't need my help at all, but, rather, simply wants me in the room with him. As we stand in front of the huge mirror, I see clearly that the difference in our heights is now pronounced—I must be four inches taller—and that his weight, judging from how the skin wraps his collarbones, is back to where it was right after the surgery. But his hand is steady as he strokes his cheeks and then, carefully, his chin, how he pauses to rinse the razor sure as ritual. Without even a glance at me he says, "Know what this apartment is worth?" I answer it must be a lot. "Probably two," he goes right on as though I haven't spoken. "Know what I paid for it?" I shake my head and he glances at my reflection in the mirror. "Forty-three," he tells me, his eyebrows up, eyes bright. "Good, don't you think?"

"You've done very well," I offer.

"I have," he says quietly.

As I reach to get him a small hand towel hanging on a bar just to the right of the toilet, I see that he hasn't flushed yet this morning and that there's a rose tinge to the water. The towel in hand, I turn around and see right away that he's aware of what I've seen. For a second, just before he looks back at himself in the mirror, our eyes lock. In this moment I think I see in his eyes that he wants to tell me something, as if he's chosen right now to pass along an important message from his generation to mine. Even turned away and patting his face with the towel, there's a depth of expression in his eyes—as though finally he'll turn back to me with serious, lasting words—that gives great comfort. He pauses, the towel held pensively to both cheeks, and looks at me again. "I was a good father, wasn't I?" he says. His tone is even and objective, as though it matters not at all that he's asked me the question. He puts the towel down and reaches for the Old Spice, has trouble getting the top off, and hands the bottle to me. I get it off and as I hand it back to him I smile and say, "You weren't perfect." He shakes some liquid into one palm, puts the bottle down, and as he presses the aftershave into his cheeks he says, one eyebrow raised, smiling and looking at me again in the mirror, "Was too."

Then he says he wants me here when the aide comes this afternoon, and adds that as far as he's concerned I can leave anytime I want. "You'll be all right, you think?" I ask.

"It'd be best," he says.

I put a hand on his shoulder that's nearer to me and, our communication now strictly through the mirror, say, "Okay."

Able takes Lillian a pretty red dress folded neatly in a shopping bag, along with a crimson belt and shoes with half-inch heels. In his pocket he's also brought a gold circle pin with small diamonds he bought her years ago. Now and again at the lawyer's, he puts his hand in that pocket or his fingertips touch and ride over it through his trousers. It's arranged by Able that I'll get a copy of the will and the codicil when it's all typed up fresh and witnessed. The lawyer asks if one's to be sent to Benjamin, too, and Able thinks for a moment, then glances at me and finally says, "Both sons." As we leave, Able tells me about a lawyer he went to years ago when he was having a will drawn, "which one I can't remember." He says the s.o.b. didn't like what he wanted done and asked Able what he thought he had to do to get to heaven. "Get another lawyer is what I told him," Able says. All the way down to the hospital, Able sits quietly, his face calm and pleased, as though his mind is in constant replay of the moment.

Lillian is thrilled to see Able but she does not know me and she has no memory of my having been here yesterday. Still, at Able's urging, she tolerates my presence. She looks at me warily, as though I've done something unpleasant to the Teddy in her mind. While Able and one of the aides help Lillian dress, I go out to the balcony. Butts and soda cans are everywhere, and in the far corner by a brick column there's a condom on the dirty cement. I put my hands on the railing to look out toward the water and right away I feel the dirt on my palms. So bright is the late morning sun that there's no visible horizon, only a great shimmering where the sky and ocean meet.

When I open the door and go back into the hall, Lillian's just coming out of the room in a wheelchair, Able, slightly bowed, pushing it. Lillian's chart in the crook of her arm, one of the nurses walks beside them until they get to the long main corridor, where she moves ahead toward the elevators. I fall in behind like a polite afterthought, someone who really has no business here at all. So absorbed is Able in leaning over and talking to Lillian that if I were to come alongside the wheelchair I'd surprise him. He does his small talk all the way down in the elevator, and there's even a giggle between them as he says something in her ear. Lillian, smiling, raises one hand from her lap and makes a gesture as if to wave him away. Whatever he's said, she loves it. I get the car and drive it around and then Able directs her rising from the wheelchair and her entrance into the front passenger's seat as though it were a major but very delicate event. Finally in and somewhat out of breath, Lillian has a moment of bewilderment and looks up at Able as though she's never met him. But then it's gone in a flash and he reaches past her to do the seat belt. She seems not to know what it is but is glad to have it tightly around her. Then Able starts around to the driver's side and I have to move fast to intercept him. I get to the door just before he does and he pauses, then looks at me. Finally, he steps around me and opens the back door. In front of the apartment building he makes the same kind of fuss in getting her out and having her take his arm to walk up the steps. I go right behind them, as close as I can get without really intruding, and toss Joseph the keys. In the elevator, he tells Lillian that this afternoon someone from the agency's coming and that from now on she won't have a thing to worry about. "I'm so glad," Lillian says.

When they're finally settled in the den, Lillian lightly napping on the couch, Able's eyes fixed on the market quotes, I go out to the kitchen and call to make a reservation to fly out tomorrow afternoon. Just after I hang up and turn to look out at the pool area, now baking in the heavy midday sun, what returns to me are the unanswerable questions of who we really are and where is it that we're going. I sit at the kitchen table and stare out at the ocean as if it's suddenly taken on some mysterious meaning, as if it has more value as a metaphor than what it really is. Is it too much to ask for a small sign that there is, after all, something true and right in this whole life, a plan, a form? I cannot take it all on faith and philosophy; I want some slight degree of evidence, a kind of proof, that I can take with me, something private and meant for no one else, something to give me peace and that I would have no desire ever to share. Isn't the best prayer a demand?

I turn away from the window, expecting to see Able standing in the doorway across the room, but there's only a sense of his presence there, as if a few seconds ago he were watching me. I feel Lillian in the living room dusting, moving from the coffee table to the ones at the ends of the couches, full of energy and routine, as if, even after they're gone from here, on some level such things will always continue. Down below children play in the pool and people lie perfectly still in the sun on the beach, waves curl and then smack silently on the sand, and I know that I am going home tomorrow, that this is the last night I will be with both my parents.

Turns out there's a misunderstanding between the agency and the aide about when she is supposed to arrive, and there's much confusion when around four-thirty I call the agency and they say one Jamaica Wellington was due an hour ago. At five a substitute comes who's already worked a full day elsewhere and she's none too pleased to have pulled dinner duty for strangers. The arrangement that's finally worked out is that Jamaica will arrive tomorrow at nine to take over a permanent position. Most interesting to me is that all of these details are taken care of by Able, and on the phone he's reasonable, even gentle and kind at times. But he is anxious about the arrangment, and it's clear that he's relieved when he knows that he's not going to be left alone with Lillian for any length of time.

Right in the middle of the dinner preparations, the substitute aide gets a phone call that nearly creates the next world war. The phone is answered more or less on reflex by Lillian in the den, and she is utterly baffled by the male voice on the other end asking is Elaine there. I get wind of trouble when I hear her say that Elaine lives in Pennsylvania. She stares in my direction as Able moves toward her to take the phone. It seems then that something goes a little haywire in Lillian's mind and she refuses to let the receiver go. Startled, Able steps back and watches as Lillian says that he should call Pennsylvania if he wants Elaine. Then she covers the mouthpiece with one hand and looks at me. "Teddy," she says, "somebody wants to talk to Elaine."

"Give me the phone," Able says, and for a second it looks like he's going to snatch it from her. Finally, she hands it to him and looks past both of us at the television as though there'd never been a call. Then her eyes wander over to mine and she asks if Elaine's all right. I tell her she is. Able, with a sudden loss of patience, demands to know who the caller is and what business might he have with this number. Just as I close my eyes in a second or two of momentary escape, I realize that nobody asked the subsitute aide her name. I'm too late to get this information to Able before he abruptly hangs up. Elaine, who has apparently been waiting for the call, then appears in the doorway and asks if someone just telephoned for her. Able and Lillian both stare at her as if they have no idea who she is. I try to take the heat for the situation by saying apparently there was a small misunderstanding, but it doesn't work. "My name," she says to Able and Lillian, "is Elaine Moore. I'm alive, too." Then she snaps away and is gone back through the living room and into the kitchen. When I say I sure hope he calls back, Lillian looks at me and says, "Who?" Do I need to say just how bad the dinner is or that a plate and a glass hit the floor on the way to the dishwasher?

The evening doesn't go like I want it to, either. I had hopes before dinner that the three of us might sit out on the balcony for a while, but it starts to rain and then Benny calls to see how Lillian is. Able verifies that she's well on her way back to her old self, and Lillian, although she hasn't the faintest idea what he's talking about, smiles proudly. Then there's a long pause while Benny talks and Able's face grows very serious. He hands me the phone and says he's going to the kitchen to finish the conversation and would I please hang up in a second. With Lillian staring at me and smiling, I hold the receiver close to my ear, worried that Benny is going to tell Able that after all he's got to have a bypass or that one of the other tests at the hospital turned up something ominous. I eavesdrop only long enough to hear Benny start with, "Listen, Dad, I've got a chance on a deal you wouldn't believe . . . ," and then I hang up. For all practical purposes, I know the evening is gone. Able will be upset and preoccupied with Benny's having asked for money, and what little energy he's saved for tonight will be squandered on his fretting over whether or not, once more, he should bankroll one of Benny's schemes.

About half an hour later when Able comes back into the den, I waste no time asking him what it is now. "Diapers," he says and lowers himself slowly into his chair. "Another chance to get in on the ground floor." I ask Able to explain what the deal is and he shakes his head and says he didn't follow all the details, but Benny wants ten grand. Lillian chimes in with, "That's quite a lot of money, dear," to which Able answers, "No, not really," and then picks up the remote and starts through the channels so fast it's impossible to tell what any of the programs might be.

Over the next half hour sleep begins to overtake both of them, Lillian first, then Able, who fights it to the extent that he shakes his head several times before giving in and letting his chin rest on his chest. Neither is in deep sleep of any kind, their breathing shallow, their eyes frantic under the closed lids. I leave them quietly and go out to the balcony, where I sit for a while and watch the rain, now a downpour so hard that the pool is about to flood, the putting green is under water, and all the cabanas have been folded down. The ocean is calm, the waves dark and small from the heavy rain, the horizon gone. Down below, a man comes out one of the lobby doors in a white beach robe and white swimming cap, a towel rolled under an arm. As I watch, he starts his laps with the breaststroke, the pool lights making him look like a big black frog. I look around at the sky, the building, watch the gray sparkling rain shoot straight down past the balcony, and nothing makes any sense, not even questions. I sit for perhaps half an hour before I come to realize that what I wanted from tonight was closure with Able, some kind of rounding off of his life that I might take with me. But now I know I'm just not going to get it and I'm going to have to live with that.

What verifies this is that when I go back inside both Able and Lillian have gone into their bedroom and closed the door. Faintly, the sounds from their bathroom filter out and I know that they're getting ready for bed. I watch some sitcom I've never heard of and after about twenty minutes Able opens the bedroom door and steps halfway into the hall. He raises one hand slightly and says, "See you in the morning," and then steps back inside and closes the door.

"Good night," I say.

What Able wants out of this last night is for it to be like any other.

When I come into the kitchen in the morning, Able's making decaf for himself and Lillian, who sits at the small table lost in a pink robe and matching slippers. Able asks if I slept well and I say yes, and that I've stripped the bed and put my bag in the hall by the door. "The girl's on her way up," Able says. "Joseph just called."

"Who's coming?" Lillian asks.

"It's all right," Able says softly. Lillian turns away as though responding to a command to go to sleep. "So, you'll be okay?" he says to me. I nod. "And you'll call?" Nod again. Then he takes a check out of his pajama pocket and gives it to me. Just as I see that it's for ten thousand dollars, he says, "The difference between you and Benny is that a year from now you'll still have yours." His eyebrows shoot up in emphasis just as the doorbell rings. He turns without another word and shuffles in his way along the kitchen floor, turns like a thin toy soldier, and goes into the living room. "Who's that?" Lillian asks, a little paranoid. I tell her it's Jamaica and she says, "I don't know any Jamaica." I turn and go out to the living room and am pleasantly surprised to see that Able has already let Jamaica in and that he's showing her where she can put her two suitcases. I introduce myself and she shakes my hand firmly, says it's nice to meet me, and then picks up both suitcases and heads off to the bedroom. Right then more important than her smart, alert eyes and her tall, strong physique is how Able looks at her as she goes across the living room. His face is soft, his eyes slightly watered, as though he knows he's just met the person who will soon be the sole caretaker of Lillian. And he likes what he's seen.

Then we both go back into the kitchen and Able motions me to sit at the table while he stops at the stove to pick up the teakettle of hot water. When he's poured a cup of decaf for me and set down a bowl of Cheerios, he then sits himself and asks when I have to leave. Of course, this catches Lillian off guard and she asks where I'm going. When I say, "Home," she stares at me, then looks to Able to clarify her confusion. Able says, "Pennsylvania," and then Lillian nods.

"But when will you be coming back?" she asks. In reponse I look at Able.

"Six months," he tells her. "Maybe sooner."

Enter Jamaica. She comes in wearing a bright red and white polka-dot top with white slacks, glances around at the appliances and the cabinets, and then comes straight across the room to Lillian. In her clipped, lilting accent she introduces herself and Lillian reaches out to shake her hand. "And how do *you* do?" Jamaica says. Lillian looks up into Jamaica's face as though she's just recognized a long-time friend. I glance at Able and see the relief pour through him. He gets up then and starts his familiar shuffle across the floor, and, as if they'd actually planned it, Jamaica takes his seat.

"Where're you going?" Lillian asks.

"To check the futures," Able says and turns the corner without looking back.

After a few moments it's clear from how Lillian and Jamaica begin to talk that I'm odd man out here, and I get up and put my empty cereal bowl on the counter and then take the rest of the coffee into the den. Able sits as he always has, as if he'll go on forever just like he is right now. He takes no notice of my coming in but after several moments gestures with a finger toward the television and says the futures are up. When I ask him what futures are, and add that I've never understood them, he says that everything in the market is speculation, and proceeds to explain about futures. I don't understand a word, really, until the end when he says the only way to be in the market is for the long haul. "All these kids jumping in and out," he says and shakes his head. Then he looks at me and adds, "Right now, right this moment in fact, I'm in it for the long haul."

When the phone rings on the table beside the couch I pick it up because I know it'll be Sidney telling me the taxi's here. It's then I tell him that it's time to go and, as if he's been waiting for it, he responds as quickly as a finger snap that he'd appeciate it if I just went into the kitchen and kissed Lillian but didn't say I was leaving. Lillian's standing by the sink watching Jamaica stack the dishwasher. I put a hand on her shoulder and then kiss her cheek. Fascinated by the process, Lillian lets out a small "Oh," but doesn't turn to see if it's Able or me. Just as I take my hand away, hers absently comes up to touch it, but we miss.

Able's standing in the small hall by the door, the suitcase between us. I stop and we look at each other, and then I say, "You'll be all right?"

"We'll be fine," he says. "Thank you for coming and doing all you did."

"If you need anything," I say.

"I know," he answers.

Then, as we begin to shake hands, he pulls me in to him—awkwardly over the suitcase—with what feels like his old great strength.

It's over in a few seconds and I pick up the suitcase and turn to the door, open it, and step out into the hall. At the elevator I press the down button and then turn to look at him. He's back a few steps in the shadows of the hall, one hand up on the door, as faint as though already he has gone into my memory. As I step into the elevator, he waves a little and I do, too, and then the door closes and I start down.

At the north entrance to the building I say good-bye to Sidney and he says he hopes I have a good trip and asks when I'm coming back. I tell him maybe in a few months, sometime in the summer for sure. Then I'm out the door and down the steps. As I cross the parking lot, it is as if I am directed to look up at the sun over the ocean and hold my eyes on it for as long as I can. It is like a huge hole in the sky through which for just a moment I am allowed to see the great blaze of all eternity.